The Eye in the Ceiling

A Novel

Julie Sampson

BookLocker
Saint Petersburg, Florida

In memory of Mary Ellen Sampson

Contents

Get your bags together,

Go bring your good friends, too

'Cause it's getting nearer,

It soon will be with you

Cat Stevens

"Peace Train"

1. The Break-In

Everything began the night of the break-in at the Ames Gate Lodge. I was out walking Hobson when the black Land Rover appeared. I had volunteered to take the dog for his evening walk — well, I didn't volunteer exactly. Ms. Montgomery emphasized that exercising the English springer spaniel was a vital aspect of my library internship duties, although that part of the deal wasn't written up in the college catalogue.

I was a freshman at Kew College in North Easton, Massachusetts, and it was my first week of classes. The library internship was part of the requirements of my Library and Information Science major. It was an Indian summer evening in the grassy town outside of Boston, and it felt amazing to be out in the fresh air. I had never heard of H.H. Richardson or the Porcellian Club that evening as I clipped the leash onto Hobson's collar, but those names and the mysteries which surrounded them would dominate the next three months of my life, and nearly kill me in the process.

Shovel Town, that's what the locals call North Easton, is a perfect place for dog walking. Usually, that is.

I remember that early autumn night so clearly...I hear the SUV coming before I see it, the engine roaring, the tires screeching. I pull Hobson onto the lawn away from the road just as the SUV peels around the corner. The car barrels across the lawn right up to the side entrance of the building. I crouch behind a rock wall to watch. Four men wearing ski hat masks, dressed all in black, jump out of the car and bash crowbars into the large arched wooden doorway. The aged wood splinters into chunks as they gouge a jagged opening. They bust through and the sounds of smashing glass follow from inside the building.

"It's over here," one guy yells. "Let's go, move it."

The men grunt as they drag furniture out of the way, slamming objects into the walls. Stacks of boxes thud onto the floor. They burst outside, hauling a metal filing cabinet into the back of the SUV. They slam the doors so hard it resonates like a round of gun shots. The SUV blasts past me but the dark-tinted windows make it impossible to view anything more as they roar out of sight.

Part of me wants to walk away, ignore the whole thing, because I have to get back to the library. But I can't just blow it off. It's my civic duty to report this intense activity. So, I call the cops — become the lone eyewitness to this epic caper — and here's where things turn weird.

"911, what's your emergency?"

At first, I can't find the right words, then I manage to say, "There's been — a break-in."

The operator takes the address and dispatches the police. "Is an ambulance required?"

"No. Nobody got hurt."

"The police are on the way. Wait for them."

I feel stupid standing in the dark driveway with the dog. Hobson has soulful brown eyes and long, curly brown ears that drape like symmetrical chandeliers. He is the library mascot owned by the head librarian Ms. Montgomery. Hobson howls at the police sirens racing toward the lodge.

The officer jumps from the cruiser. "Are you the caller?"

"I'm Paige Moore. Yes, I'm the one who called 911. I saw the break-in," I say, settling on the word *break-in* instead of robbery or burglary because stealing a filing cabinet seems more like a misdemeanor than high crime. I hold my hands up to show I'm not armed, other than holding Hobson's leash.

The cop approaches me and adjusts his peaked police cap. His thick black eyeglasses slide down his sweaty nose. He pushes them back with his finger. The lights on the cruiser flash a blinding red across my face. A second police vehicle pulls into the driveway and kills the siren. Hobson jumps toward the cop, barking at him.

"Don't worry, he's friendly," I say.

He keeps his eyes focused on me while the other cops use high-powered flashlights to survey the damage. "What happened here?"

I review the details with him while the other cops mark off the investigation area with yellow caution tape. I feel like a lousy eyewitness — not too many details to report — a black SUV, four men in black wearing ski masks, crowbars.

He pushes up his glasses. "Did they say anything?"

"One guy inside the building found whatever they were looking for. He said, 'It's over here. Let's go, move it.'"

"Were there any sounds when they moved it?" The cop is writing down everything I tell him in his wire-bound pocket notebook.

"Sounds? Some clunking around. Maybe dragging sounds, at first, but then they picked it up and carried it out."

"How heavy would you say the cabinet is?"

"I can't even guess. Three of them carried it while the other one, the driver I think, went ahead of them and opened the car door."

"Did you smell anything?" The cop flips to a fresh page.

"Smell?"

I wonder what a person might smell in moments like this. I'm guessing the cop was trained to cover the five senses in witness interviews along with the five Ws — who, what, where, when and why. "No smells that I recall. Maybe the dog picked up on something though."

"Could you tell what age these guys might have been?"

"I'd say mid-to-late twenties. They moved so fast."

"Height?" he asks.

"Tough to say. They were hunched over carrying the cabinet. The other guy I'd guess is 5-foot-10ish."

"Accents? Boston accent, for instance? Foreign?"

"I didn't notice."

"The SUV, was it a late model or a clunker?"

"It looked high-end. Brand-spanking new. All shiny."

He glances at Hobson who is antsy because this is supposed to be his walking time. The cop softens when he scratches behind Hobson's ears and says, "The captain will want to talk to you in person. Where can he find you?"

"I'll be working at the town library until it closes, then back at my dorm," I tell him and give him my phone number.

The cop points his pen toward my hooded sweatshirt — it has *Kew College Saints* silkscreened across the chest with a graphic of the college St. Bernard mascot.

"You go to Kew?"

"I'm a freshman there."

"Okay, Miss Moore, the captain will be in touch with you to follow-up," he says and adjusts his glasses again. "You're free to leave."

Back at the library, Hobson laps up a fresh bowl of water. Ms. Montgomery pokes her head in to see who is bustling in the back room. Punctuality is a non-negotiable as a library intern and Ms. Montgomery keeps a close watch on the whereabouts of her staff.

I am still out of breath from rushing back with the dog. "Ms. Montgomery, you're not going to believe —"

"This isn't story time, miss. There is work to get done, chop-chop," she says and slices her hands through the air.

"But —"

"No buts, miss."

I slip a few extra pumpkin flavored treats to Hobson before I put him into his crate. I pull off my hoodie and stuff it in my backpack in the coat closet. I have less than half an hour to set up chairs in the community room for Ms. Montgomery's town history class. I dim the overhead fluorescent lights, because they're adding to the headache that started with the flashing police lights. I am prone to migraines — the aftermath of a concussion last year — and I am aware of the various triggers such as bright lights and loud noise that cause my brain to rebel.

Ms. Montgomery bounces around the library like an aerobics instructor. Her spiked hairstyle swoops upward like a dandelion you could blow across the lawn, an efficient style that won't slow her down. She boasts that she is up early each morning for her power walk, suited up in a bright swishy nylon jogging outfit.

Once the class assembles, Ms. Montgomery makes her grand entrance up the center aisle with me shadowing behind her. I am the youngest by forty years at least.

"There are two things you should never try to figure out," announces Ms. Montgomery, pausing while the silver-haired senior citizens wonder what those two things are. Politics and religion? Death and taxes?

She scratches the answer on the portable chalkboard and wipes the chalk dust from her fingers. "Love and traffic," she declares. A collective chuckle fills the room.

I'm surprised there are so many retirees taking a night class about this small town. Ms. Montgomery teaches at a rapid-fire pace. I wonder what vitamins this woman uses and if she would be willing to give some to me. Ms. Montgomery requests that I sit front row and center in case she needs assistance. I think my time would be better spent helping the library patrons instead of passing around photocopies. Ms. Montgomery has taught this local history class for years, gaining the reputation as an expert town historian.

North Easton's industrial history began with the discovery of bog iron, Ms. Montgomery explains, which made the town an important late 17th and 18th century iron-producing region in Massachusetts. The first commercial steel generated in the colonies was made in Easton by the Ames Shovel Company, established in 1803. Ms. Montgomery speaks with pride that the Ames Shovel Company provided the shovels that dug away the earth that formed the Union Pacific Railroad.

"The Union Pacific Railroad made the states truly united," she annunciates. "Most Americans overlook North Easton, our wonderfully historic town. The Ames family shaped the town's economy, its geography and architecture. Our town is fortunate to have several Henry Hobson Richardson masterpieces, which we will discuss when we take our field trip."

She assigns an essay to the class on the history of the Ames Shovel Company. She nods in my direction indicating that I am expected to write this paper as well, because part of my internship is helping her write material for the official guide to North Easton.

"Miss, please distribute," she says, handing me a batch of stapled photocopies. As I pass around the sheets, my eyes jump past the rows of senior citizens where I see a guy my age doodling in his notebook. His bent legs press through the rips in the knees of his jeans. His t-shirt has the word Tool swirled across the chest. He must have arrived late to class because I definitely would have noticed him when I came in.

"Thank you, miss," he says, mimicking Ms. Montgomery.

I feel my face turning chili pepper hot as I restrain from laughing. On the way to my seat, I feel his eyes on me. I should have done something with my hair other than pull it into a ponytail. I look down at my wrinkled black pants and ink-stained white blouse — I must look like a waitress at the end of her shift.

As the class labors on, I glance to see his flip flops out in front of him with the frayed hem of his jeans pressed against the floor. His head is turned as he focuses on the teacher, his dark hair is slicked into a tight man bun, and his skin looks tan from the summer.

Ms. Montgomery finally dismisses class. The back-row guy pops a handful of gummy bears into his mouth before getting up.

"You're the only one in this class that doesn't have gray hair," he says to me.

"And you're the only one with a man bun."

He lets loose a loud snort. "My professor is gaga over this town's early American architecture. H.H. Richardson is his idol. A legend according to my professor. He's the only American with a style named after him, Richardsonian Romanesque." His breath smells like the gummy bears and the green color in the corners of his mouth looks like toxic waste. "What's your excuse?"

"Internship."

"What's a library intern do?"

"Basically, I'm the old lady's bitch."

He laughs harder than I expect, so I tell him about her do's-and-don'ts list, including how to properly exercise the library dog around town.

"I'm Christopher, by the way." He reaches out to shake my hand. "My friends call me Stoph."

"I'm Paige. I'm a freshman at Kew College. You?"

"Sophomore at Harvard, studying architecture. Which you probably guessed already."

He mentions Harvard off-handedly. I'm thinking, one, good looking; two, smart; three, funny; four, humble.

"See you next time, Paige, the main bitch."

"See you, Soph."

"It's Stoph, not Soph."

"I know."

I head over to the reference desk where Ms. Montgomery nods toward the archive department. She plucks a thick ring of keys from her top drawer, some regular-sized and some antique looking brass keys that she jingles with authority. She unlocks the door and I follow her down to a musty smelling dungeon. Weak light exposes cracks that run like veins in the cement floors and walls. The basement has lengthy rows of shelves and old metal cabinets. There is a solitary desk positioned against the far wall.

"Return this stack of material to its proper location. Don't touch anything else. I do not generally allow staff down here, so make it snappy," she orders and shuffles back up the stairs.

I examine the desk. Its legs are made from old shovels with the shovel blades bent to serve as feet to steady the desk. The shovel handles are screwed into the front of wood beams as leg posts. Old wooden shovel handles are welded together in snug rows to form the desktop. A thick piece of glass tops the shovel handles to make a flat work surface.

The desk is littered with scribbled notes, yellowed blueprints of buildings and piles of old books. I flip through one of the musky smelling tomes.

As I shelve the books, I notice an antique cabinet, the metal doors ajar. I open it snooping for any out-of-circulation vintage books. The cabinet is packed with old notebooks that have aged oxblood leather covers and bindings. I thumb through the yellowed pages of one notebook — it's filled with calligraphy handwriting with words and symbols, equations, arrows and slash marks. Some drawings have animal heads emerging from wild scrolls of oak leaves, ivy strands and braid patterns; there are elaborate ink drawings of fish creatures with gaping mouths, owl heads, ram heads and goat heads.

"Young lady. I believe I instructed you not to touch anything. There is a level of trust when you work as my student intern."

"Sorry," I say, my heart skipping a few beats. "I was just admiring this —"

"It's not yours to touch or admire. Put it back and finish up."

Ms. Montgomery folds her arms in front of her chest. I scurry around trying to figure out where the books belong. It is an uncomfortable five minutes where she stares in silence until I slide the last book into place. "I'm finished."

I follow her up the stairs where a police officer waits by her desk.

"Captain Biff, what a wonderful surprise. What brings you here this evening? Need a new crime novel to read?"

He puts his hands on his hips, broadening his stance. He has trimmed sideburns that fade into a buzz cut on his block-shaped head that reminds me of a Lego character. The gold captain's badge on his shirt reflects the overhead light. "I'm here to talk with Paige Moore about the break-in. She around?"

I step forward. "I'm Paige."

"I need to ask you a few questions about the incident earlier this evening." He takes his spiral-topped notebook from his chest pocket and twists open his gold Cross pen. I notice he doesn't wear a gun holster or handcuffs like the other officers investigating the break-in.

Ms. Montgomery whips her head around. "Incident?"

"B&E at the Ames Gate Lodge."

"Beeee and eeeee?"

"Breaking and Entering. Moore is reported as a witness."

"Oh, my word!" She squints at Captain Biff as if she just bit into a pickle. "How extensive is the damage? What did the criminals take?"

"Place was ransacked," he says, looking toward me. "What exactly did you see?"

I tell him about the four men, the black SUV, and the filing cabinet.

"You didn't think to come back and report this to me?" Ms. Montgomery narrows her eyes at me.

"I started to tell you when I got back, but then you did that chop-chop thing —"

"In the future, miss —"

Captain Biff clears his throat. "Can you describe any of the perpetrators?"

"No, it was too dark and it went down fast. I just heard one guy tell them to take the whole thing which I assume meant the whole filing cabinet."

Captain Biff pulls out a pair of gold wire-framed reading glasses from his chest pocket and adjusts them on the bridge of his nose. He jots a quick note and asks, "Did you see the make of the car?"

21

"It was a black Land Rover."

"Did you see the license plate?"

"It was a Massachusetts plate, but I didn't see the letters or numbers."

"Were there any other cars around, parked or moving?"

"None that I noticed."

He glances over the top of his glasses. "You said a file cabinet? You sure that's what you saw? Not a safe, a desk or storage trunk?"

"I'm positive. It was a light color, like gray or beige, had silver drawer pulls on five drawers, it was metal and about five feet tall by eighteen inches wide with deep drawers."

"And you say four men. Not women?"

"They were big athletic looking guys."

"Were they young or old?"

"Young. They looked like pros. You know, like *Ocean's Eleven*. They were fast. I mean, it was like a military operation, it seemed, almost. Experts. The whole robbery only lasted three minutes, maybe less."

"Did they use any names?"

"None that I heard."

He flips to a fresh page. "Did you notice anything else unusual?"

"I thought the whole thing was unusual. That's why I called the police."

He nods and stuffs the notepad in his shirt pocket, then buttons it closed. He hands me a business card with his name above an embossed gold badge. "Okay, if you think of anything else or hear anything give me a call. Sometimes a witness will recall details a day or two after the trauma."

"It wasn't actually a trauma. I mean, I hid behind the wall. They didn't even see me."

"The event," he says, stressing the word, "if you prefer that term."

I look to Ms. Montgomery. "Do you need anything else taken care of before I leave for the night?"

"That's quite enough for today, miss."

When I get my backpack, an old man hobbles in the rear entrance. His steely eyes glare into mine as he limps past me. I hear Ms. Montgomery say, "Homer! What on earth happened?"

He lowers his voice and says, "Cut my damn foot steppin' on broken glass at the lodge. Evening, Captain. Any leads?"

I move closer to the door to eavesdrop.

"I think the perpetrators are sniffing out North Easton again. They're probably canvassing for the compass."

"With all due respect, Captain Biff, that filing cabinet has critical research —"

Ms. Montgomery cuts him off. "Enough with your research, Homer, should we call for a meeting?"

"Definitely," says Homer.

Hobson starts yapping in his crate, so I hustle out before I get caught eavesdropping.

Back in my dorm, an ice cream social is in full swing on the first floor. The resident director lures me in and slaps a name tag on my shirt. I step into line because I love ice cream — it helps my migraines somehow — and I want to go unnoticed so she forgets the fact that my roommate never showed up. I'm hoping she neglects to arrange for a new roommate assignment to fill my double. I scoop a chocolate cone topped with colorful sprinkles.

A petite girl with straight strawberry-blonde hair and a face full of freckles points to the sprinkles. *My Name is Sheila* announces her name tag. "Just curious, what do you call those?"

Two other girls — *Melissa* and *Jill* according to their name tags — lean in to hear my response. "Ummm, sprinkles? Or is it a trick question?"

Sheila turns to her friends. "Fine. You two win."

"Win what?" I ask, licking my ice cream.

"Name game."

A girl from a different cluster says, "In Maine we call them shots."

Melissa flips her salon-fresh brunette hair from her shoulder. "Yeah, well, we're in college now and shots has a whole new meaning. Let's not confuse things."

Sheila says, "I grew up in Massachusetts and we call those jimmies. Melissa and Jill are from New York and they call them sprinkles. Are you from New York, too?"

"Connecticut," I tell them. "I'm Paige. Room 401."

Melissa, who is wearing more makeup than I wore to the prom, says, "You're at the end of our hall. Jill and I are in 417."

Sheila, from room 202, keeps the conversation rolling. "So, what do you call a long sandwich? Sub?"

Melissa shakes her head. "In New York we call it a hero."

I add, "Connecticut says grinder."

The eavesdropper from the other group says, "Hoagie."

The resident director stops by. "Good times, ladies. Just so you know, there is a new coffee shop opening in town if anyone is looking for some part-time work. My friend Tanya is the owner. She's a super cool lady. You can find a job application on the Goforth's Daily Grind website."

"Thanks, I'll check it out," I say.

"Paige, I need to find a roommate for you. It's on my list."

"Oh, it's okay. I don't mind," I tell her.

"Wait, what? You don't have a roommate?" Melissa dabs a napkin on the corner of her red-glossed mouth.

"Nope." I polish off my ice cream and think about going for seconds, but I don't because I am still up ten pounds since I stopped training for soccer.

"That's so awesome. Alone in a double! Think of the possibilities!" says Jill, who has an exotic look, half-Korean and half-Caucasian, I'd guess.

I like the idea of having the room to myself so I can read and study in quiet solitude.

Jill bumps knuckles with Melissa, then asks, "Would you mind if we hit you up to crash in your extra bed if one of us has company?"

She says "company" and makes air quotes.

"Sure, anytime." I toss my napkins in the trash and notice that Melissa and Jill throw out their half-finished cones.

We head up to the fourth floor together. At my door I say, "See you around."

"Wait, can we see your room?" Jill asks.

I swing open the door and they step inside. My dorm room is blasé in comparison to some of the other rooms that have matching comforters and pillows, posters of Monet paintings, well-stocked mini-refrigerators, televisions and stereos. The plaster walls are off-white, probably the residual grime from former occupants. My walls are bare other than a bulletin board with my class and library intern schedules. I stacked crates filled with my favorite books against one wall.

Melissa surveys the room. "Have enough books? Total fire hazard."

"They're like old friends. I can't part with them."

Jill picks up *Infinite Jest* and fans the pages. "Did you read this? It's a million pages."

Melissa sits on my desk chair. "You should take a page from each book to wallpaper an accent wall. Anything but these cinder block prison walls."

"I was waiting for my roommate, figured we'd go pick stuff out together," I say.

Melissa eyeballs the closets. "We can do it with you. I love decorating."

My bed is made in simple white sheets with a purple comforter tossed on top. I positioned high-riser blocks under the legs of the bed to create storage space for my plastic containers filled with winter clothes. Other than a few cable-knit sweaters and some soccer hoodies, my wardrobe consists of jeans, t-shirts, sneakers, flip flops, and sweats. I notice that

Melissa and Jill look stylish in designer jeans, crop tops and hard-soled mules. I should buy some new clothes when we go shopping for dorm décor, but I don't have much extra money.

"Sounds great. Saturday?"

"For sure." They respond in unison. After they leave, I wonder if that's what happens when you have a roommate: instant bonding.

I flop onto my bed feeling good that I've made some new friends. In high school I was a total *futbolista* — playing soccer every day — as if my life depended on it. My obsession with soccer started in grammar school when I discovered I had a natural nose for the goal. By the time I was a sophomore, college coaches were scouting me at all the showcase games.

The concussion happened during an elite travel game in the summer before my senior year. I was cruising toward a hat trick — pissing off the defenders with my slick juke moves — when I jumped for a head ball inside the goalie's box. Instead of driving the ball into the back of the net, I smacked heads with a defender and was knocked unconscious.

Everything after that is a blur, a heavy fogginess that lingered for a year. A neurologist diagnosed post-concussion syndrome. I suffered persistent headaches, mood swings and hypersensitivity to light and sound. The impact of the concussion trashed my senior year and the doctor determined the head injury meant the end of my soccer career. I could never play again, he said.

I went from being a top-college recruit to being a high school senior with a B-average and not much else. The college coaches dropped my name from their recruiting lists. My former teammates and friends gradually stopped socializing with me because I became a drag. I couldn't blame them. I couldn't do much. I had horrible headaches, dizziness, blurry vision. I couldn't even go to the mall with friends because the lights gave me instant migraines. I tried toughing it out, went to some house parties, but the music pounded inside my head. I couldn't think straight — my mind would tell me to smell colors and taste sunshine — and I'd know it was time to leave. I had no cast or crutches to show how hurt I was. It was an invisible injury that no one could see, and I had to deal with it alone.

I was a total jock in high school, but that didn't deter guys from asking me out. I went steady with Luke for two years before my concussion. He was the 6-foot-3 stud quarterback on the football team. Our friends joked that we were going to get married someday and make bionic babies. We felt like the Snoopy and Woodstock balloons in the Macy's Thanksgiving Day Parade — all eyes on us — the popular couple holding hands in the hallway. Then — bonk — I noticed a million stupid things about him that annoyed me, like how loud he chewed his food and how he bounced his knees with nervous energy all the time. I struggled with sleep, so I was often tired and snappy with my comments. He tried to be supportive in the beginning, but after a while, I was too much of a drag with my headaches and rotten moods. We broke up. I went to the senior prom with a guy named Melvin, an AV geek, but I was just going through the motions.

My parents made me see a therapist. The therapist told me depression is common with post-concussion syndrome. Plus, without soccer, I didn't know who I was anymore. As I slowly recovered in my quiet, dimly lit bedroom at home, I read day and night, mainly because it was the only thing I could do without getting a headache. Screens are the enemy of a concussed brain, so I read every classic from *Anna Karenina* to *A Tale of Two Cities*. I read the Bible — not because I'm religious — but the Old Testament tales intrigue me. My life without soccer became a life filled with books. That's how I chose my major and ended up at Kew College with this student internship at the Ames Free Library. Now I'm a book geek destined to be a librarian.

2. Toughy Juice

It amazes me how much time soccer sucked from my life. Although I have a full class schedule and a fifteen-hour per week internship at the library, I still have spare time. I need some beer-and-pizza money — the internship pay goes straight toward tuition.

I take my dorm director's suggestion and apply for a barista job at the new coffee shop. The Goforth Daily Grind's website features a picture of the owner, Tanya Goforth, smiling in front of a Volkswagen hippie van. The coffee shop appears to be an organic health-nut haven. One of the questions on the application asks: *What is your current mantra?*

I fill in the blank — *my body is a temple* — thinking that will impress the hippie coffee lady, and I'm correct: she hires me the next day.

Tanya Goforth hosts a staff meeting at her house near the campus. A wave of homesickness hits me when I see kids racing around their front yards, reminding me of my old soccer net in my yard where I honed my quick shot. Heading off to college is like bouncing down a rocky steep slope on a bike — I'm thrilled with the ride, barely staying on the path, not sure if the brakes will work at the bottom of the hill, and no one to clean the scrapes after a wipeout.

As I search the front of the houses for Tanya's address, a gunmetal gray Dodge Challenger pulls up beside me. At first, I think it's someone looking for the same house, but then I notice the driver is checking me out. I quicken my pace, but the Dodge matches me. When I turn up her driveway, the Dodge speeds up the street.

Tanya Goforth waves from the wrap-around front porch. A few other new barista employees sit on the porch in Adirondack chairs drinking coffee. Tanya, young and energetic, looks like she is in bionic shape with toned arms and legs. Her thick dark ringlet curls hang past her shoulders in a free-flowing mane that has no style, but it dominates her presence, lion-like.

She flashes a high-wattage smile, introduces the staff members and hands me a cup of coffee. "Try this!"

"I'm not really a coffee person."

"You are now."

The toasted-bread-and-barnyard-hay aromatic steam rises into my face. I take a sip. "Wow. That's just awful. This is by far the worst coffee I've ever had. It tastes like garden mulch."

"Exactly," says Tanya.

The staff of eight gather in her kitchen while Tanya buzzes around, maneuvering her various contraptions that resemble beakers in a science lab. Until now, I never realized how complicated making a cup of coffee could be. My parents always made instant coffee and joked about yuppies who pay five dollars for a bitter Starbucks. Tanya pours sample-sizes for us all to try.

"What you have there is liquid gold, my friends. I discovered these organic, shade-grown coffee beans in Honduras. One morning, after a long hot night camping in the rain forest, I awoke to find an elderly couple chatting outside my tent. I couldn't imagine how these old folks had hiked the difficult terrain to the spot where I was camping. They offered me coffee from their thermos. It was humid so I really didn't want it. But I joined them to be polite, and suddenly it felt like sparks shot off in my head. The old woman observed my reaction and said, *Jugo esforzado,* which basically translates to toughy juice."

"Sounds like they slipped you an upper, Ms. Goforth," says a guy standing behind the kitchen island.

"Trust me, that's what it felt like, but it was the coffee. And please, call me Tanya. The elderly couple own a farm where they grow coffee beans. They invited me to hike home with them. That's what inspired me to open a specialty coffee shop here in town."

"What's the shop officially called? Toughy Juice Perks?" the same wisecracker asks.

"Goforth's Daily Grind," she says. "The coffee beans are organic. The family farm has to be one of the most pristine places on the planet. The beans are mold free. You might not realize that mold grows rampant in coffee. The health issues it can create really suck. These are the best beans you could ever find. But it goes beyond that. Mama Hernandez taught me all the secret techniques to make toughy juice and other mind-bending blends."

A staffer raises her hand. "Do you worry that your secret blends will get stolen by other coffee shops?"

Tanya gathers her thick hair into a rubber band. Her smooth caramel face has no lines or marks. "There's no need for secrecy. I intend to share my knowledge just like the Hernandez family shared it with me."

I take a sip and restrain from making a sour face.

"There's a million things you can add to coffee. It's an art form. You can learn how to read energy. I can tweak coffee with different blends to put our customers on a higher path."

"Really?" I blurt and look around for the cream and sugar to kill the taste. This coffee racket is starting to sound like witchcraft to me. "Do you really think we should be in the mood-altering business? I mean, everyone has a bad day. It's part of life, isn't it?"

Tanya says, "I'm not talking about a bad day. I'm talking about energy. We all have these energy bubbles that we encapsulate ourselves in without even realizing it. We trap ourselves with our thoughts and what weighs on our minds and spirits. Sometimes it is a genuine positive energy vibe, but that generally only happens to those who have awareness. It's not that we need to go around like happy idiots all the time. But we should seek higher vibrations. Get in harmony with the universe."

Higher vibrations. Harmonizing with the universe. The superpower of toughy juice. I wonder if any of this will be on the menu board in the coffee shop. If she is serious, then it's possible that her time in Honduras warped her brain. Or maybe she was always funky. I'm tempted to ask her what she did for a job before she became coffee crazed, but a sudden wave of energy hits me and I feel as if I just woke from a nap. "Whoa. What's in this stuff anyway?"

Tanya pours another sample. "Coffee can be used as preventative and restorative medicine. We'll start an energy that flows into the community. If we don't make our personal health our own priority, then the pharmaceutical companies will happily continue to rake in the millions off our chronic illnesses. Do you catch my drift?"

"Groovy," I say, even though I am not sure I catch her drift.

Another staffer sucks up to Tanya and says, "This coffee is incredible. I can't wait to start learning from you."

"I have lists of the various recipe blends for you to memorize. While we infuse our health-conscious coffee into the town, keep in mind that not everyone is into health food. Coming on like gangbusters can be a turnoff."

I ask her, "Who could be against healthy food?"

"Coffee, like any whole food, is *information*. We need to put the right information into our bodies. Various coffee blends, for example, can promote health. When we gathered on the porch, I thought, what will help articulate the speech of your hearts? I tweaked the sample coffee blend with some warming tones. Now I sense higher vibrations in the room. See what I'm saying?"

"I feel the shift." And I do. The tight homesick sensation lodged in between my shoulder blades has lifted. I feel more at ease.

"That's it exactly. A shift. We can change our coffee shop patrons for the better. We can change the vibration of this whole town." Tanya collects our empty cups to rinse them in the sink. "We'll prove how polluted our food industry is, how it poisons us with Frankenfood, addictive pills, gluten, dairy, soy. We'll raise awareness."

"Epic!" I love the way she says *we*, including me in her avant-garde plan. I feel like I'm on a team again.

Tanya hands out pens and notebooks so we can write notes on grinding beans, boiling filtered water, and blending frothy concoctions. I point out that there are no stools or chairs in the kitchen.

"Sitting is the new smoking. You'll be on your feet when you're working. You'll get used to it."

I pull a face, and Tanya surveys me with a quick, wide-eyed sweep. "You, Paige, are frazzled, frustrated and fuhklempt. All Fs. I think you need an F-Bomb."

The group snickers. I feel my face redden. "It's been a while since my last F-Bomb, to be honest."

She tosses a concoction together in the blender. Then she pours the mix into a large ceramic mug.

"Drink," she commands.

I am overwhelmed by the taste of wild spices. All eyes are on me, as if they await a transformation. I take Tanya's cue to focus on my breathing, a four-count inhale through my nose, hold, four-count exhale through my mouth. Sip. Repeat.

"That's good. Breathing is good. How do you feel?"

I take another deep breath and feel heat rising in my chest. "Less F'd, I think."

"Then it's working." She pours the rest of the F-Bomb for the staff to taste. "It's impressive how Paige paused to breath in that moment. Controlled breathing is a wonderful tactic to remain calm. Remember that when the flow of customers gets hectic."

Tanya would make a terrific therapist, unlike the one I had to see when I became a loner post-concussion. The therapist seemed to make a sport out of trying to crack open my feelings. *Paige, it's important for you to see what is on the other side of social avoidance. You are dwelling so deep in this self-created solitude that it will be extremely difficult for you to see that anything else is possible.* When I told the therapist that I prefer reading books to the migraines caused by bright lights and loud noises, I was met with a blank stare. *Yes, but burying yourself in books prevents you from social forwarding.* Then when I told the counselor that I read the Bible for pleasure, she determined that I was a *budding theologian.* I am far from that.

Back in parochial school, long before my concussion, my friends joked that I had headed too many soccer balls. They claimed that all those dings to my forehead had dented my brain. No one, they said, could remember biblical facts the way I did. I can't help it. I have an unusual ability to read the Bible and retain the words as easily as learning the alphabet or multiplication tables.

Bible stories have always fascinated me, not because I'm super religious (just the opposite), but I loved the fantastical tales. It all started with the Old Testament story about Jonah and the Whale when I was nine. It blew my mind. He ignored God's invitation to serve as a prophet and instead left on a sea voyage as a peon. This angered God who raised a great storm to frighten Jonah. A whale swallows Jonah and he spends three days praying until God commands the whale to vomit him out.

In class, when an issue arose about Jonah's backstory, I rattled off the facts: that the story took place in Nineveh, the most populated city in ancient Assyria on the east bank of the Tigris River. That Jonah went to Port Jaffa and sailed to Tarshish. Everyone looked at me. I said, "The whale's mouth represents the synagogue and the pearl on its tongue provided the light so Jonah could see through the whale's eyes. The whale's eyes were the windows in the synagogue. This is the origin of Teshuva, the ability to repent and be forgiven by God."

The teacher's mouth fell open. "Extra credit for Paige."

I loved Greek myths too, but the biblical symbolism really fired me up. I read each Bible story for the hidden meaning, parallels to other stories, secret messages, signs and signals. My classmates thought my Bible knowledge was cool, so they quizzed me like a contestant on *Jeopardy*. In sixth grade they called me Sister Paige and in my junior high yearbook I received *Most Likely to Become a Nun*. That was a joke, due to my well-known tendency to curse and sneak backstage to make out with boys during play practice.

As a result of my passion for reading the Bible, I became fascinated with churches. My father is an architect so he taught me about Gothic cathedrals, Romanesque abbey churches, Renaissance basilicas and more. He could talk for hours about design, art, sculptures, and stained-glass windows while I sat there memorizing it all. I can't remember the lyrics to a Taylor Swift song, but I can tell you the Winchester Cathedral is Norman Gothic and an entablature is made up of the architrave, the frieze and the cornice.

Wherever we went on family vacations or traveled for soccer, my father and I visited the churches and other significant buildings in the area. He would point out gargoyles and mythological characters and we would talk at length about the significance and meaning of such elaborate architectural ornamentation.

After my soccer injury sidelined me, I read *The Lesser Key of Solomon* and learned about the seventy-two demons and their signs. The illustrations of the multi-headed, odd-legged demons were the coolest drawings I had ever seen. The legion of shape-shifting demons had special powers and hell districts to rule. I memorized them all partly because they were too amazing to forget and partly to exercise my brain.

After listening to me rattle off the names of demons, my father asked what I plan to do with all this knowledge of demonology. I had no answer until I was assigned a school project where we had to outline an original business idea. I drew up plans for The Demon Den, a tattoo parlor featuring elaborate inks of the seventy-two demons. The project got an A-plus.

I particularly liked the demon Onoskelis, a beautiful fair-skinned woman with the legs of a mule, because female demons in Solomon's Temple were rare. Plus, most female soccer players have thick legs and sturdy butts like me, so she was an inspiration. I plan, someday, to get a tattoo of Onoskelis on my butt, of course, so my parents never see it.

At some point I realized if I was going to beat the counselor at her own game, I would need to prove I was *social forwarding*. So, I jumped into the college application process with a vengeance, got accepted, landed the library internship, all to prove I was eager to accept the next step toward the other side of social forwarding. The therapist marveled at my resolve to break through what was blocking me.

The reality was that I was stuck in limbo without my teammates and the sport I loved. All that was left were my own demons: persistent headaches, irritability, brain fog, a pudgy physique and depression.

After I finish Tanya's brew, I realize I am super energized and in a great mood. The brain fog that creeps up on me every afternoon is gone. Maybe Tanya's coffee is what I needed all along — not a therapist or downtime in my darkened room.

The wisecracker calls out, "Hey Tanya, what do you call a sad cup of coffee?"

"Beats me."

"A depresso."

It's not that funny, but I start cackling as if Seinfeld were in the kitchen. My cackle is contagious and now the whole staff is cracking up.

Tanya grins and says, "Paige, that laugh leads our good vibe tribe. Love it!"

3. The Town Trip

"I thought you would have submitted your material for the guidebook by now," Ms. Montgomery says as I pass by the reference desk. She sits like an on-duty lifeguard, scanning the depths of her domain.

"Almost finished. Just tweaking a few things."

"Tweaking? I assume you mean fact checking, miss."

"Exactly." In truth, I haven't written a single word. As far as I can tell, North Easton is a sleepy town with a few hole-in-the-wall restaurants, one pub, a brewery, a dentist's office, a nail salon, two banks, one gas station, and a thrift store called One Man's Junk Consignment. Goforth's Daily Grind could be the pulse the town needs. There are plenty of social activities to pursue on the Kew College campus, but I'm not sure what Shovel Townies do for fun besides taking the train to Boston.

Ms. Montgomery's assignment is a pain because it steals time from my academic work. She expects me to write the essay on my own time — another detail not listed in the internship description.

The local museum is called the North Easton Historical Society, but everyone calls it the shovel museum. I don't expect it to resemble the Metropolitan Museum of Art, but still, I'm shocked by the dank corridor stuffed with rusty artifacts, as I come through the entrance.

"Looking for something?" A lanky older gentleman sits in a worn leather armchair behind a desk covered with heaps of papers.

We lock eyes for a moment. I think it's odd that he didn't say, "Welcome to the museum" or "Feel free to look around, let me know if you have any questions." Clearly, I am disturbing him.

"I'm researching the history of North Easton," I tell him. "May I look around?"

"There are seven hundred eighty-three shovels in the collection," he mumbles. "There is over fifteen hundred linear feet of manuscript material."

"Wow, who counted all those shovels?"

He remains silent. His eyes follow me while his face has no upward or downward turn at the corners of his mouth, no raised eyebrow, just a flat expression. His gray hair is scraggly. He rises from his chair and limps over to a display cabinet. He is wearing wool socks with his aged Birkenstock sandals, and his left foot is wrapped in a beige ace bandage.

"The oldest shovels start here. We close in thirty minutes."

"I thought the sign said the museum was open till six," I protest, thinking I need more than a half hour to peruse *fifteen hundred linear feet of material.*

"Committee meeting today."

"No worries. I can come back another time." I look in the cabinet displaying the oldest shovels. I imagine rugged soldiers during the Civil War gripping the handles of these shovels.

"I wasn't worried." He hobbles back toward his desk. The front of his desk has an etched nameplate with block lettering: **HOMER TREADWELL, CURATOR.**

Now that I see his name, I recognize him as the man who came to the library to speak with Ms. Montgomery and Captain Biff after the break-in.

I sense that he wants me to look and leave so he can go to his committee meeting. I linger just to annoy him. In the reflection of the glass display cabinet, I see him peering over his spectacles. It amuses me that there is a "committee" dedicated to the preservation of seven hundred eighty-three shovels. I wonder why the committee doesn't curate seventeen more shovels to make the collection an even eight hundred.

I meander through the shovel sanctuary — oldies propped on pedestals, silver-plated shovels kept in a small display room, rows of glass cases — an immortalization of shovels. Old shovels are like snowflakes, no two are exactly alike.

There are square, round, heart shaped, deep, light, flat, heavy. There are shovels to move dirt, snow, potatoes, dandelions, cotton and coffee beans. Some have handles, some just the pole top. I wonder how many jobs these shovels helped perform.

Prior to the Ames' family designing metal-blade shovels, all American-made shovels were solid wood, I read on a plaque. Oliver Ames took his father's shovel designs and built the factory to mass produce millions of metal-blade shovels.

The rotary-dial phone on his desk rings. "Treadwell here. Yes, I know. I'm on my way now." He hangs up and clears his throat. "Time's up, young lady."

"That was a fast thirty minutes," I say.

"Come see us another time."

"Will do."

As I head back to the library, I hear a low-rumbling sound from an approaching gunmetal Dodge Challenger. Two men in front check me out. The car stops and a third guy gets out from the back seat and flashes a silver badge at me. He has a stocky build and he's wearing a black leather trench coat with the collar popped. A black snapback is pulled low to his eyebrows.

"Paige Moore?" His open coat flutters behind him as he returns the badge to his coat pocket. "I have a few questions regarding the robbery you witnessed at the lodge."

"Okay. But I already talked to the police and Captain Biff."

"Right. We have a few more questions." His black on-duty boots crunch against the street sand. "Did you see any of the faces or see any defining characteristics of the perps?"

I step back. "No. It was too dark. Plus, the windows were tinted so I couldn't see in."

He glances over his shoulder. "And did you see what was stolen?"

I notice he's not writing anything down. "A filing cabinet."

"Do you know what was in the filing cabinet?"

"No. Maybe files?"

"Are you guessing or did you see actual files?"

"I just assumed that's what would be in a filing cabinet. I know they didn't get the compass, at least that's what Captain Biff told Ms. Montgomery."

His intense brooding expression freezes for a moment.

I shrug and continue, "I told all this —"

"We know. We have to double-check. You're a freshman here? What's your major?"

"Library science."

"And you're doing an internship at the Ames Library?"

"Yes. I'm sure these details are in Captain Biff's report if you want to ask him —"

"You don't have a Massachusetts accent."

"I'm from Connecticut. We don't have accents."

"Was anyone with you the night of the robbery?"

"Yes. Hobson was with me."

"Hobson? Is that your boyfriend?"

"I don't have a boyfriend," I say. "Hobson is a springer spaniel."

"Have you discussed the robbery with any of your friends or professors or the coffee store owner?"

I notice he says robbery, not B&E like Captain Biff did. "No, just with the two other cops who asked me questions. And Ms. Montgomery."

"Do you know the name of the other officer who you spoke with?"

"I don't remember." His coat covers his hips so I can't see if he carries a gun, handcuffs or a nightstick. "His name should be in the reports."

"That'll be all for now." His badass long coat flows behind him as he strides back toward the car, jumps in the back and slams the door. The hellcat roar fills the parking lot as the Dodge blasts away. Students passing by on the sidewalk turn to watch the car.

I'm frozen on the sidewalk. He flashed a badge — but I couldn't see if it was campus police, town cop, FBI, special investigation unit? I should have asked for his name and unit. I wonder how he knew so much about me and why this stupid "robbery" is so important to so many different law enforcement officers.

Ms. Montgomery hands me a clipboard and a class roster and sends me out to take attendance in the library parking lot for the bus tour of the town. As the senior citizens shuffle onto the minibus, a black Audi squeals around the corner with rock music thumping out the sunroof. Stoph pulls into the parking spot, drumming his fingers on the steering wheel. He gets out with a coffee in one hand and notebook in the other and hip-checks the car door shut. He struts across the parking lot.

"Miss," he says to me, then hooks his tortoise-framed Wayfarer Clubmasters around his crew neck t-shirt. He gets on the bus and takes a seat near the front. "I'll save this seat for you."

His slick man bun looks fresh as if he just showered and splashed on a musky-scented cologne. My walkie-talkie crackles with Ms. Montgomery's voice. "Come in, intern. Roger that?"

"Copy, we're ready to roll."

"Copy that, on my way."

Ms. Montgomery comes out of the library and power walks with long, determined strides toward the bus and climbs aboard.

"Driver, commence," she orders.

Stoph drums his fingers on the seat. I slide in next to him.

"My head is pounding," he volunteers. "I went to a kegger with some of the guys from my dorm. I'm walking wounded."

"I thought there's just serious studying at Harvard."

Ms. Montgomery fires up the microphone and begins her tour guide spiel. Our little field trip focuses on the historical North Easton architecture. Ms. Montgomery talks about the Ames family shovel company that bankrolled the buildings designed by H.H. Richardson. Ms. Montgomery fawns over H.H. Richardson's architecture like a lovestruck teen. She gets so excited she flaps her arms and looks like a bird trying to take flight. Richardson, she tells us, designed massive stone buildings in a late Victorian style using semi-circular arches that became known as Richardsonian Romanesque.

Stoph elbows me. "That's why my professor made me take this class. He's big into Richardsonian Romanesque."

She shoots a look in Stoph's direction and he turns his attention back to her. "Richardson designed Trinity Church in Boston in 1877. That church is a prime example of architecture from the American Renaissance, a time after the Civil War when the country flourished."

Richardson studied at Harvard, she tells us, which is how the Louisiana native found his way to Cambridge. After Harvard, he studied architecture at the Ecole des Beaux Arts in Paris. He returned to design nearly eighty buildings in America, including churches, libraries, railroad stations, and private homes, several of them in Massachusetts, including Harvard's campus.

"His buildings are visually striking and beautifully proportioned," Ms. Montgomery gushes. "He used forms inspired by early medieval churches, including rounded arches, massive towers, and rugged stone walls, with blocks often laid in bands of contrasting color."

I elbow Stoph. "Have you seen his buildings at Harvard?"

"You can't miss them," he says.

"I'd love to see them."

"You should."

Stoph's response is disappointing — I set up the perfect pitch for him to invite me to his campus. Steady, Paige, I remind myself. Don't be desperate. Sure, he's hot as hell, and I haven't had a boyfriend since Luke, but play it cool. This is what I tell myself but it's difficult to think straight when our knees are touching and I'm breathing in his musky man smell.

"Richardson was a towering figure, physically as well as professionally," Ms. Montgomery continues. "He loved wearing bright yellow vests to dinner parties and his unrestrained appetite probably contributed to the kidney disease that killed him in 1886. He was only forty-seven and at the prime of his architectural career when he died. When you think that his career was cut short, the influence that he had on American architecture is extraordinary!"

North Easton, she tells us, has more Richardson buildings than any small town in America with the Ames Gate Lodge, the Old Colony Railroad Station, the Ames Free Library, and Oakes Ames Memorial Hall. The tour starts with her drive-by narration, then we circle back to go inside some of the buildings.

I lean close to Stoph. "I love all the gargoyles and creatures built into the exterior."

"For me, it's the rooflines and gables."

The driver loops around Shovel Town while Ms. Montgomery works through her introduction to Richardson's buildings. Then he returns to the front of the library and we pile out for the inside tour. The main entrance features a low cavernous arch over the doorway. Ms. Montgomery rubs her hand on the lower portion of the arch, as if for good luck, like kissing the Blarney Stone. "Richardson used this type of arch for the first time in his work and this became one of the most prominent and widely imitated characteristics of his style."

At the bottom of the archway are two funky carvings, an owl and a rooster, that pique my interest. "Does the rooster represent morning and the owl night?" I ask.

She ignores my question to read from her note cards. "Richardson used a diurnal theme here. The rooster is an archaic symbol. The rooster is the symbol of the Creator and is associated with the sun because it crows before dawn. On the rooster's side of the entrance there are sunflowers carved in that section. On this side there is the owl, a bird of night associated with wisdom, books, and the moon. The owl is a patient creature, happy to wait for the right time to strike. On the owl side there are carvings of nightshade flowers."

I've passed this entrance many times but never noticed the owl or rooster. When this library first opened in March 1883, says Ms. Montgomery, there were almost two thousand books that went into circulation, a large number for a town with a population of four thousand during a period when novels were considered frivolous. "One of the first librarians to serve was Mary Lamprey, who worked for fifty years at the Ames Free Library from 1891 until 1944. She resided in the library tower apartment all those years. On her fiftieth anniversary of working here, Mary Lamprey said, 'In a library you deal with the stuff out of which eternity is made; the garnered best that mortals have thought and hoped, preserved in words of force and beauty.'"

Ms. Montgomery pauses to let that linger for a moment and some of the senior citizens nod and hum with appreciation.

Ms. Montgomery leads us to the fireplace, which is adorned by a bronze medallion of Oliver Ames Jr., the former president of the Union Pacific Railroad and co-owner of the Ames Shovel Company.

Out of the corner of my eye I see Homer Treadwell, the museum curator, limping through the side entrance. He has a crate filled with books — and I perk up because they resemble the notebooks with aged oxblood leather covers and bindings that I saw in the cabinet in the archive department. He huffs past us, giving Ms. Montgomery a quick wink and he crisscrosses his pointer fingers in front of the box before he goes down to the archive department.

"Those two are definitely banging," Stoph mutters and I crack up.

When we leave the library, I notice the archive department door is slightly open. In the crack of the door, I see Homer Treadwell staring at me, or maybe that's just my imagination. I wonder what he does in that dungeon.

We follow the sidewalk toward the town hall, next to the library. Standing at the base of the front staircase, Ms. Montgomery announces that Oakes Ames Memorial Hall was built by Richardson from 1879 to 1881, as a gift to the town from the children of Congressman Oakes Ames. The building has the Richardson arches, five of them, with a row of windows set above them and an octagonal tower in the upper right corner. The third-floor dormer stonework features a wreath with sculpted foliage surrounding the letters *OA* — for

Oakes Ames I assume — and the twelve signs of the zodiac. The crowd strolls around the outside of the building, taking pictures and jotting notes. I study the lion on the side of the building, alongside mythological animals clinging to the downspouts, cherub-like faces and scrolling etched leaves embedded in the building's ornamentation. The scrolling reminds me of the hand-drawn artwork in the oxblood notebooks.

Stoph and I wander into the building. There is a spiral staircase leading to the upstairs octagonal tower room. The base of the staircase is shielded by a thick plastic blockade. A sign hangs from the plastic shield that warns: "Closed to the Public."

The rest of the group catches up to us. I ask Ms. Montgomery about the upstairs room. "It is used by no one, miss. The top floor was deemed a fire hazard because it only has one exit, and therefore, we cannot go up there."

"Richardson designed a fire hazard?" says Stoph.

"Need I even point out, young man, that the fire code had different requirements in the 19th Century?"

She shoots a narrow-eyed look of annoyance his way before leading the group into the auditorium to point out the professional stage. Stoph pulls me toward the staircase. He pushes back the barricade and we hurry up the steps. In the attic room, a powder blue ceiling features gold stars and gold rays stretching from an ornate center medallion. On the far end of the ceiling there is a giant human eye painted with meticulous realistic detail. The attic air is musty and hot. There are piles of folded old maps and blueprints on a table in the corner. On the wall hangs a large framed vintage photograph of a bearded man with a protruding belly, his elbow resting on a desk. He is facing the camera, wearing a hooded monk's robe. The engraved nameplate below his photograph says *Henry Hobson Richardson.*

I go back to look at the eye. It's spooky and I feel like it's real.

"Hey," I say. "Check that out."

"What?"

"The eye."

"What about it?"

"I feel like it's watching us. For real."

Stoph steps in front of me, glides his hand to the side of my neck and kisses me.

I pull back.

"Sorry," he says. "It's just — you're so beautiful. I wanted to do that since we met."

"No need to apologize — but I feel really claustrophobic up here. Come on."

I need to get out of the attic. I turn, practically running down the winding staircase. I cross the street, joining the class gathered at the Memorial Cairn Rockery. I'm trembling and out of breath.

Stoph catches up with me. "What's up?"

I try to act cool. "That room freaked me out."

"You sure it wasn't me? I mean, I shouldn't have —"

"No, I liked that part."

Ms. Montgomery tells the class that Richardson worked alongside his friend Frederick Law Olmsted, the American landscape architect. Olmsted created the Rockery in 1882 as a memorial for North Easton's Civil War dead. The memorial looks like a fort with boulders heaped into a long, asymmetric mound across a rustic archway that resembles Richardson's archways.

"These wild plants growing in and around the boulders symbolize peace. It is meant to tame the horrors of war."

"Excuse me," says Stoph. "But this is a really strange memorial. It looks more like a fort."

"Olmsted used his artistic license here," says Ms. Montgomery.

Next stop, the Old Colony Railroad Station. The bus bumps through the train station parking lot. Richardson's design is a simple rectangular block, Ms. Montgomery explains, which had a central lobby and ticket office with separate waiting rooms for men and women. The building is covered by a broad-hipped roof. The eaves project over the sides, supported by plain wooden brackets, with the windows grouped under Richardson-style arches.

"Look at the windows with the wood framing. They are decorated with wood carvings of red snarling wolves' heads," Ms. Montgomery says.

She encourages us to get off the bus to make our own observations. I think they look like dragons, not wolves. "Are they protectors of the train station?"

Ms. Montgomery pretends not to hear me. Watching the dragons, I step on Stoph's foot, and he catches me from falling.

"Oh, thanks."

"That's okay. I have another foot don't worry about it."

Painted in a sharp cardinal-red hue, the wood panels stretch the length of the windows with the beastly heads facing each other, fangs exposed, nostrils flaring, eyes glaring, tongues lashing out. It's such a simple design for an old train station, yet the dragons are intense and dramatic, totally over the top.

Last stop, the Ames Gate Lodge. Here we are treated to Ms. Montgomery's jubilation as she extolls what she calls Richardson's greatest work. "This is the granddaddy of all archways, constructed with boulder walls that span the estate drive. Frank Lloyd Wright once said that the presence of a building is in its roof. Behold the Ames Gate Lodge roof!"

All visitors must pass beneath the archway on the way to the manor house. The gate lodge draws a line where the public world ends and the private innards of the estate begin.

"That long low wing over there —" Ms. Montgomery gestures with her hand — "was an indoor nursery for the gardener. It's an extraordinary piece of architectural athleticism. The rustic stonework unites man with nature, the original American *man cave*. Don't mind the restoration at that end of the building."

The *restoration* is actually the crime scene where the break-in occurred. I turn to see a rotund man wearing a hooded monk's robe, coming up the driveway toward the side of the gate lodge where I witnessed the robbery. He glances back at the school bus, then ducks under the police tape and disappears into the lodge.

"Excuse me, Ms. Montgomery? Does that man live in the lodge?"

Ms. Montgomery spins around so fast her penny loafers barely keep up with her feet. "What man?"

"The man that just went into the building."

"Miss, no one lives in this building."

Stoph whispers, "Are you feeling okay?"

"Yeah, why?"

"No one's been anywhere near the building. I've been staring at it for two minutes."

"Really?"

"Yeah, really."

I study his face to see if he's kidding.

"Too much coffee," I tell him.

But I know a man in a robe went in the building.

4. Stoph

"This is Hobson, the library mascot." The dog bolts from his crate and spins in wild circles while I wrestle with his harness and leash. Stoph reaches down to stroke his ears and help contain him.

"Can his ears get any longer?"

"Do you have a dog?"

"At home. A sloppy Bernese mountain dog named Cash."

"Why Cash? Was he expensive?"

Stoph laughs. "My mother named him after Johnny Cash. She's a big fan. But he's true to his name. He got into her handbag once and chewed up all the money in her wallet — seven hundred bucks."

Hobson pulls onto the lawn and squats to do his business. I pull a bag from the plastic roll to clean up the mess, embarrassed to be handling poop in the presence of this handsome guy.

But Stoph doesn't seem fazed. "Are you a fan of Chinese? I know a decent place not far from here."

"I love dumplings," I say, relieved that I wore my best jeans and fuchsia polo shirt for the tour earlier. "Mind if we stop by my dorm room? I just need to grab my wallet."

"On me," he says nonchalantly. "You can get it next time."

Whoa. First, he invites me out, then he indicates a follow-up date. I could get used to this. I need to breathe, telling myself it's just a quick dinner, no big deal.

Stoph turns the volume down when I get into the passenger seat. "What's your roommate like?" he asks as we zip through town.

"She never showed up. I'm on my own. What about you?"

"Chase from Oregon. Great guy. I'm in a two-room suite."

"What'd you think of the tour?"

"Loved the gargoyles and mythical creatures," he says. "Did you see the panther on the downspout? My professor told me to pay close attention to the rooflines and ornamentation. Architects don't design like that anymore. Richardson probably saw all those gargoyles when he studied in Europe and figured he'd try it back here."

"I could look at gargoyles all day," I say.

"I would love to design something using wacky creatures like that. Who knows, maybe I will."

The Chinese restaurant has patio seating out front. It is warm, so we take a table in the corner. Stoph orders a pu-pu platter for two. "Thanks for coming out with me. I needed a break tonight. I got tapped by the Porcellian Club and the punch process is about to start."

"Porcellian Club?"

"The oldest and most prestigious final club at Harvard. It's pretty archaic."

"Is it like a frat?"

"Not exactly. Candidates receive wax-sealed invitations under their doors in the middle of the night. The group gets whittled down until there are only ten left. The punch process lasts until November, right around the Harvard-Yale football game."

"Punch process? Is that like hazing? Midnight streaking across the campus?"

"Not exactly. It's an entire semester of being judged for everything I do and say with hopes that I make the cut."

"And you're into all that?"

"Definitely. I'm pretty stoked I made the invitation list. The guys who aren't selected for the Porcellian Club usually go for the Fly Club, the Fox Club, Spee Club or Delphic Club," he explains. "The Porcellian has an incredible list of former members, including Teddy Roosevelt and our man H.H. Richardson. Richardson's connections with the

Porcellian Club won him the bid to design Trinity Church in Boston."

"I get it. Connections," I say. "The good-old-boy network."

"You got it, times about a thousand."

"Richardson was a funky dude. Did you see him in that photo wearing a monk's robe?"

"Maybe he was religious." Stoph spears the last dumpling with his chopstick.

"Maybe he was kinky. What's the deal with the attic room? The Cyclops eye on the ceiling really freaked me out."

"I noticed. Memorial Hall was where the local Freemasons met back in the day."

"Freemason. That's like the Elk Club, right?"

Stoph flashes me one of his killer smiles, and I melt a little bit. He explains that the Freemasons go back to the stone masons of the 14th Century. "It's the world's oldest and largest fraternity."

"Richardson clearly liked his good-old-boys' clubs."

"For sure, but Porcellian is by far the most prestigious."

I frown. "So, at Harvard, are there any clubs for women?"

"A few, the Spees Club, for one." His eyes are a soft ocean blue that I can't stop looking into. "I admit, it's some serious sexist shit. But if I get in, I'm hoping to make my feelings known on that issue. Change the system from within."

"Heard that one before, Stoph."

"Well, to start, I'm going to need a date for a semi-formal. Would you like to go with me?"

"When is it?"

"Saturday. At Stonehurst. I'll pick you up."

I stop breathing for a few seconds and narrow my eyes, my version of making him sweat it out. Then I blurt, "Sure. Love to. I'll clear my social calendar. Semi-formal, you say?"

"I'm going to rock my black tux."

Stoph works his chopsticks like a ninja. To make conversation as he gorges, I tell him about the break-in at the lodge. "Dudes dressed all in black," I conclude, "Like CIA phantoms."

"I sorta doubt they were CIA, sounds more like crackheads."

"They took a filing cabinet, of all things."

"Maybe it was a safe," he says.

"No. Clearly, a filing cabinet. What's strange is this other cop — not with the town police — questioned me, too."

He shrugs. "Probably just following up. The building is on the historical landmark list, so maybe that makes it some kind of state or federal crime."

Stoph slides a fortune cookie across the table. I crack the cookie in half, pop it in my mouth and pull the paper ribbon from the other half: "A friend is a present you give yourself," I read.

"In bed," he adds.

"What?" I giggle.

"Haven't you played the *in-bed* fortune cookie game? Add the words *in bed* to the end of the fortune —"

"I do now."

A woman steps under the canopy with a dog on a leash. The hostess hands her a takeout order. I see it is Ms. Montgomery. Her eyes pop with surprise when she sees us.

"Miss," she says, nods at Stoph and tugs on Hobson's leash.

Stoph peels the wrapper from his cookie, then flips the cookie in the air toward the dog. Hobson snatches it midair and gulps it down along with the unread paper fortune still tucked inside.

Dogs, I suppose, deserve fortunes, too.

5. Strange Brew

I meet Tanya at her house for barista training. She's rummaging through some boxes in her walk-in pantry, organizing her spices, coffee beans, cocoa, oil, ghee, herbs and coconut oils. There's a hand-painted peace sign on the pantry wall that says *Make Coffee, Not War*.

"I memorized all the special blends," I tell her.

"Perfect. We're just waiting on the delivery of the shipping container. I had it retro-fitted into a movable coffee shop. I'm starting small with a forty-foot container, then I'll commit to bricks-and-mortar once it takes off," she says.

"A shipping container, very cool."

"Repurpose with a purpose," she says. "I've settled on twenty-five coffee blends to get the menu started."

I help her carry a few boxes out to her Jeep parked behind the house. Her backyard is hedged with tall green holly shrubs. There's a bird feeder, a bird bath and Adirondack chairs circled around a small fire pit. A small brown shed is at the end of the driveway with a two-toned Volkswagen hippie van parked next to it. I recognize the van from her website photo.

"Nice ride," I say.

"Nothing like a Jeep to handle our winters."

"I meant the VW van over there."

"Been on some great camping trips in the Peace Train."

"I bet. Why did you name it the Peace Train?"

"It's my favorite Cat Stevens song."

"I'll be sure to listen to it."

Back inside the house, Tanya demonstrates her coffee-making techniques. She has the ingredients and equipment set out on the kitchen island.

"Are there any non-coffee options?"

She pulls her hair back with a rubber band. "You bet. Tea blends. Kombucha. Goat's milk kefir. Bone broth with healing blends that are great for gut health."

She steps to the stove and removes the lid on the stainless-steel pot, simmering with chicken bones, apple cider vinegar, garlic, onion. She turns the contents with a wooden spoon, releasing a swirl of pungent steam. She ladles the broth into a ceramic bowl, adds fresh lemon and grated turmeric, and hands it to me to try.

"Ah," I hedge. "I ate earlier."

"Be brave, Paige. It's an acquired taste, but it's super healthy. It'll turbo-charge your immune system."

As Tanya talks about her all-organic policy, I obsess about Stoph. He's easy to talk to and he's not conceited. I don't want to turn him off the way I managed my high school boyfriend after the concussion. I should have kissed Stoph back instead of bolting from the attic. But things felt like they were closing in on me. My head feels okay lately, a slight migraine now and then, but why was I sensing wacky things on the field trip like seeing the man in the robe?

The blender whir snaps my attention back to Tanya. She sets a shot glass of tobacco colored liquid in front of me. "I should name this the Pensive Paige Protocol — to release what's trapped inside your head right now."

"Ah, sorry. I forgot you're a mind reader." I take a sip. It tastes like pencil shavings.

"No. It's a shot. One swig, so you don't really taste it. It's way too earthy for sipping."

I chug it and swallow hard. Cough syrup. Tanya rinses the blender and puts it back on the base. She shows me how to grate turmeric, press garlic and dash lemon zest. It doesn't take long before I sense an inner calm that's been missing since I started the semester. All at once, I feel settled.

"Wow," I say. "That stuff really works."

"Glad to hear it."

"You learned all this in Honduras?"

She nods. "And more. Would you like to try a guided meditation? You seem more relaxed now."

"What's that?"

"You follow my voice into a state of relaxed concentration. It's a great stress buster," she says.

"Sure. I'm game."

I follow her downstairs to an aloe-colored zen den with round meditation cushions on the floor and a plush chaise lounge chair. Beaded curtains cover the windows. Soft paper lanterns dangle from the ceiling and in the corner a chair swing hangs from a hook in the ceiling. She lights candles and dims the overhead lights.

"Damn, Tanya. You're a total neo-hippie."

"I take that as a compliment." She gestures for me to sit on a floor cushion.

I settle down and say, "Something weird happened today."

She blows out the match she just used to light a candle. "Tell me."

I tell her about the robed man at the lodge. "And when I went into the attic at Memorial Hall, I freaked out. It felt haunted. I felt someone watching me. I totally panicked and ran out of there."

She pauses for a moment. "Doesn't sound like stress to me. Sounds like you're tapping into your intuitive powers, Paige. You sense things that others are blind to. It's not unusual for some enlightened people to know things or see things that others don't."

"Is it? It kind of feels like I'm losing my mind."

A salt rock lamp glows in the far corner. She lights an incense stick that billows a fragrant scent. "It's dragon's blood. It takes the negativity out of the room."

I didn't realize there was any negativity in the room. Tanya adjusts her cushion on the floor across from me. She sits in lotus position with her eyes closed. She chants a low mantra: "Your shadow will only give you what you are ready for. The technology is hardwired within you to learn how to live a more aware life. You're already on the path."

"What are you talking about?"

The incense smoke causes a pounding between my head and ear drums. She hands me a small wooden cup, and I chug it. More tea.

"What is this stuff?" More garden mulch I think.

"Relaxation herbs. Turn off your mind, Paige."

"How?"

"Close your eyes. When you initially take flight, you might have a sensation that you're dying, melting or losing your mind. Just go with it. If you see a door, open it. If you see a staircase, climb it. If you meet a creature, move toward it. If you encounter another person, start a conversation. Don't be afraid."

I shift on the cushion to settle in, close my eyes and follow Tanya's soothing, hypnotic voice. There is a gradual shift in the room, or maybe the shift is within me. My feet start tingling.

"Tanya...what was in that tea?"

"Shhhh. You're doing great. Stay focused."

Then my feet heat up and melt from my legs like wax dripping from a candle. Tanya morphs into a man in a brown monk's robe. He waves scrolls of papers and unfurls the papers on a desk.

I slither my body like a snake toward him. He lifts my snake body to drape across his shoulders. My head hangs low, giving me a clear view of his sketches, which are architect renderings.

I squint to focus, but the drawings remain blurry, as if water-splotched. The ink pools swirl. Then three-dimensional structures rise from the pages like children's blocks. I see buildings that form a small town. The library, town hall, train station, lodge and the rock memorial — Shovel Town.

The length of my body shortens, and I feel pin pricks jabbing at my skin like a sewing needle. Feathers force their way through the pin holes until my body is completely covered. My arms flap like wings until I trust myself to take flight, darting around the room, weightless and joyful. A window ledge offers me a safe landing pad where I stop to briefly rest before the ledge softens into pages of old books. I sink deeper into the pages before I flap my wings to fly out.

I see my reflection in the window. I am an owl. I feel the room shift again, and when the window slides open, I launch my feathered body into thin air to take flight into the open night sky. I soar through the stars and look down at Shovel Town. My wings slice through the powdery smoke puffs until I hear Tanya's voice encouraging me to return. I land back in the room, the air reeking of dragon's blood incense.

"Holy crap, Tanya. That was trippy!"

"That's enough for tonight," she says and hands me a glass of water. "You did great. A natural."

A chalk texture is pasted to the roof of my mouth so I guzzle the water. "This isn't spiked with anything is it? Magic mushrooms?"

Tanya cracks a smile. "I don't *spike* things, Paige. I'm a professional herbalist so I know how to open a person's channels. You opened a lot quicker than anyone I've ever seen. I'm impressed."

"Did I have a choice? It just happened."

"Most of my clients put up walls, remain closed off —"

"Closed off to what?"

She sweeps up the incense ashes with her hands. "Closed off to what the universe has to offer. You'll feel tired for a bit."

"I'm exhausted."

We walk out to the front porch. "Go take a nap. You'll feel like a whole new person when you wake up."

"I was fine with the old me."

She winks. "Just wait. You'll see."

6. The Makeover

Melissa and Jill give my room the once-over. "Slide the beds together, make it a king size," says Melissa. "We can pick up sheets and a king-size comforter while we're out schwandering."

"What's schwandering?" I ask.

"Shopping and wandering at the same time. It's the only way to find cool things," she explains.

We head out. Melissa and Jill know the funkiest places to go poke around for dorm décor. The sun shines through the open sunroof in Melissa's compact green Toyota. We stop to fill up her tank.

"Need some gas money?" I offer.

She swipes her credit card without even looking at the amount. "All set. My dad pays my credit card bills."

I like her bed idea, but I don't have extra money to spend on more sheets and blankets — no one is covering my credit card bills. We park on the street, feed the meter, and stroll toward an old bookstore that sells vinyl, posters, greeting cards and an impressive selection of books. I don't care about sheets — I'd rather drop a hundred bucks on used books.

"The most happening posters are over here," Jill says and I follow her to flip through the poster rack. "This one could work for your room."

It's a print of Frida Kahlo, holding a cigarette in one hand, a cup of coffee in the other in front of her bare breast. The artist used brilliant reds, greens and yellows with birds and a blooming floral arrangement in Kahlo's hair.

"Score!" I say.

"You like it?"

"It's relevant, too. I got a job at the coffee shop opening in town. I've already started barista training."

"Then it's a must!" Jill finds a copy of the poster rolled up in plastic and hands it to me.

We continue to flip through the poster rack and arrive at large posters of individual playing cards. Melissa stops to see what we're looking at and says, "Are you thinking what I'm thinking?"

Jill grins. "The joker? For Paige's room?"

"Exactly." Melissa high-fives us.

I can't interpret their hidden language. "I don't get it. What's with the joker card?"

"Jill and I think you're hilarious. You should get the joker card. It's so you. It has another meaning, but we'll tell you later."

"I'll get it. But I didn't realize I was hilarious."

Melissa says, "Are you kidding? Your facial expressions alone crack us up."

Jill bops her head side-to-side to imitate my mannerisms and says, "Your epic eyerolls and head tilts are priceless. You don't even have to say anything. I just look at you and I crack up."

I buy the posters and we head outside. I could spend the rest of the day in the bookstore, but we're on a mission. There's a small antique store that we need to check out. "You never know what's hidden in these little shops. Let's have a looksee," Melissa says leading us up the front walkway.

I'm not really into musty smelling distressed furniture or creepy porcelain-faced dolls for my dorm décor. Melissa pulls a large weathered farm stand sign from the shelf with brown block letters that reads: *Fresh Eggs.*

"This sign, straight up over your bed…classic!"

I take the sign straight to the cash register because we all think it's funny and it only costs five bucks. We leave the store, giddy from the find, and pass a diner on the corner.

"Anyone hungry?" I ask them.

We stop for burgers and fries. They sit on the same side of the booth while my posters and egg sign take up half the seat next to me. "Need some advice."

"Dating advice, fashion advice or miscellaneous?" Jill asks.

"The first two. I have a date to a semi-formal. What should I wear?"

Melissa pops her eyes. "Where is this alleged semi-formal? I didn't hear about one."

I tell them about Stoph and mention his Harvard social club. Melissa's head nearly spins off her shoulders. "Which final club? Did he say?"

"Porcellian."

"Holy shit! Are you fucking kidding me? I mean, only the *one percent* get punched for that club. I'd give anything to snag one of those spoiled-rotten Mr. Moneybags."

"Settle down, forty-niner," says Jill. "What kind of car does he drive?"

"A slick Audi convertible. Other than that, he seems like a regular guy."

"And you're dating him?" Melissa crosses her arms in front of her chest. "How did you meet him?"

"Library internship."

"Let me guess — he's a dorky Asian dude with his nose jammed in a book twenty-four-seven." She catches herself and adds, "Sorry Jill, no offense."

Jill, who is half Asian, swats Melissa's arm. "As if I'd ever date a dorky Asian guy."

"He's — regular American. Tall, good looking, great hair, funny."

"Did you go down on him in the library? Is that why he asked you out?"

"We kissed."

Melissa cackles. "Oh my God, you're so junior high. Look, wear your best LBD. That's what everyone will wear."

I didn't bring an LBD to college because I don't even know what it is. "I left it at home."

When the waitress returns with the bill, Melissa asks her if there's a woman's boutique in town that sells Yves Saint Laurent or Tom Ford.

"Ah, not really. You'd need to hit the mall for that."

The mall is thirty minutes in the opposite direction. Melissa proposes plan-B. "Come back to our room. Between our closets we can tart you up for your semi."

"Really?"

"But under one condish. You have to introduce us to his Harvard friends."

"Deal."

On the ride back toward North Easton, Melissa stops off at Target. "If you're dating a Harvard hunk, you'll be needing king-size sheets."

We hit the home goods section where I'm relieved to find a half-price sale event on bedding. We settle on solid light blue sheets with a blue-and-white paisley comforter set.

"Grab three extra pillows," Jill says.

Melissa glances at her. "Planning a gang bang?"

"It's always good to have options."

Melissa tosses a set of string lights in the shopping cart while I find the cheapest pillows on sale. At the check-out counter I cringe at $86 total; I use my credit card and hope that the tips add up fast at the coffee shop.

Back at the dorm they help me rearrange the dressers and desks to maximize the space. Jill takes the sheets from the plastic packaging and unfolds the fitted sheet. "Not the highest thread count, but these are decent. Normally, I'd wash the sheets first, but no biggie. You'll have to wash them anyway when you break them in after the semi-formal."

"Hold the bed. I'll stand on the mattress so I can hang the egg sign." Melissa has a plastic adhesive hook that she centers over the bed to position the sign. "This sign kills me."

While Jill and I make the bed, Melissa drapes the white string lights and plugs them in. Frida Kahlo hangs above my desk while the joker card is centered on the main wall. "I'm glad we got the joker in blue. It all matches. You two are pros!"

"It's been said before," Melissa says. "Ready for us to tag-team your makeover?"

"You mean now? I've got some studying —"

"Aren't you dying to suss out your look for the semi? If it were me, I'd be contacting my personal shopper at Bloomingdales."

We go down to room 417. They have matching candy-stripe pink comforters, monogrammed throw pillows, and lace curtains in the same shade of pink. Giant playing card posters deck their walls — the jack, queen and king of hearts above one bed, four aces above the other.

"Love the playing card motif," I say.

"That's why we got you the joker. You are part of our deck now," Jill says.

"Joker's wild!"

Melissa pulls her LBD — little black dress — from her super-organized closet. The dress is protected in plastic wrap from the dry cleaners. "See if this works. It's a tad roomy on me so it should fit you fine. But listen: I want this back dry cleaned. Deal? No sweaty pits, okay?"

"Deal," I say, already sweating about whether this will fit or not.

A ceiling tapestry separates the room. She unties the tapestry and it drops down. I step behind the curtain to try on the dress, praying that it's not too tight. Melissa zips up the back and guides me in front of the full-length mirror on the back of the door. Not only does the dress fit, but I look good.

"Not bad," she says, admiringly. "You've got nice legs. Look at the definition in your calves."

"Soccer," I tell her.

"I'd go with basic black pumps," she says. "Wait. Don't tell me you didn't bring dress shoes? What size are you?"

I tell her eight and she has pumps that are a half size smaller. She tosses them to me from her closet and I slip them on. Tight, but I can make them work. Melissa tells me to spin around.

"You're butt looks good in this dress, a tad big, but if you pick up some Spanx undies it should tighten things up, especially in the gut."

"I'll get right on it."

"I'll throw in my pearls, too, but don't forget our deal — we want Harvard dates."

"If I can."

Melissa strokes the pearls. "Just say you'll try."

"I will."

Now that I think about it, I wonder why Stoph asked me to the semi-formal when there are plenty of attractive options like Jill and Melissa. In high school my friends called me Plain Jane because I always dressed in sweats or jeans. After the concussion, I went from being super toned to mush, even a couch potato. As I check my look in the mirror, I can see that I am attractive when I wear flattering clothes. I think it's time to start running again to get back into shape.

Melissa takes her cosmetic box from her dorm-issued dresser and sits me in her desk chair in front of the mirror. She tells me to look up while she strokes mascara on my eyelashes. She moves in with a clamp to curl the lashes.

"Your lashes with this Givenchy Noir Couture mascara — illegal!"

She pulls the cap off a teal pencil to run a thin line under my lower eyeline. She pours liquid foundation into her palm and uses her fingers to apply it in circular sweeps around my face. The concealer dabs away a blemish near my chin. She pops open a compact and uses a thick brush to swipe blush upward on my cheek bones.

"Pucker up," she says and adds the pink lip gloss to finish the trial makeover.

She spins the magnifying mirror toward me and says, "Simple elegance. Earthy charm. What do you think?"

Wham, bam, glam! In less than thirty minutes, Melissa and Jill have transformed me into a Cosmo Covergirl. "Wow. A whole new me."

"You look totally curvaceous," Jill adds.

Melissa works her round hairbrush in long strokes, collecting my hair into her free hand, then twists it around to gather it high on my head. She pulls a few strands free from the knot and uses a curling iron to create waves. "You need some highlights. You obviously spend zero time in the sun. We'll force some natural looking sun streaks to brighten up your blonde. I like your hair in an up-do. You need to get your eyebrows shaped up, too."

I stand in front of the full-length mirror. The heels and updo bump me up to 5-foot-10, at least, and the dress fits like a second sexier skin. Melissa fastens the pearls. "Perfect look to hang with the Porcellian boys, those dickwad one-percenters. You'll knock them on their asses."

Now I just need to practice walking in the pumps, and then I should be ready to hobnob with the elite.

7. Vintage Books

I glance at the owl in the library entrance, remembering how I grew wings during Tanya's guided meditation session and took a freedom flight, releasing the brain fog that has been stuck with me since the great soccer head clunk. I feel so much better that I start jogging again. I join Melissa and Jill in the cafeteria every evening for dinner. My laugh has returned in full force, a loud cackle that I didn't even realize was missing till now.

I find a note left on the front desk for me: *Took Hobson to the vet. DIARRHEA ALL NIGHT! Put away the returns. Focus on writing usable material for the guidebook. Ms. M.*

I worry that the canine-calming drops I gave him from Tanya's kitchen caused his sick stomach. I can't tell Ms. Montgomery I altered his water because she would freak. I also worry the fortune cookie that Stoph tossed to Hobson might have added to his digestive distress.

I very much prefer when Ms. Montgomery isn't around, so I can work in solitude without her hawk eyes watching my every move. There aren't too many returns, so I find a quiet spot to hunker down to write some *usable material* for Ms. Montgomery's North Easton guidebook.

The library is empty. I grab the keys from Ms. Montgomery's desk drawer and slink down to the archive department. I peruse the shelves looking for books on the history of North Easton. There is a locked cabinet near the shovel desk. I flip through the key ring, trying the old brass keys. After four or five attempts, the door clicks open. Inside I find a collection of vintage oxblood leather-bound notebooks.

I flip through the notebooks filled with sketched scrolling braid patterns, Celtic knots and heads of mythological animals. The back of each notebook is stamped with embossed letters *Property of AOD*. The cracked binder of an old beige book catches my eye: *Richardson's Monitor of Free-Masonry*. The title page reads: *This book is a practical guide to the ceremonies in all the degrees conferred in Masonic Lodges, Chapters, Encampments, Explaining the Signs, Tokens, Grips and Giving All the Words, Passwords, Sacred Words, Oaths and Hieroglyphics Used by Masons.* A sketched picture of a coffin with a star on the lid breaks up the text. The book is written by Jabez Richardson, A.M. published in New York in 1860.

I sense a pattern — Freemasons — the same fraternal organization Stoph mentioned at the Chinese restaurant. I stuff the book in the waist of my pants. I hustle upstairs, drop the keys back in her drawer and settle into a private corner of the library. I read through the opening chapter, which discusses being a first-degree apprentice of the Freemasons. Guarded meetings take place on an upper level of a building that the Freemasons prepare and furnish to replicate King Solomon's Temple.

The book explains the various levels of Freemasonry, steeped in mystery and secrecy for over six hundred years, revealing spiritual paths taken by inductees as they move through each initiated degree of enlightenment. The degrees (Mark Master, Past Master, Most Excellent Master, and the Royal Arch) have rituals, arcane symbols and mystical doctrines. There is a lengthy list of gestures, terms and special tools used in the ceremonial formalities of the meetings.

I search the author's name and find no information about Jabez Richardson. I wonder if H.H. Richardson wrote this book under a pen name and whether he took a biblical name — Jabez — when he joined the Freemasons. The A.M. postnominal letters stand for Accepted Mason. I conclude that it's too much of a coincidence that the author's name is Richardson and the book was published in New York during Richardson's prime.

I read through the first twenty pages until I reach the part where a senior warden discusses that all lodges are true representations of King Solomon's Temple — situated north of the ecliptic, the sun and the moon, darting their rays from the south, no light was to be expected from the north. Freemasons called the north a place of darkness.

The ecliptic, or zodiac, is the path of the sun as seen from earth, defining which constellations are part of the zodiac. Then it hits me. I wonder if Richardson, an architect and Freemason, may have attempted to build *a true representation of King Solomon's Temple*. One of the towers on Memorial Hall has all of the zodiac signs. The owl and the rooster outside the library entrance are signs for the sun and the moon.

I track down a copy of the Bible and find the story of Jabez in Chronicles. The name Jabez translates to *great pain* — his mother named him Jabez after a difficult birth. The Jabez prayer says: *Bless me and enlarge my territory! Let your hand be with me, and keep me from the evil one.*

I flip to the book of Kings to read about Solomon's Temple. King David marries Bathsheba after he sees her bathing on the roof and falls in love with her. They have a son, Solomon, who becomes the king. King Solomon builds his temple. The Bible lists the specific measurements of the temple: sixty cubits long by twenty cubits wide by thirty cubits high. The inner hall was forty cubits long. The holy of holies, the room that held the ark of the covenant, was twenty-by-twenty-by-twenty cubits. A Hebrew long cubit is an ancient measurement approximately equal to the length of a forearm, about twenty inches.

Yes, I conclude: it makes sense that Richardson used the dimensions to build his own Solomon's Temple in North Easton. Excited, I decide I need to run this idea past Stoph.

From the entranceway, Ms. Montgomery commands Hobson to sit, so I close the Bible and hide the Freemason book in my backpack. I pick up a stack of books to make myself look busy.

"How's Hobson?" I ask.

She hangs his leash on a hook and says, "His loose bowels are due to dietary indiscretions. Would you know anything about that, miss?"

"Um..."

"I thought so."

She returns to her desk, signaling that I have been dismissed.

Later, when I'm about to leave for the night, I notice the Archive Department door ajar. Treadwell must have gone down there and I hadn't noticed. I hear Ms. Montgomery's voice.

"Treadwell, damn it. You scare the heart out of me the way you skulk around here."

"I don't skulk," Treadwell snaps at her. "Why was this cabinet unlocked and the door left open?"

"I certainly didn't unlock it. You must have done it and forgotten about it."

"Absolutely not! I'm not careless like that. Is there anyone who would come down here for any reason? One of your interns?"

"Treadwell, relax. My intern is a harmless college kid. She looks like she's half asleep most of the time. She is, in essence, my dog walker."

He lowers his voice, but it is deep and resonant. "Please allow this incident to serve as a gentle reminder, my dear, that no one is allowed in the archive department unattended. I have private research filed away. After the B&E at the lodge, we must be more vigilant."

"Incident?" Ms. Montgomery raises her voice. "A cabinet you leave unlocked is an incident? I expect you'll be taking this up with the other members? Perhaps I should report your latest gaffe! Wouldn't the Order love to hear about your own carelessness?"

"I may have misused the word *incident*. Forgive me. I should be more careful around a grammarian. I'm working on a great amount of new research. I am close to a breakthrough, but since the robbery —"

"Listen, Treadwell, I have been waiting a long time for you to have a *breakthrough*. It will be a miracle the day that happens. Your research is in disorganized heaps!"

He fires back at her. "I have had multiple breakthroughs! My research is what has kept us going. I cannot afford any further disruptions. Since the robbery, I feel like I am starting from scratch."

"Maybe it's time we take this to a higher authority. We need a proper investigation. Yes, Captain Biff is investigating, but maybe we should call the FBI —"

"The FBI? Listen to yourself. We are in good hands with Captain Biff. We are not contacting higher authorities —"

My knees start trembling from standing on the top step. I slide my foot to try to rebalance, but my sneaker makes a dragging sound.

"Who's there?" Treadwell shouts.

I jump up the top step to get to the main level of the library. "Ms. Montgomery? Are you down there? I just finished up and I'm going to leave now."

"Yes. That's fine," she calls.

I grab my backpack and denim jacket and rush out the side entrance. In the parking lot a police cruiser is shining a strobe light across the back gardens, illuminating the garden water fountain. Captain Biff steps out.

"Moore!" He calls, sounding like my old soccer coach.

"Yes?" I say, waiting for him to come closer.

"About that SUV you saw at the lodge." He snaps out his pocket notebook. "Can you describe it for me again? Try to remember everything."

"Black, but more specifically, it was definitely murdered-out in a matte black."

"Murdered-out?"

"You know, like after-market detailing. It had wheels with the y-shaped spoke design. All pimped-out. Nothing glossy, everything flat black, even the spokes."

He flips back through his pages to review notes from our first interview. "You said the SUV was a Land Rover? Are you sure it was a Land Rover?"

"Positive. It said *Defender* across the front hood right above the oversized black grill. It was no doubt a Land Rover Defender with black tinted windows all around."

"Did you see the back of the SUV?"

"I caught a glimpse when they swung the door open. It had a spare tire attached to the back door. The tire said *Defender* as well. It happened so fast, sorry for being a lame eyewitness. I feel dumb that I don't have more details for all the various cops asking me questions."

"Various cops?"

"The one who asked me questions the other day. Plainclothes cop in a Dodge. Two other cops were in the car, but only one got out, flashed his badge and asked me questions."

"Can you describe him?"

I run through the details: black leather trench coat, black on-duty boots, stocky build, snapback hat, no note pad.

"And what department was he with?"

"Yours?"

"What did the badge say?"

"Dunno."

"Moving forward, I am the only law enforcement official you should be communicating with. I don't think the person you described is an officer. Please call me if that happens again."

"Sure thing."

"Have a good evening."

I'm not far from the library when I hear Stoph's thumping music coming from two blocks away. The Audi cruises around the corner and he pulls over and slides the window down. His smile makes my day.

"Hop in."

"Everything alright?" I say, bending into the leather bucket seat.

He pushes the button to close the sunroof. "Porcellian Club. You know that punch thing I was telling you about? The semi-formal?"

He's wearing pressed dress slacks, no socks, and a white Oxford shirt. There's a striped tie and blue blazer tossed on the back seat. His beef-rolled loafer taps the gas pedal.

"Did they smack your ass with paddles and make you sit on an ice block?"

He chuckles. "Something like that. We're not allowed to talk about what goes on. Top-secret society. But I got something for you."

"Really?" I peak into the back seat, but there's only his tie and jacket.

He parks outside my dorm. He pops the trunk and hurries to the back of the car ahead of me. "Close your eyes," he says, rustling some bags. "Okay, now."

I open my eyes to see an oversized stuffed fluffy purple beanbag chair. He looks ridiculous holding this squishy monstrosity. I cover my mouth from the surprise. "Oh, my God. I had one in my bedroom when I was nine."

"It might look silly, but take it from a sophomore, this is the most essential piece of dorm furniture you'll ever need. Can you grab that other bag for me?"

We trudge up the stairs to the fourth floor. I key open my door and he tosses the bean bag in the corner and plops onto it. I can't help but laugh at him lounging in the cushion. I'm still holding the bag from his trunk and he tells me to open it. There's a teal blue jewelry box with a white ribbon bow.

"What's this?"

"Open it."

Inside the velvet-lined box is a pearl bracelet. "Stoph, this is beautiful."

He takes my hand to pull me into the beanbag chair with him. He fastens the bracelet to my wrist. "Do you like it?"

"Love it —"

I tense up. I haven't let anyone get this close since my high school boyfriend. I recall my therapist telling me that I need to let people back in. Well, here it is, Stoph has officially broken through my buffer zone. He reaches his arm behind my shoulders and pulls me closer to him. He's wearing that musky cologne again and I like it. He gazes into my eyes, which I don't mind because I like looking into his eyes. He leans closer to me and presses his lips to mine. My heart pounds so hard I'm positive he can hear it. After a few minutes of kissing, he pulls away and says, "Are you psyched for the semi-formal?"

"Definitely. I'll wear my new bracelet. Anything special I need to know?"

"I'm all you need to know."

8. Goforth's Daily Grind

Tanya's to-do lists scatter the kitchen like confetti at a ticker tape parade. We are packing the last few boxes while awaiting the phone call from the trucker delivering the container. Since the town's approval to set-up the temporary coffee shop behind Ames Free Library, Tanya's been operating in overdrive.

"Are we taking all three blenders?" I ask.

"Just pack two. Use extra bubble wrap on the Vitamix." She combs the shelves of her walk-in pantry for pumpkin spice. She rubs her temples and sighs. "Paige, I want you to design the menu. Name the beverages to show some unity with the library. That's your domain."

"Like what?"

"Think, woman! Name the beverages after American writers. The Edgar Allan Poe Raven for a dark roast, or the Emily Dickinson *I taste a coffee never brewed.*"

"But it's: *I taste a liquor never brewed*—"

"Have you never heard the phrase poetic license?"

"How about Stephen King's Carrie Americano and Ernest Hemingway's The Sun Also Rises Espresso?"

Tanya tosses a pad and pen to me. "Jot it down."

I scribble away. "Let's name the bone broths as well. How about John Updike Uptake, Kurt Vonnegut Gut Healer and the Harriet Beecher Stowaway?"

She makes herself a reishi blend and glances at the clock on the wall.

I say, "How about some architects too? We are, after all, surrounded by great architecture. I bet an H.H. Richardson roast would be a big seller."

"You have a thing for him."

"If you checked out the detail in his buildings you would have a thing for him, too."

"I'll add that to my to-do list."

"Maybe we could sell books, too," I say.

"Great minds, as they say." She nods toward some boxes. "The hardcovers and bindings will look perfect tied into short stacks to hang from the ceiling. Just a few to create a literary vibe."

She demonstrates hot-gluing the books together in stacks of three. Then she uses a narrow drill bit to puncture a small hole through the center of the books. She threads fishing line through the drilled hole to hang the stack from a ceiling hook.

She takes a quick phone call. "The trucker will be at the library in twenty minutes. Let's roll."

We load a few boxes in her Jeep and take off. It's not long before the truck eases to a stop in front of the library.

"Where do you want this, lady?"

Tanya points toward the garden fountain. The container gets lowered as if it were made of precious sea glass, then maneuvered toward the back garden.

A town official is on hand to witness the delivery to ensure the landscaping is not damaged. The trucking team unlatches the straps and guides the container across the lawn. A crowd has gathered in the garden, clapping when it is finally positioned. The container, painted cherry tomato red, gleams with *Goforth's Daily Grind* painted on the front wall in bright white letters. Tanya strokes her hand across the logo that she designed and inspects the roll-open doors and windows.

A group of library patrons gawk from the large window. It doesn't take long before Ms. Montgomery emerges from the building to push her way through the crowd.

She charges toward me gripping her umbrella like a club. "Miss, what is going on here?"

"Temporary coffee shop."

"A temporary eyesore!" She marches straight to the town official, pointing her folded umbrella at him like a sword.

"How could the town board approve this catastrophe without notifying me?"

He backs away from her. "You were invited to the meetings. To be honest, I was surprised you didn't show up. There were no objections from anyone."

"I am running one of the best small libraries in America!"

Tanya steps forward. "Looks like you could use a relaxing cup of Ralph Ellison Euphoria."

"You have some nerve plopping this hunk of junk in the middle of my gardens," she screeches. "This has always been a commercial free library. Who did you bamboozle to get this approved?"

Tanya smiles, unfazed. "This might not look so great right now, but once it is all set up it will be as quaint as the lovely gardens. Plus, we will have a special tip jar to collect for your library fund."

"Look at that. Do you see that crowd inside the library? Do you think this is fair to our dedicated library patrons who are trying to concentrate on their reading and research? This is an outrage."

"Actually, I'll get you a large Albert Camus Calm —"

"I don't want any of that slop!"

Stoph pulls into the lot and hops out of his car. He jogs toward us with a big grin. Ms. Montgomery starts in on him.

"Are you part of this outrage too? It looks like scrap-yard salvage."

Stoph says, "Maybe if you give it a chance, Ms. M., you might warm to it. What's better than a hot cup of coffee?"

"Coffee is coffee. I don't know why your generation needs to make a project out of drinking coffee. Everything with you Millennials is so specialized. Nobody can do anything without a phone, a tablet, a computer, a this-and-a-that. Everything is a swipe and a swoop. Screens, screens, screens! Technology is making you incapable of holding a conversation. Do opposable thumbs not work anymore? God forbid a young person should hold a book. You have the attention span of hamsters, partly because you're so wound up on coffee! Coffee with this, coffee with that, coffee to go. Where is everyone going with their coffee and computers? What happened to the days of roll-up-the-sleeves ingenuity? As a future architect, can you imagine designing this library without a computer? The way Richardson did? He designed archways and rooflines with a pen and paper!"

"Maybe he drank coffee, too," I interject.

"I'm not talking to you, young lady."

Stoph says, "Look on the bright side, Ms. M. It's only temporary. Everything will be back to normal in a few months."

"Months!" She stabs the tip of the umbrella into the grass.

I nudge Tanya with my elbow. "It looks fabulous."

She flashes me a smile. "Opening day is in one week."

"Miss, to the library. Pronto!" I'm not scheduled to work at the library today, but I follow her inside. "I guess you have time to waste on that hippie."

"It's just a part-time job. I need money for books —"

"Books may be borrowed for free, so long as they are returned by the due date. This internship and schoolwork should be your focus. Selling coffee is a waste of time."

Treadwell waits by her desk. She spikes her umbrella into the stand and stacks her hands at right angles — the Mason's sign for distress. Treadwell swings his right hand horizontal under his chin and drives his left thumb toward the floor. They wait for me to go in the back room.

"Treadwell! Things are spinning out of control. Call a meeting tonight!"

9. The Semi-Formal

The Big Tease Salon is open for business. Melissa and Jill tag team on the finishing touches — hair, nails, eyebrows — details they claim could be deal-breakers if I don't nail tonight's semi-formal.

The red nail polish bottles are lined up on Jill's desk like an army prepped for battle.

"I guess I'm going with red tonight?"

"One hundred percent, it's got to be red." Jill picks up a bottle and taps it upside down against her palm. "I selected the shades that have cooler undertones. Your fair skin won't look so washed out —"

"Pick a color," Melissa says imitating the manicurists in the nail salon.

I try to please them both by suggesting, "How about *red-hot chili pepper* on my hands and *spice it up* on my toes?"

"You know the hands and toes have to be the same color?" Melissa says.

"How about this crimson shade? That's Harvard's color, right?"

Jill holds the bottle toward the light for color analysis. *"Berry boss.* That works."

Melissa files my nails, a scratching sensation I don't care for, before she applies two coats of crimson, a clear topcoat to prevent chipping and a protective layer for quick drying. Jill strokes a blonde color on specific strands of my hair and wraps them in foil, making me look like an alien. They take turns tweezing my eyebrows; the sting of each pluck lingers long after the miniscule hairs have been discarded.

Jill blows out my hair for what feels like hours, making it perfectly straight before gathering it into a neat updo with carefully displaced highlighted strands.

"You never pierced your ears?" Melissa looks at my lobes with horror.

"No and we're not doing that today."

The girls eye me with mouths agape — a Martian who never pierced her ears. A long debate over lipstick shade follows; until they settle on a glossy porn star red.

"I look like a stop sign," I say.

Jill agrees. "Yeah, that's a tad neon against your pasty complexion. I think plum will work better, plus it complements the crimson."

Melissa drags a plastic storage container from under her bed and sorts through a multitude of clutches. "You need a pop of bling. You can either carry this as a clutch or use the sparkly strap for an over-the-shoulder look. Keep the lipstick and eyeliner inside this pocket for periodic touchups. Make sure you use the ladies' room to check your look and eavesdrop on the other girls. It's a great way to scoop some inside info on who's who among the Porcellian crowd."

"It's a date, not a reconnaissance."

"Uh, don't you remember what you promised us?"

"Right," I agree. "I'll keep my eyes open."

They unzip the dress from the wire hanger and advise me to step into it; pulling the dress over my head might muss the updo. They clasp the pearl choker around my throat. The pumps are ready to march, and Melissa rips through her jewelry box for the finishing touch.

"You need a cocktail ring. Make sure you hold your drink so that you flash the bling with every sip. Speaking of drinks, I assume you have a fake ID?"

"Um...not exactly."

Melissa sighs and produces her fake ID for me to keep in the clutch with the cosmetics. "You need to memorize the name, address and birthdate."

I study the details on the ID and tuck it in the clutch. "Thanks, but I probably won't need it."

"Good God, Paige. It's the Porcellian Club! Order a cocktail. Just sip it if you have to. You can't go to this event and stand there like a dummy. This is a big deal! Okay? Just order whatever your boyfriend is drinking."

"Stop calling him my boyfriend!"

"If he's Porcellian, you better do your best to make him your boyfriend."

"Yeah, whatever," I say.

"Listen, Paige. This guy is a serious catch. You gotta bring you're A-game." Melissa blasts hairspray around my head. "You look smoking hot! Don't forget: we want introductions."

"I know, I know."

I wait for Stoph in the parking lot. I look up at the dorm to see Melissa and Jill gawking and waving.

At exactly six, a black Town Car rolls up. A limo driver opens the back door and Stoph gets out. He's wearing a tuxedo with a crimson-colored bowtie. He oggles when he sees me. "Sweet," he says.

He holds the door for me and I slide into the back seat. "I was expecting your Audi."

"Compliments of dear old dad. This way we can drink and not drive," he says. "Plus, dad is super stoked that I got punched by The Porc. He wants to make sure I arrive in style."

"Was he a Porcellian?"

"Oh, yeah. His proudest accomplishment. You see, you have to have some sort of accomplishment just to get punched."

"What's your big accomplishment?"

"Freshman project. I won an award from the architecture department. I used virtual reality to present the future of architectural planning," he explains.

"I'd love to see it sometime," I say and cross my legs to flash my defined calf muscle like Jill showed me. "And tonight? Are there any rules I should know?"

"Some of the guys get super high strung about all the formalities but I'm just like whatever, this is who I am, take it or leave it."

"What formalities?"

"Club rituals. You'll see."

He slides close to me and kisses my neck. "We're here. Stonehurst. Guess who the architect was?"

It's a stone monster sitting high on a hilltop, the massive boulders cover the entryway. "I'm going to go with H.H.R."

"Bingo. Stonehurst was one of his collaborations with Olmsted, who did the landscape design. This was the country estate for the son of Robert Treat Paine. The elder Paine was the Massachusetts representative to sign the Declaration of

Independence. Harvard grad, one of the founding members of The Porcellian Club in 1791."

The driver lets us out by the front entrance. Stoph escorts me into the wooded great hall. Most of the women are wearing LBDs and pearls, just as Melissa predicted.

"Martini?"

"Sounds good to me."

Stoph orders two with extra olives. The first sip tastes like an evergreen forest with pine needles tickling my nose. Stoph mingles among the other punch candidates and their dates, introducing me as "Paige from Kew College." The punchees all brag about themselves: their majors, sports, wealth, trying to one-up each other. Stoph puts another martini in my hand before I even have a chance to munch my gin-soaked olives.

Our assigned seats are at a round table with one empty chair. A dinner bell clangs and a voice bellows, "*Oyez, oyez, oyez.*" A long line of hooded men enters the room and one of the men sits at the empty chair. When the dinner bell clangs again, all the hooded men say in unison, "*Dum vivimus vivamus.*"

Four hooded men burst through the kitchen swing doors carrying a massive display: a roasted pig surrounded in ornamental trimmings of rosemary and bright yellow mushrooms. The pig's mouth holds a Granny Smith apple and its ears are perked upright as if listening to us. The roasted pig is positioned in the center table and the four hooded men use butcher knives to carve honey-glazed slabs of pork. The crowd starts chanting, *"Dum vivimus vivamus,"* until only the pig's head remains, reminding me of Caravaggio's gruesome painting, and I feel my stomach twisting.

The hooded man at our table gestures for us to sit. He is silent, which is how he remains for the duration of the dinner. The recruits must have been instructed to carry on conversations at the tables because the dining room instantly fills with chatter and clanging silverware.

Krissy, a Wesleyan English major, is one of the few dates not dressed in black. Her burnt-sienna silk dress is low-cut revealing ample cleavage. "What are you chanting?"

Stoph chimes in. "Translation: *While we live, let us live.* It's Epicurean, you know, Greek philosophy. Epicurus was an atomic materialist. He declared pleasure to be the main objective in life. And the greatest pleasure is the absence of pain and fear."

The hooded man seems to glare at Stoph. I wonder if he disapproves of Stoph explaining Porcellian philosophy. Stoph doesn't seem to care or even notice as he digs into the pork. The waiters fill our glasses with wine. Stoph lifts his glass to offer a toast: "May we get what we want, what we need, and never what we deserve!"

Everyone, except the hooded man, clinks glasses. The taste of the Malbec reminds me of pipe smoke.

"Stoph, didn't you win an origami prize for redesigning a plain brown box?" asks Calvin, Krissy's date. His buttoned shirt looks too tight around his thick neck. He has chiseled cheek bones, broad shoulders and weight-room biceps straining under his shirt.

"Actually, it was a virtual reality conference room."

"What's that?" asks Krissy.

"A space where people working remotely can utilize VR goggles to attend meetings and interact with Avatars of their co-workers. The meetings can take place on beaches or secluded mountain tops or wherever you want."

"That's cool," Calvin says. "But not quite as cool as my *actual reality* of placing in the Nationals, though. All-America as a freshman at 157."

His girlfriend rubs his flexed arm. "He's such a stud."

"Wrestling isn't an Epicurean pursuit — it's all about pain and fear," Stoph says.

Another candidate says, "While you were sweat swapping with muscle-Mindys Calvin, and you were creating fantasy land for mid-management executives Stoph, I was crushing it with Bitcoin. Cybercurrency is where it's at."

Stoph scoffs, "Crushing it? Don't you just buy and HODL? How's that considered crushing it?"

"What's HODL?" I ask.

"Hold on for Dear Life," says Stoph with a brilliant smile.

I slice my pork, but just spread it around my plate. The roasted potatoes and steamed vegetables are all I can stomach right now with the pine needle taste of the gin repeating in my mouth and throat. I feel like I swallowed a lit match. I need water, but there is only a steady flow of wine at our table. I sip the smoky-tasting Malbec, attempting to squelch the burning sensation lodged in my esophagus.

As the dishes are cleared, a voice booms, "*Oyez, oyez, oyez,*" and everyone stands while the hooded quartet lifts the pig's head and initiates a single-file procession. We all get up to follow. The guys chant in the slow procession, but suddenly all my walking-in-heels lessons fail me. As we file outside, the fresh night air hits me hard, the sky starts to spin, and I feel like I am wearing VR goggles.

I grab Krissy's burnt-sienna sleeve and say, "Quick, please, take me to the ladies' room."

She steadies me while my ankles wobble. We barely make it into the bathroom before I launch the martinis, a veritable bucket of Malbec, and steamed broccoli into the toilet. My throat is blazing as sweat rolls down my back. There's a chair in the corner of the bathroom where I collapse.

"Wow! That was impressive."

"Thanks, I guess."

Krissy gets me a glass of water. "Hydrate, blondie. Quick. You've got to pull it together."

I freshen up in the mirror with lipstick, smearing the red into my teeth and drawing a wavy line above my lip.

"Nice try, Khloe Kardashian. Better let me do it for you."

"Thanks."

She wets a paper towel to wipe the crooked plum lines, then reapplies the lipstick in a neat line. "Good as new. Feel better?"

"Much"

"I'm not surprised. You hurled about ten pounds of mush."

She breezes down the woodland path to rejoin the guys, leaving me to wobble in my pumps and sweat-soaked LBD. I catch up at the ceremonial bonfire, with hooded men chanting Latin phrases, which could be Pig Latin for all I know. Finally, a hooded man announces that all those present must drink the ceremonial brew.

I find Stoph and cling to his arm. "Ceremonial brew?"

Stoph hushes me. "Shhh. A ritual."

"I am hammered," I tell him.

"You and me both."

There is more chanting, bodhran drumming, Dixie cups passed around. There is a totem pole with carved owl heads stacked on top of each other. Then I see the pig's head with the Granny Smith still lodged in its mouth, its perked ears digging the chanting and drumming as it gets lowered into the bonfire.

The hooded leader chants something in Latin and then everyone swigs the brew. I'm still holding mine and Stoph elbows me. "Bottoms up. Can't be worse than the martinis."

I glug the liquid, which tastes like one of Tanya's earthy concoctions. More hooded chatter, the group starts swaying, singing, chanting. I feel myself getting ready for round two, so I opt out of the swaying and head back down the woodland path toward the massive stone palace.

The spinning increases, now with flashes of color. I faceplant under a pine tree, inhaling dried pine needles, which reminds me of the gin martinis — and here comes another expelling. I manage to crawl away from the mess to lean against the trunk of the tree. I look back at Stonehurst where I see two hooded men approaching me.

"You are not the first person to blow chunks at Solomon's Palace," one man says in a cheery tone. "Is that what the kids call it nowadays? Blowing chunks?"

The other man howls with laughter. "Sounds about right."

I look into the man's eyes and see H.H. Richardson. The other man is Frederick Law Olmsted.

I blink, but the apparition is still there. "What's going on? Shit, was there acid in the Dixie cups?"

Richardson says, "You need to encourage your friend to work harder at getting selected to the club. You must continue to keep company with him, no matter what. He is the key that will open the door for you."

Olmsted adds, "These gentlemen are fools. They are the selfish elite, in it for themselves. Do not trust them. Pay attention. Be smart."

The two hooded men leave before I can scramble to my feet. I stumble after them down the path, but they blend in with the returning hooded parade. I step to the side before I feel Stoph's hand on my elbow pulling me back into the procession. We march in line to the parking lot where the Town Car awaits.

"Where did you go?" Stoph whispers behind me.

"Don't ask. Did I miss the fireworks?"

"Actually, you missed the ceremonial sacrifice calling upon the spirits of Porcellian Club members past. It was kind of cool. I wish you saw it."

"Oh, trust me, I saw it."

I slump in the backseat, resting my head on Stoph's shoulder. He tells the driver to head back to my dorm. I take off the pumps and stagger barefoot, with Stoph's help, back to my room. I flop on the bed, which starts spinning like an amusement park thrill ride, only this doesn't feel amusing or thrilling.

He brings a glass of water to my side. "You'll need this tomorrow," he says.

"Did I screw up the punch party for you?" I slur.

"You did great. Belle of the ball."

10. The Bike Tour

I wake up at 2 p.m. to Tool's "Fear Inoculum" — my new ringtone that Stoph downloaded on my phone. It's his favorite song; he says it will grow on me.

But the only thing growing right now is a throbbing headache and a fat, chalky tongue.

"Ugh," I say into the phone.

"And a good day to you too," says Stoph.

"I wouldn't call it *good*, exactly."

"Maybe you just need some company."

Then a knock on my door. The door cracks and Stoph says, "Room service."

I sit up in bed, still wearing my LBD. He hands me a bag of croissants and hot coffee.

"You're an absolute lifesaver." I slurp half the coffee. "Those freaking martinis. I don't know what happened."

"That ceremonial drink clobbered me, too. Clobbered everyone, actually, so you didn't stick out at all."

"What the hell was in that? LSD?"

"Probably something like that. I passed out in the back of the Town Car."

A few parts of the night are missing from my memory. I need fresh air. "How about a bike ride?"

"Sounds awesome, but let's go to Sunday afternoon services first."

"Really?"

"If you don't mind."

Church isn't my thing — all those Hallelujahs — but I'll go along if it makes Stoph happy. I owe him one for last night. Quiet reflection doesn't sound too bad at the moment, and I can offer a prayer to the hangover gods.

We ride dorm loaner bikes down Main Street and lock them to the playground fence behind Unity Church. Stoph takes my hand as we walk up the unpaved path toward the front entrance.

"Gothic revival," he explains. "It's a 130-year-old church. Quarry stone, pinkish hue."

There is a flag in rainbow colors flapping outside the main entrance. Pushing through the front doors, the brass on the doorknobs looks worn by generations of the sinners and saved. Inside, the choir harmonizes a spunky rendition of "Lean on Me." I admire the sunlight streaming through the glass-jeweled windows.

"That's a John LaFarge, one of America's greatest stained-glass artists. That window is called *Angel of Help*," Stoph whispers and points to the window with an angel robed in pinks and reds with elegant blue wings and a pitcher in her right hand.

"Is that LaFarge, too?" I point across the church to the window of a woman with her elbow resting on a blue crystal ball.

"That one's called *Wisdom*. Incredible detail."

When the church service ends, we stop to study the Oakes Ames II memorial that Richardson designed in the foyer. "Check out the ornamental terracotta arches surrounding the white bust. Richardson drew up plans for the Ames church, but they didn't go with his bid for the project. So, he contributed this memorial. I'd love to see his designs, though."

We ride bikes through town, stopping at Richardson's buildings.

"My professor refers to Richardson so often, now I'm obsessed with Richardson Romanesque. The architects that followed were all imitating H.H.R."

"Imitation is the highest form of flattery, they say."

Stoph nods. "And Richardson was imitating what he saw in Europe."

"Actually, I think Richardson was imitating Hiram."

"Who?"

"Hiram Abiff, the chief architect of King Solomon's Temple. Richardson Romanesque. I think it is Bible architecture. I've been meaning to tell you this."

He looks at me, then back at the building. "Where are you getting that from?"

"It occurred to me the other night when I was reading the Bible. Richardson built Solomon's Temple according to the specs in the book of Kings. I looked up the building specs and applied the Hebrew long cubit. Memorial Hall is 60-by-20 cubits, the second level, the sanctuary, is 40-by-20 cubits and the attic, the holy of holies, is exactly 34-by-34 feet (20-by-20 cubits). Those exact dimensions replicate Solomon's Temple. Most people think Solomon's Temple was a single-story structure. No one knows for sure what the temple actually looked like, but the Bible says there was a winding staircase on the right side of the building. Richardson stacked the holy of holies directly above the sanctuary and connected them with a spiral staircase on the right side of the building. This masonic guide I found says that all masonic lodges should be true representations of Solomon's Temple. Let's sneak up to the attic room. I'll show you."

Inside, we wait for the janitor to go into another area. Then we slip past the plastic shield and run up the winding staircase. In the attic room, we pass through two columns topped by orbs. An altar in the middle of the room is surrounded by high-backed chairs against the walls. There are three steps up to the largest chair with a giant tapestry behind it marked with the letter *G* on the back wall. Stoph studies the eye painted on the ceiling in front of what must be the Worshipful Master's chair. I refuse to look at the eye again so I don't have a repeat panic attack. He pulls his keys from his pocket and takes a measurement with a laser-beam measuring tape.

"I was wondering what that key chain was."

"Gift from my dad. A serious architect always carries a measuring tape," he says. Stoph points the laser across the room and checks the measurements. "You're spot on. Exactly 34-by-34 feet."

"Can you measure the distance of the starry area on the ceiling?"

Stoph points his laser beam. "It's seventeen feet. Why?"

"Just what I thought, that's ten cubits. The ceiling must be the Molten Sea."

"What's the Molten Sea?"

"It's the bronze water reservoir set on the backs of twelve bronze oxen in Solomon's Temple. I've been finding more biblical connections. He used all stone on his exteriors and wood inside, just like Solomon. And the winged creature carvings resemble the cherubim."

Stoph nods in thought. He disappears into the adjoining storage room and rummages through some boxes.

"Check this out," he calls out. I find him crouched with his eye pressed to the wall.

"Don't tell me it's another eye."

"It's a peep hole."

I look through it and can see the whole attic room. "Who's the perv?"

"Your guess is as good as mine."

We sneak back down. Outside Memorial Hall, I point to the frieze on the northeast tower that has the ornamental carvings of the signs of the zodiac in brownstone. He pauses while studying that section of the building. "Why would Richardson put zodiac signs up there? We need to think this through."

We circle the building studying the details from various vantages. I say, "Each zodiac symbol coordinates with a constellation in the sky."

"I'm a Libra, by the way. A super social sign. You?"

"Capricorn. Hardworking." The detail in the tower can't be random. I say, "The constellations provide a celestial coordinate system. It travels through the sky at the same time every year."

"Right." Stoph jams his hands in his pockets and starts jingling some loose change.

"So, the zodiac is the circle of twelve thirty-degree divisions of celestial longitude. That's the path of the sun across the celestial sphere during one year."

"What about this other frieze, the lion's head?"

"It's enclosed by two columns. I think those represent Boaz and Jachin. The Bible details a mouth, a compass and a wheel. Richardson used the lion's mouth. The sun dial represents the compass and this Solomon knot design is the wheel."

Stoph says, "I can't argue with that. Wait, dude, how do you know so much about the Bible? I got the impression you aren't exactly the most religious person."

"I've read the thing cover to cover, twice. As literature. Helps me relax."

"Try smoking pot. That'll help you relax."

"I'll keep that in mind." I cross the street to the Rockery. "Remember when you asked Ms. Montgomery about the memorial? I've been thinking about it. The best explanation I can come up with is that the rockery is the altar in front of the temple. God told Moses to build a ramp made of earth and uncut stone."

Stoph nods. "Could be."

"On the field trip I started thinking there has to be more to Richardson's architecture. Then I started to connect his work with the Bible —"

"But the zodiac has nothing to do with the Bible."

"Sure it does. The book of Job refers to mazzaroth, a Hebrew word that translates to astronomical constellations. The three wise men followed the star in the north. In Genesis it says the stars are for signs. God said, 'Let there be lights in the expanse of the heavens to separate the day from the night, and let them be for signs and for seasons and for days and years; and let them be for lights in the expanse of the heavens to give light on earth.'"

"Amen."

We ride our bikes to Pond Street where we venture off the paved road about a hundred yards until we reach a private wooded area. We leave our bikes behind, so we can hike up to Big Pout, the rim of an extinct volcano. When we reach the top, we admire the view across Langwater Pond to the Ames Estate. We sit down on the craggy rock escarpment soaking up the sun, enjoying the colors reflecting from the water.

Stoph glides his hand in circles on my leg and leans in to kiss me. I kiss him back. His hand moves to my inner thigh, so I return the favor to him. He slides his hips forward; I can't help but notice he is excited.

Then we hear footsteps on the path. An older gentleman hikes past. "Nice afternoon," he says.

A dejected look crosses Stoph's face — the Big Pout indeed. He stands and offers me a hand up.

"I want to show you something," I tell him.

"I'd like to show you something too," he says, "but it looks like we'll have to save that for a more private venue."

"Can you walk with that?"

"I'll pole vault if I have to."

We hike back down the mountain and ride to the driveway of the Ames Gate Lodge.

"Ms. Montgomery calls this the original American man cave. But I doubt this whole place was made for the gardener. I wish we could go inside."

"It's a private residence. What did you want to show me?"

"You see the damage to those doors?"

"I see. What about it?"

"This is what I was telling you about when we were at the Chinese restaurant. I was here the other night when these guys, dressed in black, broke in and stole a filing cabinet. It had all kinds of research done by an old guy named Homer Treadwell. He's the curator of the shovel museum on my campus."

"And?"

"And I noticed that Treadwell has another research area in the library archive department. Locked cabinets, books about Freemasons. The books led me to figure out Richardson was designing Solomon's Temple. I'm positive the attic room was a Freemason lodge."

"Okay, but who cares if the attic room was a Freemason lodge? It's a private society, it has nothing to do with Richardson."

He steers his bike under the archway to look at the lodge from the estate side, whistling with admiration. "Look how he used local boulders to blend in with the surrounding nature. I would love to design like this someday, but no, we're taught to maximize for profit. Capitalize on the interior space — that's architecture now. Ornamentation, no."

"This seems like a lot of expense for a live-in gardener, don't you think?"

"Well, they didn't have Whole Foods back then. They needed to preserve their seeds and plants during the winter."

"Sure — but still. Anyway, I think this could be Richardson's take on one of the gates in Ezekiel's vision of the temple."

"I can't argue with that. Let's head back. I'm freakin' starved."

We push up the slight incline when a silver pickup truck momentarily slows to drive alongside us. The truck continues at our pace for a hundred feet or so before it swerves in front of us, nearly clipping my front tire. I stop so fast that I spin out in the street sand and fall toward the curb. My right wrist throbs while blood trickles down my scraped knee. I look up to catch a glimpse of the driver's face. Stoph curses the driver out as the truck accelerates away.

"Jesus. You okay? That jackass nearly hit you. He swerved right —"

"It was Treadwell," I say.

11. *Grand Opening*

Tanya and I tie balloons saying "Grand Opening!" outside the entrance to Goforth's Daily Grind.

"Paige, you look like you've been working out," Tanya says.

"I started running again. Plus, I walk the dog a lot. I'm paying more attention to what I eat, too, thanks to you."

"It shows. You look toned."

I've adopted Tanya's insights regarding the Basic American Diet, which she calls BAD. She advocates a mix of paleo, ketogenic, Mediterranean, localtarian, vegan, and vegetarian. She teaches the benefits of fasting, and freeing our diets from gluten, dairy and soy. There's no right diet for everyone she says, and we should focus on what is best for our own bodies and minds. Tanya wants the staff to radiate with good health.

She looks crestfallen when Paul shuffles in wearing flannel pants and dad slippers. He's coughing so hard it sounds like his lungs are rattling.

"I'm on gorilla antibiotics," he explains. He blows his nose.

"Antibiotics? What did the doctor say, exactly?"

"Doctor said it might be a bacterial infection." Paul's voice is raspy from the chronic cough.

"Now Paul, I'm not making an example out of you, but this is why I talk about Hippocrates' philosophy: let food be your medicine. The doctor isn't even sure what you have. Maybe strep throat? Maybe a virus? Maybe just rundown? So, here's an antibiotic to fix whatever might be ailing you. Prescriptions and the over-the-counter stuff could do more harm than good."

Paul slumps against the wall. "No offense, but the doctor went through medical school. I think he knows what he is doing. What would you do if you had a fever?"

Tanya shrugs. "I would rest, boost with supplements, and let the fever run its course. Give it some time before running to the doctor. A fever is the body's best defense against infection. I let my body handle issues naturally, and I purge the system with rest and clear fluids."

"Coffee doesn't cure everything."

"Most mainstream doctors get zero education in nutrition. Conventional medicine focuses on illness and how to treat those illnesses. People don't go to doctors until they're sick. It's a difficult paradigm. Then doctors analyze the symptoms and throw a prescription at the problem. Do you see where I'm coming from?"

"Not really." He blows his nose and shoots the used tissue into the trash can like a foul shot.

"Paul, there's a connection between what we eat and how we feel. Our gut is our second brain. If we eat crap, then we'll feel like crap. Many of us walk around with aches and pains, depression, anxiety and brain fog. Most of those problems we can cure ourselves by overhauling our diets."

"Oh, so if I ate your rabbit food instead of my usual cheeseburger and fries, then I wouldn't have gotten this cold?"

"Probably not."

"And if my grandfather ate more salad then he wouldn't have died from cancer?"

"Maybe, but maybe not. Our genetic inheritance and the epigenetic hand dealt to us from our environment play a big factor in our overall health. Being healthy isn't a contest. Our lives comprise millions of small choices, some good and some not so good, and the fight for health is won along the averages of our choices, not on any one individual choice. And who knows, my coffee could potentially trigger a health impact in this town. Maybe we could even become a Blue Zone for longevity and healthspan."

"What makes your coffee so special? I see people buzzing in and out of Starbucks and no one is going there for health advice. They just want their Joe to go," he squeaks, sounding like he has ten pounds of mucus trapped in his nose.

"Leading a fit and fulfilling lifestyle will bring them more energy and positivity. Healthy choices don't make one person morally superior to the next. What's right for me might not be right for you."

"Okay, I'll work on improving my diet," he says. "I mean, I'm with you on all this stuff, for the most part anyway."

Tanya continues, "We need to remember that health insurance does not equal healthcare, and there is no amount of health insurance that will save us if we don't switch our focus to preventing and reversing disease, rather than just managing it."

"Got it," Paul says.

Tanya adjusts the volume on the music. "Remember, top-notch customer service while maintaining a chill vibe. We don't want to appear lackadaisical while at the same time we cannot look stressed out when the line is out the door."

One staff member suggests, "Slow and steady."

"We won't last too long if we're slow. Think purposeful movement. Everyone should be in constant motion. If there is a lull between serving customers, then wipe down the counters and tables. Sweep the floor. Empty the trash."

Tanya hands out our uniforms: black t-shirts with Goforth Daily Grind printed in white across the front. We are all set to serve the first customers except Paul: he gets sent home until he is well.

We open to a steady flow of customers. Tanya offers free samples. I'm surprised to see Ms. Montgomery and Treadwell sipping coffee in the corner of the shop. I bring a fresh pot and offer to refill their cups.

"No, thank you. We have no idea what might be in some of these *special blends*," Ms. Montgomery says, winking at Treadwell.

"It's all healthy ingredients, Ms. M."

"Oh really? So, let me get this straight, that woman travels abroad, discovers magical coffee beans, pitches a basic cup of coffee as *toughy juice*. Everything is marketing. Everyone has an angle. Except, of course, the library. That's just good old-fashioned book sharing. Isn't that right, Treadwell?"

"Boy," he says and leans toward me. "You really get around."

"I guess."

When the Daily Grind closes a few hours later, Tanya pulls the staff together for a group hug. "We nailed it! Nice work all around."

"How many customers came through?" a staffer asks.

Tanya closes her eyes and folds her hands prayer style. "I didn't count. My focus was on being in the moment. I would like to express my gratitude to all of you by offering a group meditation session. Can anyone stay to join me?"

A few people need to leave, but I roll out a yoga mat on the floor to join some others. She lowers the lights, turns soft rain sounds on the surround sound and invites us to join her breathing pattern. "If you see an opening, you should feel free to pursue it without fear."

I don't know if it's lingering exhaustion from my drunken night out with Stoph or the herbal blend that tastes like juiced Girl Scout Thin Mints, but I sink into a deep hypnotic relaxation almost instantly.

Tanya says, "Here's a Tibetan dream mantra. *I am a warrior of the dream state. I stay lucid and conscious while dreaming.*"

Tanya, adorned with beaded chakra bracelets, lights a sage bundle. She circles the perimeter with smoking sage, her orange paisley skirt billowing when a breeze sweeps through the open window.

I close my eyes and sense I am embraced by a warm silver cloud. With a deep inhale and exhale, I release my body into the silvery steam; the cloud thins the atmosphere. I move through dark gray walls where a lion, a bull, an eagle, and several winged demons are held captive in the stone like animals in the zoo. They are illuminated by points of light that create the outline of their shapes that are striking against the blackness around us.

A sign appears: *Do not be fooled by false beings placed before you.*

A winged horse awaits and I climb aboard. Its wide white wings flap and we lift off the ground, creating a rush of air. The winged horse gracefully glides as we circle three times, finally easing into an area with lions; they scurry like stray cats to take cover from the intrusion of the winged horse. A massive broad-shouldered creature with a bull head takes charge, kicking up gold dust as he races toward me and the winged horse. Steam blows out his wide nostrils and his third eye, positioned vertically in the center of his forehead, bulges when he speaks.

"Why bring this human here?" he demands, and the winged horse nays a response that I cannot comprehend.

The third eye bulges and drool dangles from the corners of his mouth. There is a gold ball that hovers above his head between his horns that reflect rays of gold like a disco.

"This is the point of no return. You will remain here with me. I am the god Moloch, a supreme Canaanite deity not to be toyed with. You are a child sent to me so that I may sacrifice you for the greater good."

The winged horse bucks back to lift away from the raging Moloch. "You are a false god that I choose to deny," I shout back at him. He shoots gold rays. One ray strikes the horse in the front leg so that he jolts in pain, tossing me out of the saddle. The horse ignores the stinging arrow to collect me back into the saddle to continue our narrow escape. His great winged power lands us on a higher ground where he can safely rest, nursing his wounded leg. A beautiful winged goddess rises through the rocky terrain. I feel at ease in her presence, her fragrance attracts me to her like a hummingbird to honeysuckle. She embraces me in her welcoming arms like a mother to her child.

"I am Ashtoreth, mother of the Milky Way, giver of all life." She sings a soothing lullaby that pulls me closer to her.

Ashtoreth is surrounded by countless star children, her constellation shines for all heavenly souls under her careful watch. She invites me to stay with her, to remain under her protection for all my days and nights where I will have no pain, no worries, no problems. I want to accept her protection, but I decline her generosity because I realize I will never fully evolve as a human if I become her star child. As I pull myself back into the saddle, my horse limps forward and I slip away from Ashtoreth's maternal hold on my soul.

An overwhelming sadness beckons me to turn back, to remain where I know it is safe, a choice no one would ever regret. I tug on the reins and drive my knee into the side of the horse, so we can return to Ashtoreth. My indecisiveness has now blocked the path with a male figure who hosts a toad on his left shoulder and a cat on his right shoulder. A crown on his head symbolizes that he is a king in this land; his legs spider out beneath him while he creeps toward us.

A gust of cold wind sweeps around us, and rain pours from a cloud hovering over my head. Lightning cracks across the dark sky, a thunderous roar announces his presence.

"I am Baal, the god of seasons. My weather creates fertile land on which you walk, and now you are mine to hold forever so that I can guide you like a sailor voyaging on rough seas," he announces in deep guttural sounds. "To fight me only brings on my maddening storms, but to accept me grants you fertility to create as you desire."

I sprint away from him but he blocks my path with lightning that cracks the ground into large craters. My body shivers in his wake as his spidery legs pull me into his powerful body.

"Okay you win, I'll stay."

He yanks my arm and drags me to higher ground, where he starts bartering with someone.

"She has agreed to my terms," he growls at a strange creature sitting on a mound of rocks. The creature's body is part human female, part human male, with a horned goat head and large black wings splaying from its back.

"You will give her to me as we agreed. Your duty has been served and you will be rewarded according to our arrangement," says the goat head.

Baal puts forth a fierce storm, pelting the area with hail, that has no impact on the goat head. He then cowers and releases me with a snarl. "Baphomet, she is yours to do as you will."

Baal nudges me to move toward Baphomet. As I get closer Baal lashes out with a storm of violent winds, attempting to overthrow Baphomet. The powerful wind forces me past the reaching creature, his goat arms prove too short to catch me. Baal's swirling rush inadvertently sends me to my winged horse that pulls me away from the false gods Baal and Baphomet. We fly from the storm, soaring as high as his white wings will carry us to a mountain top.

When I dismount the horse, I am greeted by a giant rooster with snakes for legs. "Greetings," the rooster squawks like a seagull. "Abraxas at your service." He is armed with a shield and sword in case I prove to be an unwanted visitor to his corner of paradise.

"Greetings. I think I am the one at your service." I fold my hands prayer style to show I come in peace.

He squawks again, happy with my response. His wings flap and he starts dancing with head jolts and spastic limbs. He beckons me to his dance floor; I offer minimal movements around his disco-gone-bonkers display of joyful and hilarious dancing. He spins me around so we face a king on his throne with the sun blazing behind him.

"That's King Solomon. You have worked your way past the false gods who hold court in the night sky," he shouts from the dance floor. He takes my hands to cha-cha, then spins me around again where I am blinded by flashing lights.

I open my eyes to find Captain Biff shining his flashlight in my eyes. I snap out of the meditation. Tanya jumps from her yoga mat. "What are you doing here?"

"The question is, what are you doing here?"

"Meditating. Is there a problem?"

"Received a call about drug use. What's that smell?"

"Sage. It wards off negative energy. But it's apparently not working," Tanya closes her eyes and breathes. "Do you have a search warrant?"

"Don't need one if I'm just stopping by for a cup of coffee. Got any decaf?"

12. The Assignment

"How is your progress with the guidebook coming?" asks Ms. Montgomery the next evening when I arrive for my shift.

"Excellent," I lie. "Just finishing up."

I dig in writing and revising, and at times I think it is the greatest material ever produced by a college freshman about local history. Then a crashing wave of self-doubt rushes over me and I think I must be a knucklehead, and then I procrastinate by looking through the pictures I snapped during the field trip.

I focus on North Easton's Gilded Age all-star team: Richardson's buildings, Olmsted's landscapes, John LaFarge's stained glass, and Augustus Saint-Gaudens' bas-relief above the hearth in the library and his fireplace design in the lodge.

I take a break when Hobson whines for his outing; we head down the street toward the lodge. We cross the driveway and Hobson pulls me toward the entranceway. A silver pickup truck is parked on the grass and a man in a baseball hat is inspecting the boarded door with a flashlight. Hobson, spooked by the flashlight, starts growling at the man, who directs the flashlight toward the dog.

"Sorry, I hope he didn't disturb you." I startle when I see it is Homer Treadwell.

"Do you think letting the dog run loose is a good idea? You have the lead, so control him."

I tug Hobson to come with me, but Treadwell follows me. "What are you doing back here?"

"The dog was tracking a scent and he pulled me."

His eyes lock on mine. "You need to keep him under control."

I shrug and turn away, and he says, "I believe I'm speaking to you. Do you walk in this area often?"

I nod.

He reaches down to pet Hobson. "Do you know how this door got damaged?"

"Not really," I say.

"What kind of answer is that? Either you do or do not. Which is it?"

"What if I did see something?"

He relaxes his tone. "You're Ms. Montgomery's intern. Didn't you come to the shovel museum the other day?"

"Yes."

"Did you report to Captain Biff what you witnessed here?"

"Of course."

"And weren't you riding bikes around here with your boyfriend?"

"He's not my boyfriend."

"Do you often hike up Big Pout and engage in physical contact with men who aren't your boyfriend?"

"How do you know —"

He leans closer to my face; his intimidating eyes remind me of the one painted on the ceiling. "I know about a lot of things. I have my eye on you. Have a nice evening."

I head back to the library where I see Ms. Montgomery hunched over the table where I had been working. She is reading through my pages for the guidebook, which I've titled "Richardson's Revenge."

"Take the trash out," she says without looking up. "And take these pages with it."

"You don't like it?"

Ms. Montgomery slides her glasses to the top of her head. "If this were a creative writing class, it would be excellent. But all I asked was for you to write up the notes from the class tour. Secret societies? Hidden messages in Richardson's architecture? Seriously, miss, your imagination has run wild.

I expect more out of you. Your teachers and guidance counselor spoke highly of you. These surrealistic architectonic fantasies are a gross distance from the level of sophistication I expected."

After the last of the maintenance crew leaves for the night, I sneak down to the archive department to look through the shovel desk. I find handwritten meeting minutes of conversations between J.D., (junior deacon), W.M., (worshipful master), Brothers Jones, Brown and Smith.

I dig through more papers and notebooks. The A.O.D. initials are stamped on the backs of all the leather notebooks. At first, I think this is someone's monogram. Oakes Ames perhaps? Olmsted? But I can't find a match.

I have the keys from Ms. Montgomery's desk to unlock the cabinets. I find years of Freemason meeting minutes. On the bottom shelf I find a tattered copy of *The Ancient Druids Class of Instruction*. On the cover is an unusual symbol with the letters A.O.D.: Ancient Order of Druids. The pictures show groups of men wearing hooded burlap robes like the one Richardson wears in the portrait. Was Richardson an A.O.D. member?

According to the book, A.O.D is the oldest druidic order, started in England in 1781. Despite the similarities, initiation process and use of regalia, the A.O.D. is not the same as Freemasonry. Freemasonry was an off-shoot of A.O.D.

I can't find any books on the life of H.H. Richardson, only books about his architecture. But I write down what I know so far: Richardson went to Harvard, became a Porcellian; after graduation he went to England where he hung around with his Harvard buddy Henry Adams, grandson of President John Adams. Henry Adams spent a lot of time in England when his father, Charles Adams, was Abraham Lincoln's ambassador to the United Kingdom in the 1860s. It seems possible that Richardson's involvement with A.O.D. started when he was in England. Richardson and Adams remained friends and Richardson designed a mansion for him in 1885 in Washington D.C.

So what if Richardson built Solomon's Temple for the Freemasons? said Stoph. Those words have been buzzing inside my head like a fly in a glass jar. Last night I browsed the book of Kings again — and it struck me that the whole purpose of Solomon's Temple is to protect the ark of the covenant. I wonder if Brother Richardson and the North Easton A.O.D. were protectors of the ark? Maybe that is the answer to Stoph's question of, "So what?" Maybe the ark of the covenant is hidden somewhere here in North Easton.

A police cruiser is making its rounds through the library parking lot. The spotlight is surveying the area around the coffee shop. I head in that direction to see if everything is okay and to grab coffee to go.

When I pass the cruiser, the driver's side window slides down. Captain Biff nods and I nod back.

"Moore! I was just coming to see you. I have some questions."

"As always."

"Get in."

"You mean in the back, like a criminal?"

"Front seat, please."

I go around the cruiser and get in the passenger side. Captain Biff reaches toward the back seat like a seasoned parent with vacation elbow, arms that seem to unhinge to reach where the kids are buckled in. He finds a binder and flips it open to show me some photographs. He clicks on the overhead light.

"When you said the Land Rover Defender had y-shaped spokes on the tires, can you tell from the pictures which ones?"

I review the three different styles and tap on the one I think looks right. "This one, with the Vossen wheels, it says hybrid forged. The spokes were black. Looked slick."

"And you could see all that even though it was dark and everything happened fast?"

"It was parked for a few minutes when they were inside. That's when I noticed the wheels."

Captain Biff picks up the car radio. "O'Malley?"

The radio crackles. "Yes, captain?"

"Run the Land Rover Defender reports again, this time add Vossen, 20-inch, HF-2 wheels to the filter. I want a list of all registered in Massachusetts."

"Yes captain, right away, sir."

"Want a ride back to the campus?" he offers.

"Ah, no, but thanks. I'm going to get some coffee."

"What's the story with that place?" He points at Goforth's shipping container. "We keep getting calls about drug use."

"I bet I can guess who that might be."

"Well?"

"There's no drugs. Just funky coffee."

"How funky?"

I open the door and slide out of the cruiser. "Healthy funky. You'll feel like a new man if you try more than a boring cup of black decaf."

The radio crackles, it's O'Malley reporting back. "Captain, I found seven registered Land Rover Defenders in matte black. There's only one with Goodyear Wrangler tires and hybrid forged wheels registered to a company called Landrace LLC in Middlesex County."

"Roger that, O'Malley."

"Night, Captain Biff," I say and close the cruiser door.

13. The Mashup Maestro

My academic advisor reviews my course load and current grades.

"All As, nice work, Paige" Professor Mukherjee says.

"I really like my English classes."

"Mmmm, yes, you seem well-suited for your major. Are there any issues you want to discuss? Roommate drama? Homesickness?"

"Nope. All good."

"My office hours are on the door. You know where to find me. Don't be a stranger," he says and tosses his pen on his desk blotter. "Make sure you come back to review your classes for next semester."

"Thanks." I hustle to the dining hall to meet Jill and Melissa for lunch. We all get the same thing and find a corner table.

"Have you heard of the Dirty Cash Club? It's in Cambridge," I ask them.

"Of course. Impossible to get into though," says Jill.

"I have V.I.P. passes for tonight. Care to join me?"

"Wait, what?" Melissa power-blinks and says, "How on earth did you swing this?"

"Stoph. It's a Porc punch event. He told me to bring my friends. Dress like hipsters. Dance our pants off. His exact words."

"Oh my God. Break out the Coachella wear!" Melissa squeals.

"You really come through!" says Jill, hugging me.

"Coachella wear?"

"You never heard of Coachella?" She sends an eyeroll toward Jill. "It's the largest music festival in the world. I would give my right arm to go to it. It's in California and loads of celebrities go. The fashion scene there is next level."

After lunch we head back to their room to coordinate outfits. Melissa whips out a bright white flowy lace crop top and snakeskin pattern silky pants that flare at the bottom. Her closet appears to be organized in event order with sections for classy occasions, job interviews, casual outings and yes, Coachella wear. She gives me a once-over and pulls out a two-piece flowery bohemian dress with a fedora hat and a denim jacket with fringe. The dress is short with a steep V-neck and long, puffy poet sleeves. She rummages through a dresser drawer and tosses a black lacey pushup bra at me and says, "Tonight it's tits-up, girlfriend. You're going poet-wench-slut."

I wonder if she realizes that tits-up is a term that means "inoperable" or "broken." It doesn't really matter, just as long as I don't render myself inoperable like I did at the last punch event. Things have been going so well with Stoph that I'm thinking tonight's the night. The push-up bra could be the lure to hook him and reel him in.

Jill takes some clothes from her closet, puts them back, and continues the pattern until she says, "I'm not trying to copy you, but I really want to wear my crop top and bell bottoms. Would you mind?"

"Hell no!" Melissa says. "We'll look totally adorbs twinning on the dance floor."

My hair, orders Melissa, must be blown straight down so that when we dance, we can swing our heads like maniacs. Melissa tosses a pair of Doc Marten boots toward me. "Shit-kickers for the dance floor," she says.

"I'm not much of a shit-kicker," I say.

"You are tonight."

I take my outfit and head for Sheila's room.

Sheila and her roommate, Grace from Manchester in the U.K., have decorated their room with K-POP posters of Korean boy bands. They have a collection of colored plastic concert flashlights lined up like trophies on their dressers. "Sheila," I say, "I need some dancing advice."

"Like what?"

"Like everything."

"Sure," she says in her sweet voice. She turns on some music. "Let's see what you got."

Grace closes her book to watch the dance lessons from her bed.

It's a fast K-POP song, so I let it fly — pelvic thrusting, arms flying, feet spinning, booty shaking. I think I'm crushing it until Sheila kills the music.

"Paige?"

"Yes?"

"Don't ever do that again." She pushes me aside and flips the music back on. "First, feel the beat. Second, start counting one-two, one-two, one-two. Third, get your feet going one-two, one-two. Fourth, add in the hips, like this."

Sheila starts moving, then adds her torso, chest, and shoulders. She tells me to copy her, then adds her arms swaying, fingers snapping, head slightly bopping.

I add my head, rolling it wildly around my shoulders to the beat. The music stops.

"That head thing you just did."

"This?" I repeat the move.

"Mmmm, yeah. That too. Never again. Someone will call for an exorcist."

"Got it."

"You have a hot body, so lead with your hips, like this," she says and demonstrates a sexy hip move. I follow her lead. "Good. Just put your arms over your head like this and work your hips. Now add in your chest."

I get rolling again and hit a spin move.

"Did I say anything about spinning? No spinning. If it's crowded, that's potential for disaster."

"No spinning."

"You just need a little practice. Put some tunes on in your room and freestyle. You should dance in front of a mirror to see what works for you."

"Are you doing anything tonight? Because I really need you to come along."

I explain where we're going and she says, "Sure. Why not. Sounds better than studying econ."

"Hipster dress code."

"I can make that work."

"Grace, you're welcome to join us."

"Thanks. Maybe next time. I've got an art project I need to finish by tomorrow." I love Grace's British accent. "Good luck perfecting your dance moves."

I shower and blow-dry my hair as instructed. I still have Melissa's clutch with the cosmetics in the pocket; time to create my game face by applying the eyeliner and lipstick. The fedora and fringe jacket look like I'm trying too hard, but if Melissa thinks it works, then I'll roll with it.

The three of us stop by Sheila's room who emerges wearing a cheetah print figure-hugging bodycon dress and three-inch heels. Her hair is moussed to give it super volume. Melissa gives her the once-over and comments, "Rock on, Sheila. That's a hot number. Where'd you get that dress?"

We step outside the dorm looking like we are ready to rage. "Tonight, we're the Dirty Cash Quadsters," Jill suggests, and we all cackle.

The Town Car pulls up with the same driver that took me to Stonehurst, and I recall how much of an embarrassment I made of myself that night. The driver smiles at me as he opens the doors for us. There is a large crowd waiting to get past the bouncers checking IDs at the Dirty Cash Club. We pull up to a VIP spot where the driver tells us to sit tight while he makes a phone call. Within minutes a man jacked like a UFC fighter comes to escort us past the waiting line.

There is a downward ramp that feels like we are going into a subway station. The bouncer has the key to gain backstage entrance to the underground night club. The place is already packed with a crowd at the bars, loud music thumping above the chatter. I see Stoph on stage checking equipment, wearing large black headphones. The bouncer taps Stoph's shoulder and points in our direction. Stoph slides the headphones around his neck and waves to us.

"So, Paige, here's the big surprise, I'm headlining tonight." He grins and drapes his arm across my shoulders.

"I didn't even know you deejayed," I tell him.

"I'm the mashup maestro known for mixing some dance floor filth." Stoph shakes hands with my friends as I introduce them. "You ladies are going to own the dance floor tonight."

The bouncer shows us to the VIP section with full bar service, on the house thanks to the mashup maestro. We slide into comfy sofas roped off with velvet runway chords. Melissa orders Cosmopolitans for the Quadsters and the waitress returns with large martini glasses filled with the light pink vodka cocktails. These drinks taste a hundred times better than the gin martinis from the other night.

"Nicely balanced, not too sweet, not too bitter," Jill says like a seasoned Cosmo consumer.

A sign in front of Stoph's equipment table says DJ $toph. He has his baseball hat on backwards, his pants sagging for the occasion. The nightclub is at full capacity. The waitress delivers another round of drinks.

"He's adorable," Melissa says, as she downs her second drink and orders a third round. "Is he good in bed?"

"I'll let you know as soon as I do," I say feeling my face burning.

The stage lights up in flashing colors. Dry ice clouds swirl around DJ $toph, his voice booms over the sound system: "Let's go Dirty Caaaaaash!"

As if on cue, Sheila bolts to the dance floor and throws herself into gyrations, swinging her arms up overhead. Melissa and Jill pull me onto the floor and we break into a circle, but it becomes clear that Sheila owns the center, the rest of us give her room to work. The Cosmos are kicking in; I let it fly, whipping my head around like a possessed woman. I see Sheila watching me and laughing, "The Exorcist!"

As we rock out to his wub-heavy remixes, Stoph dances in place on the stage, looking like he is operating the devil's dashboard. Some of the Harvard Porcellian Club leaders silently watch from backstage.

We dance for hours. Stoph mixes on the fly. At last, the lights signal closing time. We have more drinks while we wait for him to pack up his mixer, turntables, and sound system. The bouncer escorts us to the car, and we all thank Stoph for a great time.

Sheila exchanges phone numbers with a punchee. "Call me," she giggles.

Stoph whispers in my ear, "Come with me."

I wave to the Quadsters as they file into the limo. Sheila responds with a wink, and the other two screech a goodbye. The bouncer helps Stoph load his equipment. Then we drive back to Stoph's dorm in his Audi.

He's got a huge room, a single. The space eddies with the easy chaos of a college guy living on his own: laundry piles in the corner, boxer shorts and socks on the floor, a textbook with his toothbrush marking the page where he left off. The room has high angled ceilings and a warm yellowish paint. There is a large window with a view of the courtyard by his desk and dresser. His bed, covered in a tartan plaid comforter with matching pillows, is positioned so he has a view of a massive elm. The walls are covered with music posters — Red Hot Chili Peppers, Psychedelic Porn Crumpets, Nirvana, Rainbow Kitten Surprise — and a framed photograph of him working as the deejay.

"I bet the Porcs were impressed tonight," I say.

Stoph opens his refrigerator and takes out two beers. He twists the tops off and hands one to me. "They watch my every move. It's hard to work like that. Hope they like my taste in music."

"The dance floor was the proof."

"You looked hot out there," he says and flashes a smile that makes me melt.

I sit on the ledge to admire the pretty plaza. Stoph runs his hand under the back of my dress, puts his beer down on the windowsill, and runs his other hand through my hair. He leans in to kiss me. I try to adjust myself so that I am against the wall rather than the glass as we are several stories above the ground and I don't want to die during dorm sex. He rocks against me so hard I imagine the window shattering and the two of us falling through the night sky in a starry blast of glass.

So, I steer the mashup maestro to the bed.

14. Sever and Austin

At first light, I wake to find Stoph is snoring loudly, so I pull on a pair of his sweat pants and go searching the campus for coffee.

There's a line at the deli. The smell of food frying on the grill — what Tanya calls *greasified Frankenfood, the curse of America* — teases my head and stomach into thinking I stepped into heaven. Several students are recapping their night out. I hear one of them talking about Dirty Cash. "Dude can mix. His transitions are next level."

I want to step in and say, *Hey guys, I'm the one he went home with*, but I doubt anyone would care or be all that impressed based on how I look in oversized sweats. I wonder at what point I can refer to Stoph as my boyfriend and whether I want that title. When I return to his room with the food, my clunking awakens him. He smiles when I hand him his breakfast.

"Some fan boys at the deli were raving about you." I scarf my sandwich and chug my coffee. "How did you learn how to mix like that?"

"In high school. My parents bought me all the equipment to get me started. I just played around with it until I got good."

"Most boys do sports."

"I do that, too."

I toss my empty cup in the trash basket. "Show me around campus?"

"Those sweats look a little big on you."

He finds me a t-shirt and Harvard shorts, which fit a little loose but comfy. He combs his fingers through his hair and puts on a baseball cap.

We stroll down Massachusetts Avenue, where Stoph points out a black door with the numerals 1324 under the arched window. Above the window, a profile of a boar's head is fixed to the brick building.

"The Porcellian clubhouse," he tells me. He points out an arched brick entryway with a wrought iron gate. "That's the McKean gate, built in honor of the club's founder Joseph McKean."

Above the gate is a limestone carving of a boar's head, the club's emblem. "The club began with a roast pig dinner — it was originally called the Pig Club — until someone decided to upgrade the name."

"Have you ever been in the clubhouse?" From the outside the building appears bland, nondescript.

"It's off-limits to non-members, except for the main level. They keep the shades closed all the time to prevent anyone from seeing inside. I read somewhere that the inside is no big deal, there's a bar and billiards, but not much more. I find that hard to believe, though. It's got to be more interesting, right?"

"I hope so, after all you've been through."

Farther down Mass. Ave. we enter Harvard Yard and I notice a Richardson Romanesque brick building. Stoph says this is Sever Hall. He positions me under the left side of the arch with my ear pressed to the brick wall, then goes to the other side twelve feet away and speaks into the wall, "Paige Moore!" His voice carries through the archway. It seems silly, but I like hearing him say my full name instead of the usual *dude*.

"Super cool," I say into the brick arch, so my voice carries back to Stoph.

Stoph comes around to my side. "The acoustical oddity is total Richardson. He always had a trick or two up his sleeve."

I study the ornamental detail. There is a triangle pediment above the back entrance with a big-eyed owl inside surrounded by oak leaves and acorns. The owl's eyes remind me of the carved owl heads stacked on the totem pole at the Porc bonfire. The swirling oak leaf patterns, like the ink sketching in the notebooks, resembles the woodland path at Stonehurst.

The north entrance detail shows the Harvard coat of arms with more oak leaves on one side and mistletoe on the other. "That plant combination as used by the Celtics in druid ritualistic ceremonies," I say.

The south entrance has two cherubim and pomegranates. Then I see it, a sprawling tree carved above the main entrance, surrounded by leaves, fruits and flowers. If Richardson's designs were inspired by the Bible, then this must be the Garden of Eden.

"What do you make of this?" I ask. "Tree of life guarded by cherubim? Those dolphins look like mythological creatures to me."

"I can't argue with that," he says. "I've been thinking about your insights into Richardson's biblical designs. I researched Richardson — his style with archways and rooflines — but found nothing about his life and influences."

I nod in agreement. "I noticed that too. No diaries, no monographs or significant articles about his life. He's an American icon. You'd think someone would have written his biography."

Stoph pulls off his hat to scratch his head. "I'm considering a design schematic of a Virtual Reality experience using Richardson's architecture. I think it would be epic to prove your theory that he built Solomon's Temple."

Stoph takes me to another Richardson building on the campus, a law school building called Austin Hall. It has all the Richardson Romanesque details with a triple arch, asymmetrical tower, and checkerboard stone patterns. I am intrigued by a detail in the ornamentation — plants swirling around the faces of terrified men.

"I think those two columns are Jachin and Boaz, the pillars that stood on the porch of Solomon's Temple," I say. "Solomon captured demons and put them to work on building his temple. One of the demons is Obizuth, a woman who strangled newborns, who had an invisible body and wild hair like Medusa. According to the Testament of Solomon, Solomon had her bound by her hair to the front of the temple for all to see. Check out the top of this column next to the entrance, I think it's Obizuth."

Stoph looks up, shielding the sun from his eyes. "That looks like her. Demons. What else?"

"Solomon captured the wind demon Ephippas, who placed the heavy cornerstone to the temple entrance. The demon Abezethibou was the one who hardened the pharaoh's heart to contain the people of Israel. Abezethibou was with the Egyptians at the Red Sea and he was trapped under a pillar. Ephippas helps Abezethibou carry the pillar but then Solomon seals them to the temple to carry the pillar forever. Check out the cornerstone over here, it has the compass and square symbols. Right above it, the two demons carry the pillar for eternity with Obizuth on top of the pillar."

Stoph whistles in admiration. "How do you know so much about demonology? You're like a walking encyclopedia on hell hounds."

"Post-concussion I sat in my room reading everything I could get my hands on. The weirder, the better. I read *The Lesser Key of Solomon* and became fascinated with demons. It all just stuck in my head for some reason."

"You amaze me."

"I think you should get a demon tattoo. Put it right here," I say and squeeze his butt.

"As soon as you get one."

"Maybe I'll get a tramp stamp," I joke, then rub my hand against the stone wall. "Richardson influenced a lot of architects, including Frank Lloyd Wright."

"I can't see Wright. He has a completely different style."

"At first glance. But Wright designed his living rooms to have a grand fireplace, just like Richardson, in a 20-by-20-cubit room. All of Wright's houses are 60x20, 40x20 and 20x20 cubit blocks in different arrangements. Wright promoted prefab construction because the Bible says no tools were used at the construction site of Solomon's Temple. The Bible says that the temple's winding got wider as the height increased. I think that was the thought behind the unique design for the Guggenheim. Wright was asked to build The Spirit of the Temple. Did that mean Solomon's Temple? The Guggenheim's main cylinder has a height of 60 cubits and a diameter of 60 cubits. The bottom of the spiral is five cubits wide and finishes seven cubits wide with the exact spiraling as described in the book of Kings."

Stoph stares at me wide-eyed. "Mic drop," he says.

"This is just the tip of the iceberg," I tell him. "The more time I spend looking into this, the more I realize nothing in early American design was random. Every detail has meaning."

Stoph leans his shoulder into mine and brushes his hand down my arm. "About last night," he says. "I loved everything about it."

"Trust me, it was my pleasure," I say and squeeze Stoph's hand. "There's plenty more of where that came from."

15. A.O.D.

It's a slow night at the Daily Grind with only a few customers braving the downpour. I wipe off the counters and stop to answer the phone.

"If you're inundated just let me know. I'm only checking in," Tanya says. It's the third time she's called tonight.

"No. It's dead."

"That's not good. Maybe we need to enhance our menu."

"Really? I think we offer a lot of choices."

"We do, but I've been holding back. I should release my latest find."

"What's that?"

"Mushroom coffee."

I freeze for a moment before I say, "Are the meditation trips sparked by mushrooms?"

"Not the illegal kind. Healing varieties, like reishi. Reishi are grounding mushrooms that put you into a deeper sleep, they cleanse the liver, have antihistamines and they help to balance yeast. If we do a deep dive on reishi, we can add years to our lives."

"So, whatever you used in the pre-meditation drinks was non-hallucinogenic?"

"Absolutely. I would never dose you, Paige."

"And now you want to add reishi mushrooms to the store coffee?"

"Definitely. And chaga, lion's mane, turkey tail."

"Sounds like a trip to the zoo."

Tanya chuckles. "Chaga is the king of the mushrooms. They have super-oxide dismutase, an anti-inflammatory. They're high in melanin, which is great for your eyes, skin and hair. Chaga is a great force field against daily pathogens. And the fruiting bodies in lion's mane supports creativity that's a high-powered nootropic when mixed with coffee."

"Nootropic?"

"Improves cognitive function. Then there's cordyceps that enhance physical energy."

"How about Joyce Carol Oates Cordyceps, because how else did she get the energy to write all those books. Maya Mane for Maya Angelou, Reishi Roth for Philip Roth, and Toni Turkey Tail for Toni Morrison."

"Write all that down. I'll finalize the mushroom coffee blends. You can close for tonight, Paige."

It's creepy being alone in the shop at night because the library is closed and no one is around. Memorial Hall is also closed, but there is a hint of light coming from the attic room.

I cross the street to the Rockery to get a better view of the two narrow windows below the half circle with the OA etched in the stone. Shadows seem to be moving across the attic ceiling. I cross the street to find the doors locked. Around the back of the building is another door that I find unlocked. I enter the dark building, listening for any activity. I go to the winding staircase and slip through the plastic blockade. I creep up the stairs. Halfway up, I hear footsteps behind me, so I race ahead to hide in a closet, with the door slightly cracked, just enough for me to peak out of the darkness.

The person reaches the attic level and raps five distinct knocks on the main door, pauses and five rapid knocks follow.

"Password?" A man's muffled voice comes from the other side of the door.

"Beezlebub," a woman responds. A moment later her silhouette enters the room and the door closes behind her.

I creep out of the closet and move to the storage room. I quietly slide the boxes away from the peep hole and crouch to see what's happening in there. A tall person in a hooded robe stands near the table in the center of the room. There is an animal fur altar covering, four pillar candles, a gold chalice, and a thick book.

"You're early, Enlightened Master Montgomery," the man says.

The woman swipes a feather duster on the wooden arms of the formal high-backed chairs. The red crushed velvet seats look worn and faded. The tops of the chairs are detailed with gold A.O.D. lettering inside an oak leaf wreath.

Their voices are muffled through the wall, but I can decipher what they are saying. "Have you observed any suspicious activity?"

"I have my eye on the intern. That paper she wrote was revealing. Did you read the copy I left on your desk?"

"I wonder how she can be figuring things out. It doesn't make sense that she could be doing it all on her own. By the way, she doesn't keep Hobson under control. She allowed him to growl and jump on me. With my foot injured from stepping on the broken glass at the lodge, I could barely keep my balance." The man flips the hood off his head. It is Treadwell, shuffling around in his Birkenstocks. "What about the robbery? Someone is on to us and we still have no leads."

"It could be the Porcellians sniffing around again. We will get to the bottom of this, Master Algorithms. How is your foot?"

She lights a three-wicked candle and sets it in place on the center table near the pillar candles.

"My foot is fine. I've barely slept in days because I'm canvassing every square inch of this town looking for clues."

A set of sequenced knocks announces the arrival of another hooded figure, who is greeted as Master Lexicon, who drops a pile of books at the foot of the altar table.

"Well, there you have it. That's all the books I could find."

Treadwell — Master Algorithms — reviews the titles on the book bindings. "The answers aren't in these books!"

"Settle down, Master Algorithms," she says.

Treadwell paces, taking deep breaths. More hooded figures are allowed entrance into the room, voicing the password, offering incense at the altar. When twelve members are present Enlightened Master Montgomery lights the rest of the candles. At the far end of the room a lantern glows toward the ceiling that illuminates the hand-painted eye. Treadwell grinds a pestle until there is a fine powder. Master Lexicon pours hot water into the ceramic cups to help make the ceremonial drink before the members hold up the mugs and recite: "We honor the sun as the source of all life. It connects us to the higher universe. The sun sustains us, we are made whole through its powers and mysteries."

Each member peers at Treadwell from under their hooded robes with double-headed eagle pendants draped around their necks. Treadwell raps his gavel three times and calls the meeting to order. "As you have most likely heard by now, the Order has been violated. Our meeting minutes and some of my research were stolen. I call upon Senior Warden. What say you?"

Senior Warden steps to the altar. "As the sun sets in the west to adorn the day, so presides the Worshipful Master to open and adorn his lodge. As Brother Richardson, like our chief architect Hiram Abiff before him, set his craft to work with wholesome direction, we must unify to protect the Order. The three wicks on the altar candle represent our three great lights: The Holy Bible, the square and the compass. The Holy Bible is given to us as a guide for our faith and practice, the square is to shape our everyday actions, and the compass is to keep us in due bounds with all those we interact with."

All the members of the Order angle their hands upward like referees signaling a touchdown. Senior Warden motions his right hand and says, "At ease."

All hands lower. Senior Warden removes his hood and I see it is Captain Biff. He turns and bows toward each corner of the room. After his final bow, he says, "At this juncture we have one eyewitness who reports to have seen four athletic looking men use crowbars to break into the Ames Gate Lodge. They stole a filing cabinet containing Master Algorithm's extensive research, our meeting minutes, and other documents. They drove away in a matte black Land Rover Defender with a Massachusetts license plate. No plate letters or numbers were obtained by the witness. Forensics verified the tire tracks at the crime scene are a match with Goodyear Wrangler tires. The witness verified the vehicle has hybrid-forged spoke wheels. Based on the description, there is only one registered matte black Land Rover Defender X with spoke wheels in Massachusetts. It is registered to

Landrace LLC which is an anonymous corporation in Wyoming. We are working with Wyoming officials to pierce the anonymous veil, although they do not seem to be in any rush to offer assistance. Landrace LLC used the address 1234 Massachusetts Avenue in Cambridge to register the vehicle in Massachusetts. The apartment is vacant and has not been rented in two years. It is above a Chinese restaurant and the landlord says it is vacant because the apartment smells perpetually like moo goo gai pan. While the lodge was ransacked, it does not appear that anything other than the filing cabinet was stolen. The witness also disclosed that she was approached by a man in a Dodge who flashed a badge and peppered her with random questions. The witness has been advised not to speak to anyone about the B&E except me. There has been no further reported incidents or suspicious activity aside from the B&E."

The room remains silent. Treadwell clears his throat. "Master Scribe, what say you?"

Master Scribe steps to the altar, bows to the Senior Warden and raises her arms overhead. The others raise their arms and after a few seconds they all drop them. Master Scribe says, "Truth is a divine attribute, hypocrisy and deceit are unknown amongst us. My investigative journalism has only this to contribute: the eyewitness to the B&E is a freshman at Kew College. Let it be known: the eyewitness is a wild thing. She spends more time partying than studying. She is dating a sophomore at Harvard who has been punched by Porcellian. She has attended two punch functions with him, one at Stonehurst and one at an exclusive night club in Cambridge. The eyewitness works at the new coffee shop in town. I arranged to interview the shop owner for a new business feature article; she's a new age hippie who seems harmless, but I am surveilling her house and the coffee shop. I will continue to accumulate information."

Treadwell steps forward, bows to Master Scribe and calls out, "Keeper Boots-n-Paddles, what say you?"

"Roight then," says the owner of Boots-n-Paddles Olde English pub. "There has been no suspicious activity to report. I will remain on the lookout."

Treadwell steps to the altar. "We need to step up the search. I sectioned off the town map and we will each take an area. Leave no stone unturned. If the slightest thing crosses your mind, we need to communicate with the group. Look at every townie and visitor as a potential suspect."

"What if someone beats us to the compass?"

"Master Scribe, we'll find it. Senior Warden will get to the bottom of this."

Master Lexicon points toward the books she brought. "Master Scribe and I have been doing some reading in the newsroom archives. Maybe we haven't been looking in the right places. Yes, we know Richardson returned from the United Kingdom with the compass for the Ancient Order of Druids. We have a photograph to prove his allegiance to the A.O.D. and not to Porcellian. It's been a hundred years since anyone has seen the compass. Just because there was a robbery and your research was stolen, that doesn't mean anyone will find it before us."

"Well, we *had* the photograph. It was in the filing cabinet," he says.

"And you never thought to make a copy?"

Treadwell fires back, "And risk having extra copies get in the wrong hands? If anyone figures out what the compass looks like or what it's for, then we'll have a problem. Let's settle down. My research has verified that Richardson's true allegiance was with the A.O.D. Somewhere within our order we have the answer to where the compass is located. Other A.O.D. members knew where Richardson hid it, but that information is lost. The A.O.D. remains vigilant about protecting the artifacts to keep them from the Porcellians who want it for money and power."

Captain Biff says, "The A.O.D. must find the biblical artifacts to protect them as God intended. Richardson left us the signs. We must figure it out before Porcellian does."

I tiptoe past the door and pad down the stairs. It is pouring again and a crack of lightning lights up the sky. I forgot my umbrella at the coffee shop, but I need to get out of here, so I run down the sidewalk not stopping until I get back to my dorm.

16. Suspicions

The next day, Ms. Montgomery fixes her owl-eyed stare on me when I arrive a few minutes late; her cheeks inflate like a pufferfish.

"I know, I'm sorry —"

"I don't need excuses, young lady. You are exactly seventeen minutes overdue and you will have to stay after to make up that time. Look to the stacks of material that need your immediate attention."

I fill up my cart with returned books. Her gaze follows me up and down the aisles. When I shelve the last book, Ms. Montgomery instructs me to set up folding chairs in a circle for a middle school program.

"Writing can be a painful process," she tells the kids. "The English language has evolved into slang, abbreviations, and choppy conversations. I know sometimes when writers dig into their heads and hearts to produce fresh writing it can feel like running five miles barefoot in the snow. I think that the written word helps to expand the recognition of the soft voice of a protected interior life."

I wonder why, if she is so knowledgeable about the writing process, she doesn't write her own guidebook.

After she assigns a prompt for the group, Ms. Montgomery visits the archive department. I lean against the closed door, but I can't hear anything, so I open the door and creep onto the top step.

Ms. Montgomery says, "It's time to question her. She knows something."

"Maybe the Porcellians have the boy feeding her information."

"Shouldn't we leave it to Captain Biff? He has more experience —"

"Nonsense. I will handle it."

"Alright, but take it easy. We need her —"

"Will you listen to yourself! She's running around with a future Porcellian. She's already on the wrong side of this."

Toward the end of my shift, Ms. Montgomery hands me a batch of periodicals. "These materials need to go down to the archive department. When you are done with that then you can leave."

The archive department is dark except for a desk lamp giving off just enough light so I can see my way down the steps. The bulb at the bottom of the steps must be burnt out. I kneel by a cabinet to replace a book on the lowest shelf when I feel I am suddenly grabbed, then shoved face first toward the cement floor. A bony knee drives into my back pinning me to the ground.

"What are you doing?" Treadwell leans close to my ear.

"I'm putting away—"

He doesn't wait for an answer. "Get up. I thought you were an intruder."

"Ms. Montgomery sent me. What's wrong with you?"

"Sorry. But you might not realize that you've been sticking your nose into some serious business. A matter of life and death. You could find yourself in trouble if you aren't careful."

"I was an innocent bystander. I wasn't sticking my nose into anything. There is no need to —"

"Has your boyfriend mentioned anything about the Porcellians looking for a compass?"

"No." I say, "but there was another person —"

Treadwell steps closer. "Who?"

"I'm not sure," I say and tell him about the guy that flashed a badge and asked about what I saw.

"And he specifically asked about the compass?"

I can't tell Treadwell the truth — that I was the one who referred to the compass when I was talking to the fake cop — so I say, "He asked me if I heard anything about the compass and I told him no."

"What did he look like?"

"Stocky. He had a hat pulled low."

"How old was he?"

"Not sure."

"Was he college aged or older?"

I shrug. "I don't know. What's the deal with the compass?"

"There are people that want to steal it from us."

I lean closer to Treadwell's face. "Who's us? Your committee?"

"What committee?"

"The one you had to go meet with the day I was in the shovel museum and you closed early."

"Listen, young lady, I'm the one asking the questions. Did you take something that doesn't belong to you?"

"You mean the compass?"

"No one has the compass! I'm talking about books from the archive department. Did you take books?"

"No. And if this compass is so important how come no one knows where it is?"

He lowers his voice. "I see you all over this town on your bike, walking the dog, driving with that Harvard snot, poking around the library. I read your paper. How do you know so much about H.H. Richardson? Solomon's Temple?"

"Ms. Montgomery asked me to write a report —"

"There is no research anywhere that says he built a replica of Solomon's Temple. Where are you getting this information? Is that owner of the coffee shop —"

"No! I figured it out myself. Deductive reasoning."

"I've heard enough. And please understand: You can call the police to complain, but I think you'll find it a bit unrewarding. I have a certain standing in this town. It's in your best interest to keep this conversation between us. Don't tell your boyfriend or his Porcellian thugs either. If you do hear anything else about the compass, come tell me, Ms. Montgomery or Captain Biff. Got it?"

"Got it." I stagger up the steps toward the main library.

"You're still here?" says Ms. Montgomery, lowering the book she is reading. "You stayed well beyond the seventeen minutes you had to make up."

When I arrive extra early to work the morning shift, the library is empty. Hobson is not in his crate, so I peer out the large observatory window toward the back garden where I see Ms. Montgomery strolling around the reflection pool with Hobson. She stares into the fountain for a few minutes, then looks over at the Daily Grind.

Tanya comes up the soggy turf to prop the chalkboard easel outside the shop announcing the daily specials. Hobson pulls his way toward Tanya to sniff for treats that she usually has for him. Hobson's water dog tendencies emerge as he dives and rolls in a mud puddle in front of the coffee shop. Ms. Montgomery struggles to control him.

Inside the library I notice something new: a large banquet table with a coffee making machine and coffee pods, disposable cups and lids, plastic stirring straws, and creamer. There's a sign with a yellow smiley face that says: *Enjoy free coffee from the Best Small Library in America.*

Ingenious. Montgomery wants to sabotage the Daily Grind. The backdoor slams, her library hush voice rises to a high decibel as she disciplines filthy Hobson. I venture to the back room where she is punishing the drenched dog by shoving him into his crate.

"What happened?" I ask, feigning ignorance about the splashdown in the garden.

"What is going on in that hunk of trailer trash out there? I demand an explanation right now!"

"I'm not sure what you mean."

"It's not a coffee shop, it's a front for that crazy woman's drug den! I see you college punks paying homage to that coffee kook, sitting on the floor, smoking and drinking. She's not brewing coffee — she's brewing a counterculture revolution. I will not tolerate this drug ring in my backyard!"

"It's just coffee."

"Miss, I can see it with my own eyes. College rebels hallucinating in circle time. Nothing gets past me. And now, and now, she is advertising mushroom coffee? Psychedelic mushrooms! She has no license to distribute narcotics. It's illegal. I'm contacting the FDA."

"Ms. Montgomery, the smoke is natural sage and incense. The nutritional mushrooms are all FDA approved."

"I've been around a lot longer than you, miss, and I lived through the 1960s. I know all about tuning in and dropping out. Your *friend* is just another Timothy Leary!"

I keep my voice level. "Tanya Goforth promotes healthy food. Mushroom coffee is just another healthcentric idea she has for turning Shovel Town into a Blue Zone for healthspan."

"Healthcentric Blue Zone for healthspan? Whosie-whatsie? I see you drank the Kool-Aid, miss. Take this dog and give him a bath. You should have been here to walk him earlier instead of leaving the mud wrestling to me."

I lead Hobson back to my dorm because I don't know what else to do with him. In the bathroom at my end of the hallway, I give him a coconut shampoo and shower. He loves it. When he's done shaking, there are mud splatters all over the tile walls.

Melissa steps out of the other shower. "Gross. What's that creature?"

"This is Hobson."

She flares her nostrils as if smelling rotten eggs. "Call animal control. I wouldn't name a stray; you don't want to get attached to that thing."

"It's the librarian's dog."

"What a mess," she says and wraps her hair in a towel.

"Yeah, I know, sorry I'll clean it up."

I grab paper towels to wipe the mud off the shower walls and run the water until the stall is clean. I towel dry him as best I can, then rev my handheld hairdryer on his undercoat. Hobson is impatient with the grooming session, so he shakes off coconut water around my room, then curls up in the bean bag chair.

While Hobson snores, I pull out the books I took from the archive department. I need to figure out what the deal is with this compass and if it has anything to do with Richardson's Solomonic Temple in North Easton.

Ever since I arrived at college, I've felt like I am under a spell. I lived out my high school years entrenched in the world of novels. Now, I feel like I have become one of those characters. An eyewitness to a robbery, a secret druid society, a mystery compass, a trail of clues from a dead architect, and a dreamy boyfriend.

This can't be my life.

17. Ecole des Beaux-Arts

At the next Daily Grind staff meeting Tanya announces, "I don't want to be an alarmist, but I need to make you all aware that I was followed last night after I left here."

"Did you see who it was?" asks a new addition to the staff.

"No. I didn't pick up on it until I was almost home."

"Maybe we should install security cameras," Paul suggests.

"That's not my style," Tanya says. "Just be aware of your surroundings." Then she shares that the coffee shop has earned a small profit since opening, and we all cheer.

Tanya works through a list of small improvements that will help boost customer service. Then she dims the lights and instructs us to roll out our yoga mats for a group meditation. The room fills with woody scented patchouli incense.

She serves a freshly mixed herbal tea drink which smells like burnt orange peel and sage. "Herbs for dreamwork," she says. "Tell your minds to get out of the driver's seat for a while. Remember: ask and the universe will answer."

I try deep breathing to create some space in my head, but the thoughts of my recent insights crowd in with loud jingling sounds. The jingling intensifies into clanging gears rotating on a moving wall that slides toward me. Flashing colors transition from emerald green to whale gray to a deep purple. I reach for an empty mirror on the wall that my hand moves through like water. For a moment I remain in one dimension while my hand waves through cloudy moving air on the other side, then my body follows my hand.

I wallow knee-deep in a silvery stream of thick fog in the courtyard of an old European building with rows of ground level archways. Posed in each archway are white statues of gods and goddesses. A high marble pedestal in the center of the courtyard supports a robed female figure with her hand outstretched toward the heavens. I spin 360-degrees to absorb the statues of naked gods and goddesses, stopping to fixate on her hand pointing toward the heavens. The statue moves as if she is a pantomime, then she looks down at me.

"What are you looking at?"

"Your hand," I say.

"What about my hand?"

A sign by the entrance reads *Ecole des Beaux-Arts*. "I am pondering the human situation in greater cosmic order. Your finger pointing to the heavens symbolizes the microcosm of human existence in relation to the macrocosm of the universe. I think we are all just a spot of dust in this vast universe."

Unimpressed, she stiffens back to her statuary self.

I know she can hear me, so I continue, "I'm wondering what relationship we have with the universe."

"You're overthinking it."

"I am?"

"I'm pointing in a direction."

"Like a compass?"

I catch a whiff of something familiar in the breeze, Tanya's mugwort, reminding me that I am in a deep meditative state. Three students dressed in brown robes carry stacks of books through the courtyard clouds. One student has the face of an eagle, the other has the head of a lion and the third has a dolphin head. They are speaking French as they pass me.

The lion looks back at me and says, *"Puis-je vous aider?"*

I should have studied French instead of Spanish. "Sorry, I don't understand."

"Eh, parlez vous anglais?"

"Oui." The eagle head joins us. "Are you lost?"

"No. I'm thinking about the universe and Solomon's Temple."

The eagle erupts into French with his friends, who join in his merriment. "Here we study how to design according to the biblical presentations of Solomon's Temple."

"Is it safe to say that there is creative leeway from one architect to another on how to recreate the temple?"

The eagle squawks, "You could say that. Provided the biblical dimensions are properly applied."

"The cubits and measurements, yes, but —"

"Eh, but what?"

"H.H. Richardson built Solomon's Temple in a small town in Massachusetts."

"Who?"

"Richardson. He's one of the founding fathers of American architecture."

"I see. And why would he build Solomon's Temple in America?" The eagle erupts with laughter, then says to his friends, "*Arche de l'alliance cache en Amerique.*"

"What's funny?"

"America is the last place Solomon's Temple would be built." The eagle raises his beak and continues. "American architecture lacks depth. There is nothing in America suited to house a French croissant, let alone the ark of the covenant."

Solomon's Temple was built to protect the ark of the covenant, a sacred chest made by the ancient Israelites according to instructions from God. The chest stored the Ten Commandments written on two stone tablets. The ark was housed in Solomon's Temple where it remained protected in a special room called the holy of holies. It was off-limits to all except Solomon, the high priest. The ark served as an archive for the tablets, a golden jar of manna and Aaron's rod. The cover of the ark was painted with an image of Anubis, an Egyptian jackal god, for protection.

"You are not familiar with Richardson? He is a graduate of this school. His talent and education enabled him to create like the European greats."

The statue on the pedestal claps her hands and shouts, "Bravo!"

If Richardson built Trinity Church as a Solomon's Temple replica, and North Easton is another replica, he was designing with biblical dimensions to protect the ark. There is another Richardson building called the Ames Monument in Wyoming, which is located at the highest point on the transcontinental railroad. The monument is a granite pyramid, sixty feet tall, standing alone in a ghost town. Perhaps Richardson built several temples in case the ark needed to be moved and hidden in different locations. I need to take a closer look at Stonehurst, the Buffalo Insane Asylum, Albany City Hall, the Allegheny County Courthouse, and his other buildings.

Tanya's soothing voice eases me out of my meditative state. "How did it go? Could you get into it?"

"I got in, all right. Definitely cool. Feels deeper than dreaming. It's like watching a film in my head. These meditations help me to sort out my ideas."

"You're getting good at this." She opens a window to let some of the incense escape.

Two police officers step inside the coffee shop. Tanya says, "Are you here for coffee or…?"

They do a visual sweep of the staff sitting in lotus on the yoga mats.

"We received a call about suspicious activity going on in here," one officer explains.

"It's a group meditation."

"We had a complaint of underage partying."

"This is the second time this happened. Captain Biff came last time."

"I see."

Tanya says, "Certain members of the library staff have a vivid imagination."

"Right," says the cop. "Got it."

The other cop reads container labels in the kitchen and jots down the herb names. He picks up the ashtray, sniffs the patchouli remnants, and sneezes. He opens the cabinets and refrigerator, and he glances in the trash can. He holds up a jar of turkey tail and scrunches his nose as if it smells foul.

The other cop shines his flashlight in our eyes to check our pupils. He steps on my yoga mat as he crosses back toward the door. The officers exchange glances in a partner commentary the rest of us are not privy to. "We're all set here. Sorry to bother you."

"It won't happen again," says the other cop.

After the staff leaves, I say, "You have to forgive Ms. Montgomery, she's — ah — old."

"I have no ill feelings against her. I just wish she'd drink one of our calming blends."

"Any idea who might be following you?"

"A guy in a grayish sports car, the other day. Then I thought I heard footsteps on my front porch in the middle of the night, but no one was out there when I looked out."

I sweep the floor even though it looks clean. "Are you feeling freaked out?"

Tanya twists the tie around the full trash bag. She shrugs. "It's a small town. People don't like change or anything that disrupts the status quo."

Tanya shuts off all the lights except the one behind the counter. She decides to hang some string lights in the kitchen area. We are a two-person assembly line, admiring the whimsical glow around the cabinets. As Tanya steps back to survey our work we hear voices outside, followed by clunk-clunk-clunk sounds.

"Shut off the light."

My heart starts racing as I duck to creep toward the window with Tanya. There are two bodies silhouetted by the moonlight, darting around the reflection pool.

They have a lengthy hose and a pool pump that makes a humming sound when it is turned on. They drag the hose as far as it can stretch straight toward the coffee shop; the gushing sound of backwashing water surrounds the shop.

"You see anything?" asks the woman.

"Nothing."

Once the water fully drains, they crawl on their hands and knees feeling around the base of the pool. The man starts tapping around with a rubber mallet moving from side to side until he works his way into the center where the fountain stands.

Tanya calls the police. We crouch under the window and wait for the cops.

"There's supposed to be a trap door in this pool." They shine flashlights searching the concrete floor.

"There's not."

"Hook up the hose and refill this thing." She retrieves the end of the hose. "Call for an A.O.D. meeting tomorrow night. This was a miserable failure."

After they leave Tanya steps outside into ankle-deep swampy grass. "Were they trying to flood my coffee shop? Does someone want me out of here that badly? Where's the cops?"

When Captain Biff arrives thirty minutes later, Tanya flips on all the lights. She explains what she saw. He glances at me. "You again?"

"Me again."

"Do you have anything to add?"

"Not necessarily."

His wet shoes squeak as he walks through the shop. "Are you being followed as well?"

"Not that I'm aware of," I say.

"You still have my business card?"

"In my wallet."

"You may need it."

18. Sushi for Four

I pick up the bohemian dress from the dry cleaners and stop by Melissa's room to return it. She's sitting in front of her mirror, applying a hot iron to her hair. "I got five Porcellian phone numbers from Dirty Cash."

"You want to try for six? Stoph is bringing his friend to go out for sushi. He wants to introduce you. Can you join us?"

"When?"

"Tonight."

"Oh my God, we need to get *prepared*." She pops her eyes and power blinks a dozen times.

"You mean, coordinating sushi outfits?"

She points to my crotch. "I'm talking about being prepared down there. You know, a bikini wax?"

My face flares from embarrassment.

"You cannot date a Harvard guy if you're rocking a full sailor's beard. That's a hard no. I've seen you in the shower,

Bigfoot." She tosses the hairbrush in disgust. "Let's go get this over with. There's a nail place in town that does wax jobs. I mean, not New York salon waxing, but it will have to do."

"Seriously? Don't you think this is a double standard. I mean, I doubt he gets his balls waxed."

"Trust me," she says and takes out two shot glasses and a bottle of vodka. "It won't hurt as much if we pre-treat."

I guess this is part of the female bonding experience, so I toss down two shots of vodka and chase it with a beer. "Fine. Let's get this over with."

On the way into town, Melissa asks, "How was the after-party when you left Dirty Cash?"

"There wasn't an after party. We went back to his room."

"Hello, that's what I mean by after party," she cackles. "Well, does he?"

"What?"

"Wax his balls?"

I want to tell Melissa that it's none of her business, but I recognize this might be one of those *letting people into my bubble* situations that the counselor talked about. "It was too dark to tell."

"You went all the way?"

"Most of the way."

"That boy doesn't take his eyes off you. He's totally obsessed."

The nail salon is empty. The woman behind the counter shouts, "Mani-pedi?"

Much to my embarrassment Melissa announces, "Bikini wax. I just need a touch up, but she needs the full monty. We're talking Sasquatch."

"She hairy? Big bush? You come sit. I fix."

I glare at Melissa. "Do you have to call me Sasquatch?"

"Come, big bush college girl. Sit here and I wax. No more coochie-poof. No Sasquatch."

"Couldn't you go with some other animal? Maybe Bambi?"

"Bambi not so hairy. Sasquatch."

The woman closes the door and instructs me to remove my pants and underwear. She hands me a chart and asks what I want as if I am ordering ice cream. The chart has graphic drawings of hair patches that are groomed into shapes called the martini glass, the happy hoo-hoo, champagne, postage stamp, half moon, full moon, and the landing strip. The aesthetician prepares the hot wax and looks at what she must work with. Then she comments, in broken English, "You Amazon forest. Scary."

"I'll take the martini glass."

I sit on her operating table and she gets to work applying hot wax with a fat popsicle stick, then presses the paper down. Then the forest ranger shreds away one section of overgrowth at a time. All the vodka shots in the world couldn't dull this pain. I hold onto the table with a death grip and grind my teeth in agony.

"Wax bush for boyfriend?" She asks casually, as if we've been friends since middle school.

I look at the aesthetician in disbelief. This is no time to start a conversation.

"Sort of," I respond, and wonder who I am doing this for.

When she finally finishes, she leaves the room so I can get dressed. I slide off her table with my inflamed crotch stinging. I pull up my underwear and jeans and limp to the cash register. I can't believe I am paying someone for making me this miserable.

"Not so bad, right? Now you're set for three weeks," Melissa says as we shuffle back to the dorm.

"Three weeks, my ass."

"You can get your ass waxed next time. That's called a Brazilian."

"There is no next time. Stoph can bring a weed-wacker for all I care."

"That's no way to treat a one percenter."

"I don't care if he's Jeff Bezos. My crotch stings like a murder hornet."

I retreat to the safety of my own room where I press an ice pack on my throbbing coochie-poof. Frida Kahlo, drinking her coffee and smoking her blunt on the poster, stares back as if she completely understands me for who I am, with or without the waxed martini glass. By the looks of her unibrow, she's not one to pluck or shave a single hair.

I stop by Melissa's room to see if she is ready. She rolls her eyes. "Is that what you're wearing?"

"I suppose you have Asian inspired silk kimonos stashed in your closet?"

"I guess jeans and a t-shirt are fine. Try this top? Step it up a notch. Make sure your toes are done because you will be asked to take your shoes off if it's traditional Japanese," she says.

"Thanks. Come by my room whenever you're ready," I say.

There's a light tap on my door and when I open it, Stoph is standing there with sunflowers. He pulls a bottle of champagne out of his backpack.

"What are we celebrating?"

"I made it to the next round." The flowers are in a purple vase, which I set on top of my dresser. Stoph pops the champagne and I offer travel mugs from the coffee shop.

"This next punch round is different. They won't give us any details, but they indicated we will be MIA for at least twenty-four hours."

"Seriously? They expect you to just fly off the radar for a whole day? What about your classes?"

Stoph shrugs. "Part of the program. We are sworn to secrecy for life. No one in the history of the Porcellian Club has ever disclosed what goes on during the overnight."

The champagne goes straight to my head. I lean over to kiss him with an intensity that surprises him. "What's got into you?"

"You're complaining?" I kiss him again and he puts his cup on the floor. His hands move in unison under my t-shirt.

There's a knock and before we have a chance to react, Melissa barges in.

"Didn't know you read Braille, Stoph."

"Champagne?" I offer, adjusting my top.

"I never say no to some bubbly," she says, dropping into the beanbag chair.

She swigs down a glass and helps herself to another. "Where we going? Atomic Sushi?"

"How did you guess?" he asks. He passes the rest of the bottle to Melissa. "Actually, we should get going. Chase is meeting us there."

Melissa waves a t-shirt at me. "You should switch to this," she says.

I hold up her plain white V-neck. "What's so special about this shirt?"

"Try it on and you'll see."

I turn my back and switch shirts. She's right. It feels wonderful and fits perfect.

"Is that a Prada?" asks Stoph.

"Of course, darling," says Melissa.

I'm a little jealous how easily Stoph gets on with Melissa, and he seems to sense it. He pulls me in close and whispers, "She's processed. You're a natural beauty."

When we arrive at the sushi place, he requests a private booth with sliding *shoji* screens. We remove our shoes and slide into the booth to face each other. He orders *sake* for the table. The *sake* is syrupy and tastes sweet like plums. We sip it until Chase's swift strides cut across the restaurant and he slides into the seat next to Melissa. He is short with blond hair, horn-rimmed glasses, and sits ramrod straight-backed. I see Melissa eye his golf shirt with the Shinnecock Hills Golf Club logo. He says, "My lab ran late."

"What's your major?" Melissa asks.

"Pre-med."

"Nice."

"Intense," he says.

"Let's start with some rolls and sashimi," Stoph suggests. He slides his foot on top of mine and playfully strokes my toes.

"I've never had sushi before," I say.

Melissa feigns a spit-take. "You're going to love it."

Stoph pours soy sauce in a small dish, so I do the same.

"This is the wasabi." He points with his chopsticks toward the green mound of Play-Doh. "Just take a pinch and make a slurry like this."

I feel like a robo-date doing whatever he tells me. After I stir the brown puddle, I see him dip a rice roll into his slurry and pop it in his mouth. I do the same and grab for my water to wash down the stinging sensation.

Stoph squeezes my hand. "Dude, you made it too strong. Wasabi can blow out your sinuses if you use too much."

I wipe the tears from my eyes and wonder why he calls me dude. I already have a one syllable name, so it's not like he needs to shorten it. I take a piece of sashimi but I don't enjoy the texture of raw fish, so I chase the salmon piece with more *sake*.

Chase shares a story about going to a party with Stoph first semester freshman year. He can barely get the story out because he and Stoph are laughing so hard. "It took three of us to carry Stoph back to the dorm! My dad's a firefighter so I know the fireman's carry, but what a mess."

"He saved my ass," Stoph says, laughing. "I'll take credit for being the inspiration for him to become a doctor."

"My first patient," Chase says.

I notice while we are laughing at Chase's story, Melissa politely smiles, but barely looks at him. She twirls her hair around her finger and sips her *sake*. She excuses herself to the ladies' room, and side-eyes me to come along.

While I pee, Melissa reapplies her makeup in the mirror.

"He's short and his dad is a firefighter. He hasn't been punched, right?"

"Dunno. Is that a problem?" I flush the toilet.

"We would look ridiculous together. I would tower over him."

"And that's a deal breaker?"

"Hello? His dad is a firefighter. Does that sound like one percent to you? Obviously, his golf shirt is false advertising. His family doesn't belong to Shinnecock."

"You're so shallow."

"Money and looks, Paige. It's all that matters. We're Kew College. They're Harvard. I want a Porcellian. Think about it. If we marry a one-percenter, then we become one-percenters. Ever hear of MacKenzie Scott?"

"No, who's she?"

"Jeff Bezos' wife. Was his wife. She scored fifty billion dollars in the divorce."

"Are you thinking that far ahead?"

"You bet I am."

"What if Chase finds a cure for some disease? He'd make a lot of money and do a lot of good. A winning combo."

Melissa brushes her hair. "True, that could happen. Or — now hear me out — or I can hook up with an existing Porcellian and not wait while Chase struggles to make the winning combo happen. I'd have to work my ass off to help pay his medical school tuition. Old money is where it's at Paige. Stoph is old money, I can tell, with one look at his dimples."

"I don't care. He's a nice guy and so is Chase. I think you should give him a chance."

"I don't do blue collar."

"His father saves lives! That's too blue collar for you?"

"Then you date him if he's so heroic."

"You're a gold digger."

"Guilty as charged."

When we go back to the table dessert awaits. Stoph says, "I ordered *anmitsu* for us. I hope you like it."

"Looks delicious," I say and smile at Chase.

The *shoji* screens slide open as the waiter returns to collect the dishes. When we leave the booth, I feel the *sake* go to my head and I start giggling. Stoph opens the car door for me and before I get in, he kisses me and squeezes my butt. Melissa power-sighs as she gets into the back seat.

We drive back to our campus where Melissa hops out, says thanks, and leaves us alone.

"Want to take a walk?" Stoph asks.

"Love to," I say.

We head into town, stroll past the Boots-n-Paddles Olde English pub. Stoph says, "Care for a pint?"

"Sure."

The brick-walled interior has a large mahogany bar and red nail-head leather bar stools. We sit at the bar and watch the soccer game while the bartender pulls two pints of Bass Ale from the tap.

"Man U or Man City?" asks the bartender with a British accent. He places two paper coasters in front of us followed by the beers.

"Man City," I say, raising my glass toward the bartender. "I'm basically A.B.U."

"That a girl," he says. "Anyone but United!"

Stoph shrugs. "I don't follow soccer."

"I won't hold it against you. Have you ever been to England?"

"Nope. You?"

"London. For a soccer tournament with my travel team. It was a blast." I sip the beer. "When Richardson was in England after Harvard, hanging around with Adams, I think he was part of the Ancient Order of Druids."

"How did you arrive at that conclusion?"

"The druids wear those hooded robes like the one Richardson has on in that formal portrait. Plus, I discovered there's an active Ancient Order of Druids secret society in North Easton."

"Seriously?"

"Yep. I spied on one of their meetings. They're up in arms about the break-in at the lodge. And they want to find the compass. They said there was a photograph of Richardson with the compass that was kept in the filing cabinet that was stolen."

"You spied on druids?"

"The meeting was in the Memorial Hall attic. Remember the peep hole? I watched the meeting as if I were at the movies. They all wore robes and they had wacky names for each other. Do you know what I think?"

"I'm listening."

"I think Richardson brought the compass back from England and it's a relic that belongs to the druids."

"Sounds like an episode on the History channel. Unsolved mysteries," he says in a fake British voice.

"Exactly. But there has to be more to it. Why would Richardson hide it? He hid it so well that no one has found it in over a hundred years? Someone has been trying to steal it. Why?"

"Maybe it's valuable? Like a rare diamond?"

The bartender wipes the area in front of us with his white cloth. "Another round?"

I slide a twenty toward him and say, "No, thanks, we're all set. Keep the change."

"Roight, then," he stashes the bill in his shirt pocket.

"I want to show you something," I tell Stoph. He slips his hand in mine as we meander through town. I take him to the side of Memorial Hall where there is a lion's head and a patina sundial.

"It's a diptych-dial," I explain.

"A what?"

"A combination of a sundial and a compass. Remember when you showed me the trick in the arches with our voices carrying from one side to the other? We agreed that Richardson had a lot of tricks up his sleeve?"

"Go on."

"He studied engineering at Harvard. I think Richardson engineered his own diptych-dial right here beneath the lion's head. The book of Kings says there were lion carvings on the steps leading to Solomon's throne. The cross below is a Knights Templar cross, which is a symbol of the Temple of Solomon. This sundial will lead to the compass everyone is looking for. I'm sure of it."

"Why?"

"A diptych-dial is supposed to hinge open. I think if we can get up to the pointer of the sundial and physically move it—"

"Quick. Hop on my shoulders." Stoph stoops so I get on his shoulders. He slowly rises and leans toward the wall. I stretch high enough to grip the pointer, but Stoph shifts and I pull too hard.

"Shit! It snapped off."

Stoph lowers me down. "Okay, just act casual."

My heart is pounding. "It just snapped off so —"

"Let's see it."

Stoph steps under a street lamp to analyze the pointer from all angles. "The edge is grooved like a key. The pointer — the gnomon — is usually flat."

"That does look like a key. A diptych-dial is hinged and opens. This is Richardson's way of opening something —"

Stoph pauses. "Maybe it opens one of his other buildings? Something in the library?"

"The attic room, I bet, the holy of holies. Memorial Hall is Solomon's Temple. We need to go up to the attic."

The door is open — choir practice in the auditorium — and the singing makes enough sound to cover our footsteps as we creep up the winding staircase. I start looking in the main room while Stoph rummages through the side room. I run my hand along the walls, searching for a secret door. The floorboards are all intact with no trap doors. Richardson would not make this obvious, so I keep searching. The altar used in the meeting is pushed to the side. I run my hands along the sides and across the top.

Stoph joins me in the meeting room. "Anything?"

I shake my head. I stand under the painted eye to engage in a staring contest. The eye is peeking through a hole in a blue sphere. Is it God looking into his universe? Solomon looking down at his temple? The paint around the eye is slightly crackled with age. The gold rays encircle the eye with more sunrays stemming from the outermost circle.

"Can you bring one of those chairs?" Stoph carries a high-backed meeting chair and I stand on it to look closer and gasp. "There's no way —"

Stoph says, "Yes, I think I see it too — a hairline crack."

"Here, take the pointer, see if you can reach."

Stoph gets on the chair. His long arms stretch just far enough to slide the pointer into the crack. "It fits. Try turning it," I say.

When Stoph turns the pointer, paint chips fall to the floor. Nothing happens. "It's stuck! I can't turn it back or get it out."

"But it fit in there like a key. It has to turn —"

We hear a cracking sound.

"What the fuck!" Stoph dives from the chair. "The ceiling is opening!"

A fault line stretches across the ceiling as large chunks of plaster crumble to the floor. A dust cloud kicks up around us. We both start coughing. Then I see it, a gold square object tucked inside the nest of wires near the ceiling beam.

"Stoph, can you reach it?"

He slides the chair and steps up to snatch the gold object. "Let's get out of here."

Oh, beautiful for spacious skies...the choir is in full patriotic harmony drowning out the sounds of us hustling down the stairs and out the front entrance.

I look in every direction. "Coffee shop."

We run down the sidewalk, across the sloped landscape until we reach the Daily Grind. Paul — now recovered from his cold — is working the night shift. He waves when he sees me. "Why is your hair white?"

I swipe the plaster dust from my hair and Stoph does the same. "Messy art project. I'll have a large Truman Capote Reishi Cappuccino."

Stoph says, "Make that two, please."

"Good choice." Paul blends Reishi, almond milk, He Shou Wu, cacao powder, coconut oil, cinnamon, chocolate stevia and Xylitol for added sweetness. "Enjoy."

We regroup at a corner table. I act casual, reading the menu board's new healing blends — Ray Bradbury Brain Fog Cutters, Robert Frost Fire Cider, James Fenimore Cooper Maca Bomb and Alice Walker Beauty Elixir.

"Let's see it," I whisper.

He takes it from his pocket and hands it to me. The case is slightly larger than a pack of cigarettes and two inches thick. Two gold latches pull outward to release the cover. Inside are two glass circles — a sundial and a compass — with etched lines of latitude and longitude. A string connects to a hook at the base of the sundial. The top of the sundial has an eye etched into the gold. It's an antique unlike anything I've ever seen. The needle on the compass points to the letter W. I close the box and hand it to Stoph.

"You better handle the safekeeping. I feel like I'm being watched ever since I witnessed the robbery. I don't want to take any chances by keeping it with me."

"Good idea. I have a safe deposit box at the bank. I'll put it there."

"Don't compasses usually point north?"

He puts the compass in his pocket. "Always."

"This one points west."

19. The Punch All-Nighter

Five days pass. I have not heard from Stoph. He didn't show up for the library class and he hasn't replied to any of my messages. I'm trying to hide my concern, but Melissa is perceptive.

She folds her lean body into the beanbag chair. "Did he dump you?"

"I'm not sure." Her question is like a punch to the gut because yes, it does feel like we broke up.

"Don't give up yet." Melissa seems sincere, but there is part of me that wonders if she would be happy if I broke up. I think it blows her mind that a plain Jane like me is — or was — dating a one-percenter.

"Stop by his dorm for a surprise visit. No guy can resist a little —" she gestures with her hand.

"I have no way to get there."

"Take my car. Just fill it with gas," she says as she digs through her bag and flips me the keys.

I am amazed by Melissa's generosity. "Seriously?"

"Just remember our agreement — but someone taller and wealthier."

"Deal. You really are a gold digger."

"I take that as a compliment." Melissa pops out of the beanbag chair and hugs me.

"Remember, guys like it when you —" she makes another hand movement, more complex.

"Got it," I say to humor her.

I blow off my afternoon class. I stop by the bookstore looking for a gift for Stoph. There's a poster of a chimpanzee wearing headphones with the plug-in end of the cord in his mouth, perfect for deejay Stoph's dorm décor. Melissa's Toyota is equipped with a decent sound system. I take 95-North listening to Stoph's playlist that he turned me onto. I worry that something happened to him, or worse, that he wants to break up with me.

There is such a buzz in North Easton about finding the compass that I feel stupid that I was so quick to hand it over to Stoph. I found the compass, so technically it's mine. What if he took off with it? Or gave it to Porcellian to secure his acceptance? Or sold it at Sotheby's Auction House? Why does a college student have a safe deposit box? My stomach twists every time I start thinking about my carelessness. I'm pissed at myself and pissed at Stoph for the silent treatment.

I find a parking spot on the street and walk through the campus with a sinking sensation in my gut. I wait outside

Stoph's dorm until someone lets me in. His door is closed and there's no answer when I knock. One of the guys on his floor tells me he's playing Ultimate Frisbee, and gives me directions to the field. I am surprised to find an official game, with uniforms and referees. I expected a couple stoners tossing a disc back and forth, drinking beer. There is a paper roster on the ground that I check: Stoph is number seven. He's on the field running back and forth, diving. I feel like a stalker and just as I think about leaving, the game ends.

Stoph looks exhausted. I feel like I don't belong here, but it's too late; he sees me. He tells his teammates he will catch up with them later.

"Where did you come from?" His blank expression is not the reception I was hoping for.

"I have something for you," I say and hold up the rolled poster.

He doesn't take it from me, he just glances at it. "What is it?"

I unroll the poster and hold it open for him. "I thought it would look cute in your room."

"Oh, okay." He's unimpressed and looks over his shoulder to see who's around. He struts away from me, so I figure I'll follow him.

"Sorry, I guess you're busy." But why can he pop in on me whenever he wants, if I can't do it to him? "Did everything go alright with the Porc overnighter?"

"It was the most powerful experience of my life. Otherworldly, life-changing stuff."

"Then I guess you made the final cut?"

"Initiated and then some! I've got a lot to do for the brotherhood now."

"Congratulations, that's great news."

"Getting accepted is practically guaranteed financial success for life. But it goes way beyond that. My life was totally transformed in one night."

"Oh wow. How was it so transformative? What happened?"

Stoph heads up the dorm steps and I follow him to his room. He sits on his bed, covers his face with his hands, and rubs his eyes. "I'm super tired. I'm not allowed to say anything to anyone. You know, Porcellian secrecy."

"You can trust me. I'm not going to tell anyone."

Stoph lays on his back and stares at the ceiling. He has grass stains on his shin. He smells sweaty and his laundry pile adds to the aroma of foot odor in his room. "I can tell you some of it. They took me to the crypt under Sever Hall. I was served a drink, some kind of ceremonial brew, and had to lay in what felt like a stone coffin. I was left alone in the pitch dark for the entire night. That's when it got wild."

"You must have been freaked out," I say.

"Dude, *freaked out* is the understatement of the century. I was laying there and this giant red-eyed serpent slithered around me and over me. It wrapped itself around my ankles, started to pull me down into a dark landscape of spongy bog loaded with earthworms. Then men wearing white swished through the walls and reached out to me. They took my arms to lift me straight through the heavens into another dimension where I saw colors that don't exist on earth. I'm telling you; we are not alone. There is life beyond the here and now. I'm part of the Porcellian brotherhood now. It was so realistic that I can't shake it. In fact, I don't want to shake it. The range of emotion from terror to bliss was like I died and was reborn into the brotherhood."

He closes his eyes and pulls the pillow over his head.

"Do you want me to leave?"

"Actually, yeah. It's important that I rest. I never know when I might be called upon by the brotherhood. I'll see you another time."

I leave the monkey poster on his desk and shut the door behind me.

20. The Porcellian Club

A couple of days later, just when I thought I'd never hear from Stoph again, his car comes zipping into the library parking lot. He struts toward the Daily Grind as I hand a customer a J.D. Salinger Lion's Mane. I wipe down the stainless-steel surfaces, pretending that I don't see him waiting to order.

"Excuse me, are there any specials today?" His tone makes it hard not to smile.

"Check the chalkboard by the entrance, sir."

"I'll try the pumpkin latte."

"What size?" I'm not giving in this easily, just because he seems jovial. I will not let my world revolve around his moods. Not to mention, his silent treatment has left me ruminating about the compass.

"Big."

I roll my eyes and say, "There is no big. It's either small, medium or large."

"Surprise me," he says.

I put his pumpkin latte in a to-go cup as a hint. I slide the coffee toward him and start rinsing the utensils.

"Okay, you're mad at me. I get it."

"Why would I be mad at you?"

"I came here to apologize. I know I have been distant lately but getting punched has been super stressful and time consuming."

"That's what I figured."

"So, you're not mad at me?" His broad smile makes me cave.

"Not anymore," I say, drying the utensils.

"Cool. I was worried that I ruined things between us. It was nice of you to come to my game. I wasn't in the right frame of mind that day. Sorry if I seemed distant. Anyway, do you want to come to a party at the Porcellian Club? I'm going to deejay again."

I shrug, forcing a *whatever* attitude. "Can I bring my friends? I promised them more fun like the Dirty Cash night."

"Of course. I'll leave their names at the door."

He steps around the counter to offer a hug. He'll send the car service to pick us up.

"You still have the compass, right? Put it in a safe place?" I ask.

The energy drains from his hug. He steps back. "There's a situation with that."

"What?"

"I didn't have a chance to get to the bank. I kept it in my jeans pocket because I didn't trust leaving it anywhere—"

"Don't fucking tell me you lost it?"

"Not exactly. The night we went underground for the last punch, I had it in my pocket. They made us strip naked —"

"And?"

"And I don't know where it went after that."

I feel heat rising from my gut. "What the fuck is wrong with you?"

"I had no idea —"

"Just shut up. It totally makes sense. I am so stupid. The meeting I spied on — they referenced Porcellian as the potential rival over finding the compass."

"This is the real reason why I haven't called you. It's a colossal fuckup. I should have hidden it in my room."

"Are we being played?"

"What do you mean?"

"Who told you to take the class about Richardson's architecture in North Easton? Think about it. If Richardson is this great early American architect — one of the founding fathers — then why isn't Harvard teaching the class? Who sent you to sit in on dumbass Montgomery's class?"

Stoph stares wide-eyed. "One of my professors."

"Any chance this professor was a Porcellian? Is he a Harvard alum?"

"I don't think so."

"And why did he send you to take this class?"

"He was impressed with my winning VR project and he thought I should learn about Richardson."

I wipe my cleaning rag in fast circles. "You realize Richardson and your futuristic projects are eons apart? Does that make any sense?"

"It doesn't sound like a conspiracy to me —"

"Open your fucking eyes, Stoph! Everyone, including Porcellian, is after that compass!"

I toss the rag in the sink.

"Sorry. I should've been smarter," he says.

"We have to be smart."

"Agreed." He holds open his arms for another hug.

He leaves his big pumpkin latte behind, so I drink it.

After work, I call for a meeting of the Quadsters in Melissa's room. The girls are wild about going to the Porc party and so it begins again, the great outfit debate. Jill thinks we should dress like hipsters, Sheila doesn't care as long as there's dancing, but Melissa is coming down hard with her opinions.

"Fuck it, I'm going all in with tight and sexy body-con. You guys can look flowy bohemian, but not me, I'm going tits-up." Then she studies me. "You look like you've dropped ten pounds with all your sulking lately. Here, try this on."

I pull the black top over my head and adjust it, so it sits off my shoulders. The neckline is nowhere near my neck as it dips so low it barely covers my cleavage. The material spared in the body of the shirt was sewn into dramatic bell sleeves. The skin-tight houndstooth miniskirt is more mini than skirt and I make a mental note to avoid bending over. Melissa reaches past the dance floor shitkickers and whips out a pair of clingy black suede boots that stretch past my calf muscles.

Melissa whistles a construction-worker approval. "Go figure. You can totally rock that fuck-me outfit. Make sure you play hard-to-get, though. He'll want to tap that big time."

Melissa directs me to sit at her desk; it's time for *big hair don't care*. She heats the curling iron while teasing my hair to ramp up the volume, then blasts a keg of hairspray like a fire extinguisher. At this rate, I think my hair will be cemented in place straight through graduation day. When she finishes Operation Paige, I stand in front of her full-length mirror appearing a foot taller because of the boot heels and maxed-out hair. The person in the mirror isn't me, it's a badass Wonder Woman with big boobs, a skinny waist, and no one to save from harm's way.

Jill succumbs to peer pressure and ditches the bohemian outfit for a short skirt and long boots. Sheila goes with the same style dress that she wore to blow up the dance floor at the nightclub, only this time the pattern is snow leopard instead of cheetah.

Melissa insists that we pre-game with tequila shots. Then we head for the car idling outside the dorm. Two girls pass us in the stairwell hissing, "You look like hookers."

Melissa, uninhibited from the tequila, says, "You look like asshats." We all start cackling and don't stop until we reach Mass. Ave. where there is a crowd waiting to get into the Porcellian Clubhouse. We get in line; this time there is no VIP usher.

We give our names to the guy at the entrance and he lets us into a small room known as the bike room, with a forbidden stairwell. No one is allowed upstairs unless you are accompanied by a member, so we follow the crowd across the green and white checkerboard floor. The Porc emblem is inlaid in black in the center of the floor and I drag my boot heels across it to deface the obnoxious all-male country club vibe.

The music is thumping a techno beat, but I don't see deejay Stoph. We work our way up to the bar and get beer, Corona the only option.

"Where's Stoph?" I ask the guy standing behind the vintage bar stained in a rich golden brown. I wonder how many famous Porcellians leaned against this bar. I rest my elbow near where I imagine H.H. Richardson bellied-up. The shelves hold old books, antique trophies, and aged single malts.

The guy looks me up and down. "What's your name? I'll let him know you're here."

"I'm Paige. They're Melissa, Sheila and Jill."

"How about a round of shots ladies?" Gordy, our new friend, doesn't wait for an answer.

"Only if you have one too," Melissa says with a flip of her hair.

Gordy grins at her, pours his shot, tosses it back and says, "The rest in your hair!" Then he turns the empty glass upside down over his head. We figure this is a Porc thing, so we do what Gordy did.

"Can you make the next round Jager Bombs?" asks Melissa with a wink. "Or should we save that for later?"

"No Jager Bombs before midnight," says Gordy trading winks back at Melissa.

"Good, I'll be the first in line. I'll save the first for you." Melissa leans her elbow on the bar next to mine.

"Can't wait," says Gordy and hands her another Corona.

Sheila and Jill move to the dance area while I stay with Melissa who has captured Gordy's full attention. We have more shots and another beer before Stoph finally saunters through the crowd.

"Have you been here long? I barely recognized you in that outfit." He glances down my half-shirt. "I see you met Gordon Preston already."

"Yes, Gordy's been taking good care of us," Melissa chimes in. "Best bartender I've ever met."

He catches Gordy's eye and gestures with his head toward the stairwell in the bike room. Gordy nods twice, more coded sign language. Stoph takes my hand, says he wants to show me around.

He whispers in my ear, "I can't believe Melissa just referred to Gordy as a bartender. He runs Porcellian. That bro comes from the wealthiest family in the mountain west, if not the country."

"Then she's definitely his future ex-wife."

He leads me upstairs and I can feel all the eyes in the room watching me. On the top floor we come to a spacious Greek banquet hall, which resembles the Parthenon with white Corinthian columns evenly aligned. At the head of the room there is a marble pig statue with a banjo near its feet. Stoph's deejay equipment is set up near the pig. He puts his headphones on and switches up the music that is cranked throughout the clubhouse sound system.

Stoph starts a wild dance, swinging his arms overhead as if he is orchestrating a multitude of devils. I start thinking that the phrase *dance like no one is watching* is not always meant to be taken literally because he looks like he needs an exorcism. His feet fly out from under him to kung fu toward the pig's head. His headphone chord extends far enough for him to swing over to me, then he pulls me behind the deejay table. He shifts behind me and wraps his arms tight around my waist and grinds himself into me. He's sweating and moving fast as he clamps his hands under my Wonder Woman suit of armor, squeezing until I practically pop out of the half-top.

Stoph, breathing hard, drops the headphones and puts the music on autopilot. He grabs my hand and pulls me across the banquet hall, down a flight of stairs to the mid-level of the clubhouse. There are guys in the lounge area that hardly notice when Stoph brings me into a yellow room and locks the door behind us. We start making out, our tongues exploring excitedly like deep sea divers searching the bottom of the ocean floor. Stoph pushes against me and I step back to steady my balance which is not easy considering the boots and the tequila shots. He grabs my ass and pulls me closer while he kisses deeper and harder. We move across the room as if we're auditioning for Cirque du Soleil. We start laughing when we plow into a bulky armoire. My shirt slides down and Stoph breathes harder when he sees my bare tits.

The miniskirt suddenly exceeds all superlatives — it's now the miniest-skirt in all of Cambridge. He reaches around to latch onto my ass while the other hand gropes for the waxed martini glass. I wrestle with Stoph's belt buckle, then unzip his pants. His breathing sounds like he is running sprints. He pulses his hips toward the miniest-skirt with a force that shoves me hard into the armoire. I pull him toward me and at first, I feel the dresser rocking, or maybe it's me rocking, but more thrusting and grinding topples the dresser and sends us sprawling onto the floor.

Someone begins pounding on the locked door. Stoph zips up his pants and rushes to the door to reassure the guys that things are totally cool in the yellow room. I readjust my clothes — the topless titty-committee meeting has been adjourned. He rushes back toward me to see if I'm okay, but I am not paying attention to him. Underneath where the dresser stood, there is an emblem painted on the floor, a flaming sword, that I can't take my eyes off. The floor around the logo has a squared-off seam with a small knob that I pull up to reveal a hidden staircase. The cobwebs are thick as this door hasn't been opened in a long time.

"Holy shit," he says.

"Follow me."

"No way. We better close this and get out of here. I need to go deejay," he stands and tucks in his shirt. He picks up my handbag and hands it to me.

"In the Bible, the flaming sword is what was used to mark the Garden of Eden. Don't you want to check it out?"

"This building has all sorts of hidden passageways. I'm still a newt so I think we should close it and just leave it alone. Take the night off from architecture?"

"A newt?" I squint at him.

"Short for neophyte. The new guy."

He heads toward the door, but I won't budge. "I want to see what's down there."

"It's not cool to go without permission. Trust me, this isn't a casual place."

"There has to be a connection between Porcellian and the compass and the Ancient Order of Druids."

"I don't know." He fidgets with his man bun.

"Stop fussing with that douche donut and come with me. Grow some balls already!" I bolt down the steps in my suede boots and miniskirt, hardly the proper outfit for an adventure in a crypt. At the bottom of the steps is a pull string to turn on a single light bulb.

"You are out of control," he says, but I'm already way ahead of him, and I hear him racing after me. "Wait up."

"Keep up!"

The bulb sheds sparse light into a wine cellar, with jugs of unlabeled vintages, hundreds of bottles, preserved within the cool rock walls. A glass door opens to another room filled with more jugs of wine and a long banquet table in the center of the room with twelve chairs surrounding the table.

"What goes on here?"

Stoph says, "No clue. Never seen this place before."

"This isn't the underground they took you to?"

"No."

I pull a wine jug from the rack. Then I pull out a few more.

"I think we should leave these bottles alone."

"Some of these bottles have liquid — wine, I presume — and others are empty," I say.

"It's a clubhouse, loads of alcohol gets served here."

I pick up one of the empties and crack it against the stone wall. The glass shatters.

"What are you doing?"

"When we broke through the ceiling in Memorial Hall, you acted all cool. But when we mess up your precious Porcellian Club, you shit your pants."

"I have a lot on the line."

"You're already in. Don't sweat it."

There's an opening that leads down a hallway; a pull string to a single lightbulb that sheds enough light to see into a storage room that hasn't been touched in many years. I walk through a spider's web and stop to brush it off. Rodents scurry in the corner of the room. There are dusty boxes filled with wine glasses, empty bottles, a vintage label-making press. Then it catches my eye — a thirty-one drawer flat file wide wood credenza with metal drawer pulls. I open the drawers.

"Stoph, this is it. Get over here." There are architectural blueprints, landscape design plans, and correspondences between the designers and their clients.

And Richardson's blueprints.

"We need a year to look through all this," he says.

We rifle through the drawers. Stoph whistles and says, "Whoa, Nelly."

We roll the blueprints to hide in my boots and Stoph's pant legs.

"That's some wild shit right there. Let's take it and get out of here."

21. The Blueprints

The shrill of the alarm clock is painful. I look toward the bean bag chair — a lump shifts under a striped pink comforter. It's Jill, she crashed in my room, after we stumbled in last night.

"Shit, I have to work at the library. I think I'm still drunk."

"That sucks."

My feet are blistered from the boots and I peel off the Wonder Woman outfit. I put on baggy jeans, a flannel shirt and sneakers. My hair is still cemented in place.

"Can you shut the light off on your way out?"

"That's the sun."

"Close the curtains, it's blinding."

"I don't have curtains —"

"Whatever," Jill says and pulls the pillow over her head.

At the library, I go in the back door to take out Hobson. We head for the coffee shop where Tanya is helping with the morning shift. "Oh, my goodness, what were you up to last night?"

"Isn't it obvious?"

Tanya shakes her head and dumps green tea, plain Greek yogurt, banana, orange and ginger in a blender. "Here's an OGHC. It'll help."

"What's an OGHC?" The thought of eating anything is repulsive.

"Orange Ginger Hangover Cure. Plus, drink this glass of Topo Chico with fresh lime. You look dehydrated." She flips a treat to Hobson who catches it midair. "If you're going to trash yourself like this, I hope you had a good time."

"From what I remember —"

"I don't want to know."

I chug Tanya's hangover buster while Hobson pulls me around to the front of the library. Two police cruisers are parked in front of Memorial Hall. I turn back to get away from the cops. Ms. Montgomery, bundled in a wool coat, is doing all the talking as her breath puffs against the cold air. Treadwell's brown barn coat is unbuttoned, his hands are stuffed deep in the pockets. They look in my direction, so now I can't avoid them.

"Good morning," I say trying to slip past them.

"There's nothing good about it," Ms. Montgomery says and looks at my drink. "You Millennials with your smoothies! Does anyone eat food with a knife and fork anymore? Everything's pulverized in a blender like baby food. It's all pablum to you."

I force a smile.

"Do you know anything about what happened in Memorial Hall?" Treadwell goes into interrogation mode.

"What happened?"

"A room was vandalized."

"How so?

"A ceiling was bashed in. An original mural was destroyed."

"That's terrible," I say.

Treadwell asks, "Where were you last night?"

"At a party in Cambridge."

"By the looks of your bloodshot eyes, I'll accept that statement as true."

He turns back toward Ms. Montgomery. "Captain Biff better get to the bottom of this before more damage is done."

I plow through the work Ms. Montgomery left for me. I wait until I'm sure no one is around, then I lay out the blueprints on the table. The first page is a drawing labeled Profile of the Grades in Sherman, Wyoming showing the highest elevation marked for the Ames Monument. The monument is three hundred feet south of the highest elevation of the Union Pacific railroad line. The monument is sixty feet tall and sixty feet wide at the base, a towering pyramid. I look up where Sherman is to find it is in the middle of nowhere.

I unroll the next set of drawings, sketches for the actual pyramid. What catches my eye is that the pyramid was designed to be hollow on the inside with a crude layout of granite stones jutting out. Keeping the interior hollow reduced the cost of construction, but it also allowed for an interior room. There are no doors to enter the pyramid. What fascinates me is the plan for an underground tunnel straight underneath the pyramid with access to the interior space.

I roll the blueprints and put them in my backpack. I finish writing about Memorial Hall and bring the pages to Ms. Montgomery for her review.

"Where was the mural in Memorial Hall that was damaged? I don't recall seeing a mural on our tour."

She glances over the top of the book she is reading. "In the attic room. We didn't go up there on our tour."

"Who would have access to the attic?"

"No one has access. It's off limits. Therefore, it is considered a B&E. A crime. It makes me sick to think some thugs vandalized our historic space."

After my shift, I head back to my dorm for a power nap. I see Melissa coming up the hallway and she pops into my room to chat.

"So, I met a great guy last night. We had a blast. He's totally my type."

"Rich? Tall? Big dick?"

"All of the above."

"I'm going back to Cambridge tonight to meet up with him at a party. Want to join?"

I agree to go with her, but first, the nap. I forewarn her that I am going casual, jeans and a sweater. When we meet up later, she eyes me, but keeps her opinion to herself. She is dressed in tight jeans and a green cowl-neck cashmere sweater with a puffy coat draped over her arm.

There isn't a line to get into the clubhouse; it's a smaller crowd, hanging out drinking beer and chatting. I take a beer and swear to myself that I am going to take it easy tonight. I have a full day of classes tomorrow so I can't be hungover again.

Melissa introduces me to her new friend Lance — tall, handsome, preppy — and we get to know each other. I told Stoph I would be here, but he's not at the clubhouse.

"Have you seen Stoph around?" I ask Lance.

"Earlier. I think he had an Ultimate Frisbee game," he tells me.

I feel like a chaperone on Melissa's date, so I tell her I'm going to see if I can meet up with Stoph. She barely grunts a response, she's so gaga over Lance. I left my coat in her car, so I borrow Melissa's puffy coat to head down the street to look for the address 1234. There's a Chinese restaurant with apartments above. I go inside the apartment entrance and look at the row of mailboxes in the foyer at the bottom of the stairs. I check if anything says Landrace on it, but there's nothing labeled on any of the mailboxes.

I head upstairs to find the Landrace apartment at the end of a dark hallway on the top floor. The door is locked. I get down on my hands and knees to look under the door, but I can't see anything. When I stand up, an Asian man is standing there staring at me.

"Sorry. I was just looking —"

"Looking for what?"

"I thought this was my friend's apartment. I guess I got confused with her directions. She said she lives near the Chinese takeout place."

"No one lives here. Too smelly."

"Oh really? Hadn't noticed," I say and head back down the stairs. He follows me and watches me until I disappear onto the campus. Stoph's not answering his phone, so I wait outside his dorm until a resident lets me in.

Stoph's door is open and I hear voices in his room. "This is unbelievable," I hear one guy say. "It's so realistic."

"Now watch this part of the building. That creature crawls down the drain spout."

I tap on the door. "Hey, got room for one more?"

Stoph smiles when he sees me. "When did you get here?"

"About an hour ago. I was at the clubhouse with Melissa and Lance."

Stoph glances at Chase and says, "Sorry, dude. Guess she's got a thing for married men."

"Wait, Lance is married?" I ask.

"No, I'm just joking. He's got a serious girlfriend, though. She goes to Brown. But you didn't hear that from me."

"What are you guys up to?" I ask.

Stoph hands me the goggles. "My latest virtual reality designs."

It's a romp through a desert on the back of a camel. The camel caravan takes me to a temple where creatures carved into the stone suddenly shift and come to life. A panther slithers down a drain, owls fly off the wall and lions sit on the steps. It's not long, but it feels as if I am right there.

"When did you make this?"

"I've been working on it all semester."

Chase says, "Later, dudes."

"Later," Stoph says.

"Do you recognize the panther on the drain?" asks Stoph.

"The one on Memorial Hall?"

"You're good!" he says. "I hope you don't mind, but my professor encouraged me to create a VR experience using Richardson's architecture in the form of Solomon's Temple."

"Why would I mind?"

"It's your idea."

"I'm flattered you think it's that good, but just one thing."

"What's that?"

"You can't put in the sundial to open the painted eye."

"Why not?"

"Memorial Hall is a crime scene. The cops were there this morning investigating a B&E."

"Oh crap. I hope there weren't any cameras up there."

"I don't think so."

"Listen, I was waiting for Chase to leave to tell you some exciting news," he says and gets his backpack from under his bed. "I found the compass."

He takes it out and hands it to me. I feel like he just proposed marriage. "Where was it?"

"In the pocket of a different pair of jeans. I went to do laundry and there it was. I forgot I changed before I went to the Porc overnight. I feel like a dope."

"Thank God!" I hug Stoph.

"Sorry for the stress about it. You should hang onto it. I lose shit all the time. There's a better chance that you'll figure out what it's for than anyone else I know. No one else seems to have insights like you do."

"Perfect timing. We're going to need this. I think I figured it out; the ark of the covenant is hidden in the Ames Monument in Wyoming."

"Wyoming? Seriously?"

"The pyramid is at the highest point of the transcontinental railroad in Sherman, Wyoming, which is in the middle of nowhere. I think the pyramid is hiding a 20x20x20 cubit room, which is the oracle holding the ark of the covenant. There are no doors. So, what exactly is this monument? I think there's an underground tunnel leading to a hollow room inside the pyramid."

"Wild."

"It's weird that the compass doesn't point north. See here? It points west. Richardson engineered this compass for someone to find the ark of the covenant — west to Wyoming."

Stoph stares at me. "Amazing."

"Road trip?" I ask.

Stoph high-fives me. "Interstate 80 all the way!"

22. The Tailgate

"Quadster meeting in my room in thirty minutes," Melissa announces when I pull the shower curtain back from the stall. She steps in and plunks her shower accessory bucket on the tile floor, barely waiting for me to towel off.

"Great boobs, by the way," she adds. "No wonder Stoph is all over you."

Since she met Lance, she's been organizing our Quadster outings to the Porcellian clubhouse as if it's a volunteer activity to include on her resume. This meeting will be about the Harvard-Yale tailgate.

As I pull my damp hair into a ponytail, I find the door to their room open. Jill dashes her yellow highlighter across the page of a textbook. "Political science exam," she says with a sigh.

"I have tons of work. I'm so far behind," I say.

Melissa returns after a minute and says, "Where's —" just as Sheila appears.

"Sorry, my class ran late," she says, dropping her enormous backpack by the door. "Did I miss anything?"

"Just getting started," I say and make room for her to sit.

Melissa props a dry erase board against her bed and writes *The Game*. "The Harvard-Yale football game is at Harvard Stadium this year. But the tailgate is where it's at. This could make or break our whole semester. In fact, it could impact our future."

"Make or break it how?" Jill asks.

"If we do this right, we could each secure Porcellian boyfriends before the end of the game. Then, if we nail it, we're looking at receiving significant gifts before Christmas break. We're talking Tiffany's jewelry under the tree, ladies. From there, it's invitations to the Vail ski chalet for New Year's Eve. The next thing you know, we're bridesmaids in each other's weddings."

The three of us look at Melissa in awe. So much for burgers and beer and football. Sheila says, "You mean, we're going husband shopping at the tailgate?"

"You bet. Let's get focused." She writes the word: *Uniforms*. "We need to get official game jerseys. I can pick them up at the Harvard bookstore. You can pay me back later. What numbers should we get?"

"How about we go with our bra sizes. We'll be the *titty-committee* like Paige calls it," Jill jokes, but we decide it's a great idea. Melissa claims 34, Sheila 36, Jill 38, and I captain the team with 40.

"Next," says Melissa, and she writes the word: *Refreshments*. "We need to bring a signature cocktail. Any ideas? Cosmos?"

"Can we adjust the Cosmos to a crimson color? Maybe use cranberry juice — call them Crimsontinis?" I say.

"Sold!" Melissa continues. "How about appetizers? Need a crowd-pleaser. Maybe pigs-in-a-blanket? It goes with the Porcellian theme."

"That works," Jill says.

"Finally," Melissa says, and writes the word: *Attitude*. "This is it, ladies. We're bringing our A-game to the big game. This is the day the Quadsters bag the lions. If all goes well, we'll be set for life. We'll be talking about it in Malibu twenty years from now when we're rich and divorced and living in mansions micro-managing our sexy pool boys. Who's with me?"

I'm not exactly with her, but we all laugh and put our hands in the middle and cheer, "Go Quadsters!"

"Meeting adjourned until game day," Melissa says and replaces the cap on her marker. "In sum, go big or go home on Saturday, titty-committee."

Stoph tells me where to meet for the tailgate — a good thing because Lance has not communicated with Melissa about the Game. We meet outside our dorm by her car and she rolls her eyes at me.

"Jeans and sneakers? God, Paige — what did we talk about? It's game day."

Melissa and Jill are wearing leggings and Chelsea boots with wool socks that have a burgundy stripe around the calf. They have black turtlenecks under their game shirts and their hair is in pigtails with crimson ribbons, like Pop Warner cheerleaders.

"We're going to be standing all day. I'm doing sneakers," I insist.

Sheila shows up with L.L. Bean boots and a wool ski hat with a pompom. She has rolls of crimson streamers that she borrowed from the dance studio supply closet. "We should decorate the car with these. It'll look like a party on wheels."

This wasn't part of the plan, but we tape streamers all over the car and steer the pep-rally mobile toward Cambridge. The campus stadium parking lot is already mobbed with Harvard and Yale fans. It takes half an hour to park and work our way through the crowd, hauling our cooler filled with pre-made Crimsontinis and tin trays of miniature hot dogs.

As we approach the Porc tailgate, I see it is a first-rate operation with an official Harvard party tent, a trailer with grills and smokers, and Stoph with his staged deejay equipment.

"Let's ditch this cooler," I say.

"Hell no. All they have is horse-piss Budweiser or Heineken. We have classy-ass signature cocktails," Melissa insists.

Stoph steps away from his maestro-mashup gear and I think he's coming over to greet us, but he stops at the keg to fill up his red SOLO cup. He hangs out around the keg, cracking jokes. One of the bros looks over at us and then turns back to say something to the other guys. They all start laughing with a mocking vibe. Melissa struts over to the keg, oblivious.

I whisper to Stoph. "What was that all about?"

"What?"

"The joke at our expense?"

Stoph plucks an empty SOLO cup from the stack and holds it under the tap. "What joke?"

"Give me a break. Your bros made a comment and you all laughed at us —"

He hands me the beer half-filled with foam. "It was inappropriate. I'd rather not —"

"Nope. Tell me or we're leaving."

He hesitates, then says, "Fine. They made a dig on Melissa because she looks like a flat-chested version of Brandi Branson."

"Who's Brandi Branson?"

"Porn star known as BeeBee. Lance actually refers to Melissa as his *BeeBee*."

"Really, Stoph? Porn star humor?"

"It wasn't me, but what can I say? They're guys," he says, shrugging his shoulders. "Nice jersey. Why 40?"

"My lucky number."

"Time to get this pre-game bumping," he says and heads for his equipment table.

I want to protect Melissa from the bros' mockery, but she has her heart set on this day, and, well, she can handle herself that's for sure.

"Let's ditch the beer and go with the Crimsontinis," Melissa says and before we can respond, she whips out clear plastic cups and starts pouring. "Did Stoph mention where Lance is?"

"No. I barely spoke to him. He's doing his deejay thing."

Some of the guys come over to chat with us. I know a few of them, friends of Stoph's, and introduce them to the Quadsters. Melissa says, "I already know Saul and Malik. You're not the only one who hangs at the clubhouse."

I let her snarky comment slide.

"Care for a pre-game cocktail — a Crimsontini? Don't worry, the cups are recyclable. Totally green. I'm a huge climate activist." She offers, batting her eyelashes. This is the first I'm hearing about Melissa caring about the environment, then I realize, it's part of her gameday shtick.

They look at their full SOLO cups and say, "Hell, yeah. Save the planet one drink at a time."

She flips her hair from her shoulder and pours the cocktails. "Have you seen Lance?"

"He wasn't up yet when we left," Malik tells her.

Stoph is playing less club vibe, more get-psyched music. He's air drumming eye-of-the-tiger style and bopping around behind his equipment. Melissa is way ahead of us with her drink count, so I say, "You better pace yourself. It's a long afternoon."

"Don't be a lightweight, Paige. Go take a nap if you can't hang. Then rebound for the Game. Get with the program, girl."

"Where would one take this alleged nap?"

She makes a horse sound with her lips and says, "Duh, with one of the Porcs preferably. Lance, if he ever gets his ass over here."

Malik asks us what year we are in. I tell them we go to Kew.

"Oh, I thought because of the Harvard shirts —"

Melissa blurts out, "We're wearing our bra sizes."

"Seriously?" he chuckles.

"Totally. The cup sizes are on the shirt's reverse side. You have to take them off to learn that information first hand." She slurs her words and cups her hands around her boobs. "But I'll give you a hint. It begins with a B. Full B."

He glances at his friends and they crack up. "I always thought the bigger the better."

"Then you better get up your stool next to Paige."

I whisper to Melissa: "Total overshare. The jersey numbers are supposed to be our little secret."

"You're too uptight. You should be proud of that rack. Show off those girls. Own those chobes!"

"Chobes?"

I head toward Stoph, who's adjusting his music to auto-pilot.

"Want to take a walk? Check things out?" I ask him.

"Sure. My Ultimate Frisbee team has a tent. I should pop in anyway."

The tailgate area is a sea of tents, kegs and barbecue grills. Fans are dressed in Yale blue or Harvard crimson and the Yale bulldog is making his rounds for photo ops. I keep an eye for anyone else who might be wearing number 40.

The Ultimate Frisbee team tent is at the end of a long row with some room to toss around a disc. The guys are running around in shorts and t-shirts despite the chilly wind. Stoph jumps in to intercept a toss. One of his teammates offers me hot chocolate. He's a rugged guy with a chiseled jaw line and massive shoulders. His sweatshirt says Harvard crew with oars criss-crossed behind the Harvard crest.

"I'm Axel. Just so you know, the hot chocolate is spiked with peppermint schnapps."

I take a sip, finding the candy cane and chocolate combination heavenly. Or maybe it's this hunk of a guy that I think is heavenly. "Wow, this is delicious. Did you make it yourself?"

He grins. "I'm a bit of a mixologist, if I do say so myself." His eyes are aqua blue and when he smiles, he reveals a row of perfect glistening teeth.

"Me too, but with coffee and teas. Have you heard of Goforth's Daily Grind in North Easton?"

He shakes his head. "Any good?"

"Best coffee shop anywhere. I work there, part time. The owner is the queen of mixology with all types of healthcentric coffee drinks."

"When do you work? I'll have to check it out," he says and smiles in a way that warms my insides along with the hot cocoa.

I tell him my schedule. "Free coffee if you visit."

"Deal." Axel holds up a tray of brownies. "But only if you try my brownies. Baked them myself this morning."

I missed breakfast, so I take a brownie and chase it with the spiked hot chocolate. The brownie has chocolate chunk surprises in each bite. I smile at Axel. One, good looking. Two, Harvard-smart. Three, he bakes and mixes.

"Delicious," I say and take another from the tray. The chocolate is irresistible so I snatch another when no one is looking.

Stoph flips the disc to me and I run to catch it. I flick my wrist to return it in his direction but it flies toward Axel. He catches it and flips it back to me. Then, running to make a catch, I start seeing fireflies, which is strange because summer is long over and fireflies only come out at night. I suddenly can't manage to catch and my throw is so lame that I decide to return to my hot chocolate. I see this nerdy looking guy pass by the tent wearing a pilgrim outfit.

"It's not Halloween," I call out to him.

"Excuse me?" he says.

"Why are you dressed like that?"

"I'm John Harvard, the pilgrim," he says and shakes my hand like a dork.

I check out his legs in white stockings and see the dark hair on his legs matted underneath resembling clumps of Brillo. "Has anyone pissed on your shoe today? I hear it's a tradition." I feel my tongue getting fat and heavy. The twisted look on his face shows he's not used to being disrespected.

"You're a bit crude, has anyone told you that before?" he says in a huffy tone, but it seems like he might be about to cry.

I hear a deep laugh next to me and Axel is cracking up.

The pilgrim storms off, but I call after him, "Wait. I was just joking. Come back."

He stops, so Axel and I pose for a photo with him. Stoph is smiling at us until I kiss the John Harvard pilgrim on the mouth, and then give him another one with full tongue, because I feel bad I almost made him cry.

"Paige, what the f—"

"Chill out, dude." I flop down on the grass. "Head rush."

"Wait, dude, how many of those hash brownies did you eat?"

"Did you say hash? Ah, that explains the fireflies." I close my eyes. I am in a cozy place and Stoph's nagging voice is aggravating. I hear him yelling at Axel for giving me the brownies.

"Help me get her back to the clubhouse. She needs to sleep this off. You made those hash brownies way too strong," he says to Axel.

"I thought she knew. She only had one," Axel says.

I wake up alone in a bed in a room I don't recognize. I find a note on the pillow, telling me to come back to the tent when I can. I feel like I've slept for a week, although I am still exhausted. I need the bathroom — the first three steps out of the bed feels like a carousel ride. I head downstairs and realize I am in the Porcellian clubhouse. I go through the bike room, past the bar to find the bathroom. There's another woman in the rest room washing her hands at the sink.

"Going to the Game?" She dries her hands and checks her hair in the mirror.

"I was tailgating earlier, but came back here to regroup."

"I'm heading over with my boyfriend now to catch the end of the first half. You can come with me and Lance."

I look at her Barbie doll figure and silky brunette hair. Her eyes are doe-like and she smiles easily. She squirts perfume on her neck and wrists.

"Lance is your boyfriend?"

"Yes, do you know him?"

"Sure, I do. He's friends with my boyfriend, Stoph."

"Oh, the deejay. He's such a great guy," she gushes. "I'm Sharon."

I go out with Sharon and Lance chuckles when he sees me. He pulls Sharon closer and smells her perfumed neck.

"I see you two have met. How's it going Paige?"

"I'm doing better, I think."

We head to the Porc tailgate. The smell of grilled hamburgers and hot dogs makes me hungry. The music is loud and the crowd gathered under the Porc tent is in full swing. I scan the crowd looking for the Quadsters — I need to warn Melissa there will be no nap time with Lance — but I don't see them anywhere. I wave to Stoph who is rocking the tunes and he gestures back to me *Are-you-okay*? I reply with a thumbs-up and work my way over to the grill where I quell my classic case of the munchies with a burger with melted cheese.

We head into the stadium to watch the game from the Porcellian section at the fifty-yard line. Yale takes the lead late in the first quarter, but misses the kick for the extra-point attempt. The first quarter ends 6-0, but it doesn't diminish the spirit of the Crimson crowd.

A bottle of Scotch gets discreetly passed around. I pass it on because I still feel strange from the brownie experience. I see the John Harvard pilgrim mascot leading the crowd in a rally cry and I start laughing at him again.

"Dude, what's your deal with that guy?"

"He makes me giggle; I don't know why."

"Because you're still high."

The gray skies release white flakes, and a pretty New England snow flurry scatters across the stadium packed with fans for the last game of the season. The stadium reminds me of a Roman coliseum with its arches. Charles McKim, an architect who joined Richardson's firm in 1870, designed the stadium. Olmsted handled the landscape details.

"You can see Richardson's influence in the stadium."

Stoph sips the Scotch. "Definitely."

The crowd goes wild when the Yale quarterback gets sacked for a loss. Yale is forced to punt and the Harvard return man scrambles for a crowd-pleasing twelve yards. Harvard settles for a field goal ending the half, 6-3.

The teams head for the locker rooms and the marching band takes the field. Cheerleaders kick and wave and the fly girls get tossed high into the air. The bottle gets passed around again and this time I take a nip to diminish the chill in my body. The spirit boosters line up to lead the cheering as the players and coaches charge back onto the field for the second half.

A group of students, several with megaphones, storm the field ahead of the players.

"What's going on?" I ask Stoph.

"Halftime protestors. Total losers."

The students link hands to form a human chain, demanding that both universities divest their billion-dollar endowments from fossil fuels companies. Police and security personnel try to disband the protest while the players retreat to their sidelines. The game is delayed twenty minutes.

Suddenly, in the Crimson end zone, I spot the Quadsters screaming and yelling with the other protestors. Sheila and Jill pump their fists in the air. Melissa switches from her anti-plastics focus to fossil fuels.

"Dude, check out your friends!"

"Melissa is totally shit-faced."

Then it happens: Melissa goes all-in. She rips off her 34-football jersey, turtleneck and *full-B* cupped bra, spikes them to the ground, and salutes to the erupting crowd. The end zone fans go ballistic with cheering as Melissa streaks bare-chested across the field shrieking on the top of her lungs. The entire stadium erupts. Some cops chase her, but she circles back and runs the other way. Someone in the crowd starts chanting *Rudy, Rudy, Rudy* and it catches like wildfire.

The cops catch up with her and cover her with a blanket. The crowd starts booing as she gets escorted from the field. I look at Stoph, "Shit. Now what?"

"We'll have to get bail money."

23. Trinity Church

"Sunday Mass. You joining me?" asks Stoph. He rips through his dorm dresser drawers looking for clean clothes.

"All I have is the football shirt I wore yesterday," I say and glance at the trail of my clothes that start by the window and end in the middle of the room. "Aren't you hungover? Let's skip church."

He tosses a white t-shirt and cashmere navy crew neck sweater toward me. "Wear this with your jeans. I want you to come to Trinity Church with me. Check out Richardson's Boston masterpiece."

"As long as we get breakfast afterward." I pull the sweater over my head and arrange my hair with my fingers.

He folds my clothes and puts them on the end of his bed. "Going braless to church, number forty?"

"I could kill Melissa for blabbing that."

"It wasn't exactly a surprise for me. I mean, I've seen the goods."

"I know Lance overshares about Melissa, but you better not be saying anything about me!"

"I'm a gentleman, my dear. A gentleman never reveals his private affairs."

We take the red line and then stroll to Copley Square. At first sighting, Trinity Church is classic Richardson with arches and towers. The detail in the exterior stonework is astonishing: men's faces, double-headed eagles, and endless cherubim. There are also druid-inspired panels with oak leaves and acorns similar to Memorial Hall.

"That's a Templar cross." I point it out to Stoph. "The Knights Templar cathedrals in France have a similar style, including the three entrances with the largest in the middle. The double-headed eagle reminds me of the Scottish Rite Masonic sign."

Clinging to the corner of the church is a dog with a long s-shaped tail. Stoph says, "I'm guessing that's not Snoopy."

"Think about it. Richardson was all about the night sky. That's Canis Major."

"Canis Major?"

"The alpha star of Canis Major is Sirius, the dog star. It rises with the sun at the peak of summer. That's where the expression *the dog days of summer* originates."

"How did you not go to Harvard?"

"Didn't apply. There are always two towers in front of Templar cathedrals. The towers represent Jachin and Boaz of Solomon's Temple. Typically, there are symbols for the sun and the moon. Just like the rooster and owl at the Ames Library. You can see Richardson put the owl right here, and he used Canis Major, the dog, to show the sun."

Stoph says, "You should become a private tour guide."

"The checkerboard pattern at the top of the columns is a Solomon's Temple detail straight from the book of Kings where it details nets of checker-work and wreaths of chain-work upon the top of the pillars."

"That's an interesting detail. But what's your take on all the cryptic male faces?"

"Ezekiel says that the temple has the faces of men on one side and the faces of lions on the other side. I bet if we look on the back façade there are young lion faces," I say.

We are late for Mass, so we sit in the back of the church. All I can think about is food. Stoph follows the readings in the missalette and sings every hymn. I can't help but think just a few hours ago we were partying hard at the clubhouse. I notice the church doesn't have a typical dome but a giant cube above the altar. When mass is over, I ask Stoph to take out his measuring tool. Just as I expected, the cube is 20x20x20 cubits. From the back of the cube to the entrance is 60 cubits. Hidden within this elaborate church is the basic formula of Solomon's Temple.

After church we stop for a bagel and coffee. Then we pass by the Brattle Square Church while we finish our coffee. "Tanya should open a coffee shop in Boston. Her coffee blows this away."

"The Daily Grind would do well in the city," he says, stopping to look at the church. "Richardson designed this as well. The tower frieze is carved by the French sculptor Bartholdi, who designed the Statue of Liberty. Look inside the panels. He carved Emerson, Hawthorne, Lincoln, Sumner, Longfellow and Garibaldi."

"That's an interesting cast of characters. Were they all Unitarian?" I ask.

"I don't think so. They were probably Freemasons. Garibaldi was an Italian Freemason and he's in the center of the frieze posing as the priest marrying the couple."

"And Lincoln is kneeling and resting his chin on his hand as if he's a guest at the wedding. Wild stuff!"

We decide to stroll back to Cambridge along the Charles River. The autumnal colors shimmer across the water where rowers slice their oars in unison. Stoph says, "The crew guys are a dedicated bunch. Their training regimen is brutal."

The boathouse is crowded with rowers hauling their shells off the water. We cut through the building to use the restrooms. When I come out, I see Stoph chatting with one of the rowers. Stoph nods in my direction and the rower glances over his shoulder at me. He turns when he sees me coming and starts laughing.

"Please don't kill me!" Axel's broad smile lights up the boathouse.

I feel my face blush. "I'm so embarrassed."

"My fault. I should've warned you. I thought you tasted —"

"Not when I was chasing it with peppermint schnapps spiked cocoa. That was a trip-and-a-half."

Axel reaches his long arm around my shoulders and gives me a half hug. "Deepest apologies."

Stoph draws his shoulders back. "Dude, do you even remember playing tonsil hockey with the mascot?"

I want to shoot Stoph for mentioning that, but then he whips out his phone and shows us the picture he snapped of me and Axel with John Harvard. Axel chuckles and says, "Great shot, Stoph."

When Stoph leaves us to go use the bathroom, Axel asks me where the Daily Grind is located and when I'll be working again. I tell him my schedule. "I'll definitely stop by. I love indie coffee shops."

"We serve mushroom coffee, so it'll be right up your alley."

We are both laughing when Stoph returns. Axel heads to the erg machines to workout. I watch him peel off his sweats and notice he is ripped.

"You two really hit it off."

I shrug. "He seems cool."

"If you like total stoners."

"How could he row crew and be a stoner?"

"Dude, there's always a work-around."

A few days later I'm working the evening shift at the Daily Grind when Sheila and Jill stop by for lattes on the house. The shop is quiet so I pour myself a black coffee and hang out at their table.

"Where's Melissa?" I ask.

"Doing her community service. At the rate she's going, she'll be ringing the Red Cross bell in front of Macy's right through Christmas. She'll meet us here in a few."

The door swings open. Axel looks around the shop, then waves to me.

"This is a nice surprise," I say, my heart skipping a few beats. I get up to hug him and introduce Jill and Sheila.

Axel says, "This is a happening joint."

He follows me to the service counter to read the menu board. I give him a minute and say, "What do you want to try? Some mushroom blend? It's on me."

"Oh please, Paige. I should pay double after what happened the other night —"

Jill and Sheila rest their chins in their hands as if they're watching television. I hear Jill mumble, "I wonder what happened the other night?"

Axel leans his elbow on the service counter while I pull out the ingredients. My back is to him, but I see his reflection in the glass backsplash. He's checking out my ass. I take my time making his drink. "I just invented this — The Boys in the Boat Cordyceps Buster."

"Extra special," he says. "You should transport this coffee shop to the Head of the Charles. It'll be a big hit."

"I'll suggest that to my boss. Then I'd get to see you row, too."

Slow down, Paige. Breathe, I remind myself.

"So, are you and Stoph, like, exclusive? Sorry to be blunt. But, I mean, I felt a vibe. Still do. I hope I haven't overstepped the boundaries —"

"It's okay. Um, I dunno, exactly —"

Melissa comes in and calls from the door, "I need something warm, Paigester. It's so cold I have NFO."

"What's NFO?" I ask.

"Nipple freak out!"

"You weren't too worried about NFO when you went streaking," I say.

Axel spins around. "Rudy? Is that really you? That was epic!"

She bats her eyes. "And you are?"

I interject, "Melissa, meet Axel."

She eyes his Harvard crew hoodie. I hand her a cappuccino and she joins the girls.

He whispers to me, "I can't believe she's the halftime streaker. She was bombed."

"Axel. Come sit," says Melissa. He pulls a chair up to their table. "Are you a Porcellian?"

"No, I'm on the crew team. Maybe you can go streaking at the next regatta," he suggests. "For carbon reduction, of course."

"I just might."

"Paige, I'm loving this blend," he says. I like hearing him say my name.

"Isn't that Stoph's favorite as well?" blurts Melissa.

I shoot a look at her. "He's a pumpkin latte guy."

Melissa leans close to Axel. "Did you like my halftime show at the Game?"

Axel cracks up. "That took guts, Rudy."

"Oh, I'm full of all sorts of surprises. Give me a call sometime."

Axel finishes his coffee and says, "It was nice meeting you all. Thanks, Paige. Next one's on me."

After he leaves, Jill says, "So what happened the other night?"

Melissa whips her head to look at me. "Wait, what? You and him? Seriously? He's so hot."

I clean up the table, tossing out the napkins. "You told everyone about our football jerseys, so it's your own fault. Being number 40 brings all the boys to the yard. Can you imagine if I went streaking?"

Melissa sighs. "Go figure. I hoisted my own petard."

"I don't think you said that correctly."

"You get the gist."

24. The Peace Train

I take Hobson for a stroll to Tanya's house and find her in the backyard washing her hippie van. She's wearing thick Buffalo plaid lounge pants with Sherpa-lined waterproof boots. Her hair is piled in a top knot.

"Paige? Everything okay?"

"Awesome van Tanya."

"Come see." She opens the door. It's pimped-out with shag carpeting and a paneled interior. "Meet the Peace Train. I drove this bad boy cross country, camped the whole way. It's a great ride, good on gas, too."

"Can I borrow it?"

"Borrow the Peace Train? Seriously?" She tugs the garden hose away from the front tire.

"I need to go to Wyoming."

"That's 2,000 miles one way! I thought you were going to say New Hampshire or Vermont—"

"Listen — I'll work a million extra shifts at the coffee shop for free. Anything. I really need to go there for some research. I'll take my boyfriend and a few friends to share the driving. I promise I won't let anything happen to it."

Tanya shrugs and smiles. "Why not? If you plan this properly, it could be the road trip of a lifetime. I've got plenty of camping equipment you can use. A six-person tent, sleeping bags, cooking gear. You would just need to pack food and water. And one other thing: no drugs."

"Definitely, no drugs. I promise. We don't do that."

"Really? You came into the Daily Grind the other morning looking like you paddled up shit's creek. I'm not trying to bust your chops, but maybe try to keep your partying in check? Booze is a drug, too."

"Understood."

"When do I get to meet your boyfriend?"

"Before we leave, for sure."

There's enough room in the van for four, five tops. I head for Melissa and Jill's room to see if they're game for the road trip. Since the streaking episode, Melissa has been extra busy serving her one-hundred-hour community sentence.

Melissa takes no time to decide. "Fall break road trip, hell ya! But Wyoming? How about South Beach instead?"

"It has to be Wyoming for a project I'm working on."

We make the plan to leave Thursday after classes. I cash my paycheck and count my tips to budget for gas and food. I stop at the convenience store in town to pick up a few items. I'm craving potato chips and chocolate, which reminds me to pick up tampons. While I'm in that aisle I see condoms with endless options of ultra-thin, ultra-ribbed, bare skin, nirvana, and lubricated. I choose the jumbo pleasure pack and stash it at the bottom of the pile.

When the cashier gets to the pleasure pack, she holds it up and says, "Looks like someone has big plans. And would you like a bag too?"

Should I walk around with the tampons and pleasure pack fully exposed? Probably not. "Yes, I'll take a bag."

The only other thing we need are shovels. I make a note to visit the hardware store before we leave. The way I analyze Richardson's plans, we'll need to dig into the tunnel to access the room inside pyramid.

I stop by the library to remind Ms. Montgomery that I won't be in for a few days.

"Fall break? Didn't the semester just start? I swear you Millennials are the laziest generation. Everyone gets a trophy for participating. There are more days off than days on the school calendar. Where are you going on this *fall break*?"

"Wyoming."

"Why there of all places?"

"To check out the Ames Monument."

Her eyes pop open. "The pyramid?"

"Yes, the one Richardson —"

She stares long and hard at my face, then says, "Take lots of pictures. We can put them in the guidebook as an appendix."

I wait inside the library until I see Stoph pull into the parking lot. I take him into the coffee shop to properly introduce him to Tanya. He was around the day the container was delivered, but with Ms. Montgomery's tantrum, I never had the chance to introduce him.

Tanya greets us with insulated Daily Grind travel mugs filled with a new blend: *Travels with Charley Chaga*.

"So, you're the lucky guy dating my best employee. It's nice to meet you, Stoph."

He shakes Tanya's hand and sips the coffee. "Delicious. Thank you."

The Peace Train is parked near the coffee shop. Tanya demonstrates how everything works with the van and camping equipment. She holds steady eye contact with Stoph, assessing his energy. Then she tosses the keys to me and winks.

"You're the best," I tell her and give her a big hug.

"Take care of this old boy," she says. At first, I think she's talking about Stoph, then she knocks on the hood and I realize she's referring to the van.

"You bet," I say.

Stoph gives Tanya his keys to keep his car at her house. "Go straight home. No drag racing," he says.

She smiles and takes a visual inventory of Stoph. I wonder what she thinks of his energy.

We pull outside my dorm and beep. Stoph has one duffle bag and a brown paper bag. I look inside and see a stash of bills. "What's this?"

"I stopped at the ATM. Two thousand bucks just in case we need cash. I took it out of my allowance."

"You have a two-thousand-dollar allowance? Every week?"

"Something like that. Does that change your opinion of me?"

"Not really. I already knew you were loaded."

Jill and Melissa come out with matching luggage. I'd reminded them to pack light, but they've already brought enough crap for a month's safari to Africa.

"This could be our first problem and we haven't even hit the road yet," I tell them.

"Problem?"

"There's not enough room for all this. I just have a duffle bag and a cooler for food. We'll be roughing it. That's what camping is."

Melissa rolls her eyes. "There's camping and there's glamping. You can camp. We'll glamp."

"We have to fit Sheila's stuff, too. You need to scale this back."

We lug the bags out to the van. Sheila is leaning on the hood wearing a cheetah print faux fur bomber jacket. Stoph helps load the rest of the bags in the back and says, "Okay kids, does anyone need to use the bathroom? We're not making extra stops for potty breaks."

"Okay, Dad."

We pile in. Stoph drives the first leg of the trip. "The driver gets to choose the playlist."

"That works," Melissa says. "Stoph, is it true that there's three things Harvard students try to do before they graduate?"

"There's probably more than three things, but what are you referring to?"

"Lance told me about one, peeing on John Harvard's foot, two, doing the primal scream and three, having sex in the Widener stacks. He's already got two under his belt."

"Oh yeah, which two?"

"That's my secret, but after the clubhouse party he climbed up on the statue and pissed all over John Harvard's shoe. It's gross that tourists stop there to rub his shoe for good luck."

"It's true. The bronze on the shoe is all worn off. Not sure if it's from the piss or tourist rubbing."

I look at Stoph — wool ski hat, Wayfarers, bubble coat — tapping on the steering wheel to the beat. "Have you pissed on the shoe yet?"

"Of course. It may sound gross, but it's super funny when you're doing it."

Stoph drives for another hour, then pulls off at the next rest stop. "Quick stop then you're up, Paige."

I buy cheeseburgers and fries for us to share and the van smells like road trip bliss. I wipe the grease from my fingers to turn on my music.

"Dude, what's this?"

Sheila says, "It's totally folksy."

"It's for good luck," I tell them. "Peace Train."

25. Glamping

Stoph and I wrestle with the tent. It seemed simple enough when Tanya showed us, but we've got massive entanglement of poles and nylon at our feet. Melissa wheels her large suitcase near us and sits on it to watch the show.

"Could you get off your ass and help?" Stoph says.

"I'd rather watch."

There's a paper with instructions, so Sheila reads through it, looks at the scattered parts, and says, "You have it upside down."

Stoph throws up his hands and says, "I don't see what difference it makes, but let's flip it."

After that, the tent assembles with ease and we roll out the sleeping bags. "It's every man's dream," Stoph says. "In a tent with four beautiful women!"

"You wouldn't know what to do with all of us at once," Melissa says.

"I can dream, can't I?"

Crickets sing their night anthem as we fall asleep. Suddenly, a loud crashing wakes us.

"What the—" Stoph scrambles to his feet.

He unzips the tent window and the Quadsters gather around to watch a hump-shouldered bear scavenging our campsite. "Who left the McDonald's bag out there?" Stoph grumbles.

"Grizzly's got the Cheetos," I say.

"Oh crap, sorry guys," says Jill. "I left the cooler behind the van. I figured we'd just load it back in the morning."

We watch the bear feasting on all our food we packed. I'm thinking about how much money was wasted feeding the bear, when Sheila asks, "He won't attack us for dessert, will he?"

"He'll be stuffed after he finishes the jerky. Let's just go back to sleep and keep quiet," I say.

In the morning we unzip the tent and inspect the damage. Not only did the bear wipe out the food, but he clawed open Melissa's designer suitcase and ripped through it to get to her coconut infused lip gloss. Her panties, bras and tampons litter the grounds. Stoph picks up a strappy bra.

"We should make a slingshot in case the bear returns."

"Yeah, we'll use your banana hammock. Put it down, Stoph!" Melissa yells, as she scurries around cursing and collecting her belongings.

"I'm starving," he says. "Let's blow this popsicle stand and get some chow."

At the next town we file into a diner. Everyone orders coffee and scrambled eggs. "I can't believe that bear," Sheila says.

"At least he didn't drink our beer," Jill says.

"We should get gas and more food at the convenience store," I suggest.

It's Melissa's turn to drive and she pulls the van back onto I-80. I slump over on Stoph's shoulder to nap.

"Love birds, gross," she says, looking in the mirror at us, then turns up her music.

I wake when the van starts bumping onto gravel. "Why are we stopping —"

"License and registration please." There's a state trooper by the driver's window. Melissa asks for her handbag from the back and we pass forward her Chanel clutch. She scrounges through the glovebox until she finds the registration. The cop takes the paper and her license back to his cruiser.

"Why did he pull us over?" I ask her.

"No clue. He's just being a prick."

"Cops don't usually pull people over unless there's reasonable suspicion," I say.

"Oh my God, I haven't shampooed in two days. Is that reasonable suspicion?"

The cop returns. "Who is Tanya Goforth?"

I roll down the window. "She's my boss. She lent us the van."

"Okay, everyone out. Let's go."

We get out and line up on the side of the road. The cop and his partner search the Peace Train. They pull out all the bags and camping equipment, empty out the side compartments, search through the food.

"Where are you all going?"

"Wyoming," I say. "We're on fall break."

He looks at Melissa. "Why are you doing 87 in a 55?"

"No way," says Melissa, batting her eyes. "Was I going that fast?"

"That's what I clocked you at." He rips a piece of paper from his pad and says, "Slow down."

"Thank you, officer," she says. We shove everything back in the van and Melissa launches a stream of curse words. "What's the big deal with 87? That's not that bad. Cops should be out fighting real crime."

"87 is a tad lead foot, especially in this ancient bucket of bolts," Stoph says.

"You drive then. And you're all pitching in to help pay this ticket."

Stoph hops in the driver's seat and starts thumping his club music. When we reach the middle of Iowa, we stop to set up camp. I pass around the six packs and chips while Stoph and Sheila set up the tent. Coors has never tasted so good.

I build a small bonfire and we huddle together to keep warm. "I'd kill for a pizza right now," I say.

"Totally," Stoph says. "I doubt anyone feels like driving to get it."

"Do they even make pizza in, where are we, Iowa?" Melissa says.

We down the beer, chips and beef jerky and watch the fire burn itself out before we turn in for the night.

The sound of rain tapping the tent is peaceful, at first, like a relaxation sound machine, until it turns to a downpour. The tent roof collects water and begins to sag. Thunder rumbles in the distance. It doesn't take long before our sleeping bags absorb the water seeping through the floor of the tent.

"I bet it's not raining in Florida right now," Melissa whines.

"That's not helpful," I say. "I think we need to pack up fast and get into the van."

Stoph pushes the ceiling of the tent to drain the pooling water and prevent the tent from collapsing on us. "I agree. Let's break down the tent and hit the road."

The drenched gear gets stuffed into the van. Then we hear crunching sounds coming through the woods. A pack of guys in gray sweats emerges through the woods, running at a mean pace. One of the sweatshirts says *Iowa Wrestling.*

"Damn, they're training before sunrise in this shitty weather," Stoph says. "Impressive."

"This is wrestling country," I say. "I don't know how those guys do it — the way they train and compete on limited calories. If I had to weigh in before every soccer game I never would have survived."

"Wrestlers are weirdos," Melissa says. "Men rolling around in onesies."

"They have hot bodies, though," Sheila says.

"If you say so." Melissa opens her mouth, pretending to gag.

"Okay, so which athletes have the best physique?" Jill climbs over Melissa to take the middle seat.

"Ultimate Frisbee players." Stoph flexes his arms.

"Ooh-la-la, look at those guns." Melissa elbows Jill and they giggle.

The wipers can't swipe fast enough to deal with the torrential rain. I drive the van with limited visibility. "First diner I see we're pulling in whether they have French toast or not."

The Bluebird Diner welcomes us with its blue and white retro vibe. We all order coffee and pancakes. While we wait for the food, we take turns using the bathroom to do everything short of showering.

An elderly woman steps out of the stall and watches Melissa tossing her hair under the hand dryer. "This isn't a beauty parlor, hon," she says.

I hold my breath, anticipating a snide remark from Melissa. Instead, she smiles at the woman, then apologizes for being in the way. She steps aside to make room for her to wash her hands, then heads back to our table without saying a word.

Stoph catches up with me outside the restrooms. His hair is wet, slicked back in a fresh man bun. "Do you have a plan once we get to the Ames Monument?"

I grab Stoph's ass to make him laugh. "Yes. The plan is, we dig."

26. The Pyramid

We cross the Wyoming state line. The welcome sign has a silhouette of a cowboy, riding a wild bronco, raising his hat with one hand.

"Pull over — photo op," Melissa calls from the back seat.

The Quadsters huddle together under the sign while Stoph snaps the picture. We park the Peace Train in front of the sign and take more pictures to commemorate the trip.

"You two sit on the hood. Act like love birds," Melissa orders, taking over the photo shoot.

"It's a sexist sign, don't you think?" I say to Stoph as he poses with his arm draped across my shoulders. We sit on the hood of the van and flash the peace sign at the camera.

He takes a longer look at the sign. "Maybe. There should be a woman on the horse as well."

"Forever west," I read the words beneath the cowboy and bronco. "As if people need to be reminded that they're roaming the wild west."

"It's just tourism marketing. Don't overthink everything."

Despite all the recent rain, the ground feels rock solid. We get back in the van and continue through Albany County, admiring the clear skies and Rocky Mountains, so different from the changing foliage we left behind in Massachusetts.

"This is beautiful," says Jill.

I slide behind the wheel to bring us along the final stretch into Sherman, a town that technically no longer exists. Sherman was created when train tracks came through the area to complete the transcontinental railroad. The tracks were later moved a few miles south, eliminating the town. The only remaining thing in Sherman is the Ames Monument.

I ease the van over the rough terrain, trying not to jostle everyone. I pop on a version of Peace Train, by Dolly Parton and Ladysmith Black Mambazo, to create a funky country vibe.

"Goes with the theme." I glance in the rearview mirror at their three heads bopping up and down.

We bounce along the dusty road, washboarded with freshly laid crushed granite, until we find a private spot in the Vedauwoo campground. We are surrounded by gorgeous rock formations — pink feldspar rising five hundred feet — with giant pines and big sky.

The place is empty, probably because of the five-day forecast of unrelenting rainstorms and a cold front. I travel far enough to be sure no one will camp anywhere near us.

"Remind me. Why are we glamping in freezing Vedywahooyou?" Melissa whines from the back seat.

"Check out the rock formations. They're said to have been created by playful spirits. Young Arapaho men travelled through here on vision quests to experience the outlaw spirit."

"Oh. Now I'm totally into it since you shared that tidbit you memorized from your dildo travel guide —"

"Dude, there it is. You can totally see the top of the Ames Monument from here," Stoph shouts from the escarpment he climbed onto.

I scramble up to see the limestone pyramid, standing alone in the outstretched prairie. It towers over the remains of the one-time railroad town of Sherman. I return to the van and unroll the blueprints that we took from the Porcellian clubhouse wine room. Stoph climbs down and looks over my shoulder.

"Based on Richardson's site plan, I've figured out the GPS coordinates of the tunnel entrance. He shows the pyramid marked in the square right here, and then he shows these track marks that lead here, to the side of the mountain."

Stoph sorts through the pages. The first page has the perspective drawing of the pyramid. It's not drawn to scale; it's only meant to show what the pyramid was meant to look like once it was finished. Then he flips to the site plan and nods his head. "I think your calculations are correct."

We all take the mile-long hike to see the pyramid up close. There is nothing around for miles: The terrain feels moon-like as we stand on the wind-blown treeless summit. Approaching the monument, I think this must be the weirdest structure Richardson ever designed.

The monument has two nine-foot-tall bas-relief portraits of the Ames brothers sculpted by Augustus Saint-Gaudens. They resemble the bas-relief in the library above the fireplace. I notice a few bullet holes in the Ames brothers, their noses shot off, as the monument served as someone's target practice.

"I guess pissing on the Ames brothers isn't a thing," Stoph jokes. "Would be a tad difficult to climb up there."

The monument is regarded by some architects as Richardson's greatest work. I am not so impressed. Workers cut the stone from a granite outcropping a half mile away. Oxen teams skidded the tons of granite blocks to create this monolithic curiosity that resembles an alien space ship.

I can imagine the mumbles between the Quadsters — *Can't believe she dragged us here! She's lost her mind!* which I ignore to study the compass readings.

"If the original tracks stopped here, I think the tunnel should stretch back to where we're camping," I conclude.

"Wouldn't it make more sense to just dig around the base of the pyramid? Enter this thing more directly. Why would Richardson have tunnels?"

"Because Solomon's Temple had tunnels," I explain. "Richardson had to include a tunnel system, just like the cavernous tunnel that ran from the Old City of Jerusalem toward the Temple Mount. That was the biblical escape route: that's how they secretly moved the temple treasures. The Ames Monument is at the highest point of the transcontinental railroad just as Solomon's Temple was built on the mount. The parallels cannot be a coincidence."

Stoph paces in front of the pyramid. "So where do we dig?"

"If we dig by our campsite, then we could find the corridor as Richardson intended. It will be less obvious if someone drives by. Otherwise, it looks like we're vandalizing the monument."

"Fine by me."

"And look: No matter which way we go, the compass points directly to the center of the pyramid. No doubt something valuable is inside there." I flash the compass toward Stoph.

Stoph takes the compass and heads in various directions. "You're right — the center of the pyramid is where it wants us to focus."

The Quadsters listen while Stoph and I discuss the options.

"What's the big deal about this thing?" Jill flicks her thumb toward the monument.

"The reason why we are here is to make an archeological dig. Based on my research, I think the ark of the covenant is buried in this monument. We are going to find it."

"The ark of the covenant as in Moses? The Ten Commandments? That ark? The one that's been missing forever?" asks Sheila.

"Yes. That ark," Stoph says.

"Oh puhleeeze," Melissa shouts. "Why didn't you tell us this was why we were jackassing all the way to Westbumbfuckwyoming?"

"You never asked." I get the shovels from the van and drop them on the ground.

The Quadsters groan.

"Let's start digging. We are about to become famous," I tell them.

Melissa's eyes bug out. "Famous? I don't see the Kardashians digging in the middle of fucking Wyoming."

I break the ground first and the others follow, all but Melissa. Stoph unloads the rest of our gear for it to dry in the sun. He takes photos of the Quadsters as we slowly make a dent in the earth.

I'm cranking away, sweating and feeling parched under the dry sun that just poked through the clouds for the first time in days. My skin turns pink, so I stop to get a hat. I find

Melissa sprawled out on the hood of the van. She's drinking beer and holding a glam magazine four inches from her nose.

"You tricked us into coming out here." She flips the magazine page.

"If I invited you to come find the ark of the covenant with me, you would have blown me off. Listen, this could be one of the greatest discoveries in the history of the world."

She tosses the magazine to the side and shields the sun with her hand. "I'm in the digging photos. That's all the proof the historians should need."

"Well, when you're done lounging around, we would appreciate your help."

"Be right over, Sister Shovel." She swigs the beer.

I want to bash my shovel over Melissa's head, but then I think, maybe she has the right idea. I grab some beer from the cooler and pass them around. We stop shoveling to relax for a few minutes.

"To Moses," Sheila says.

"To Solomon's Temple," I say, tapping my beer against hers.

The ground is rock hard. If we are struggling with our modern-day shovels, I wonder how they did it a hundred years ago — maybe dynamite or nitroglycerin? I stroll to the front of the van and slide onto the hood next to Melissa.

"You're right. This sucks," I admit. "Sorry I dragged you out here."

"This is the worst idea in the history of bad college ideas."

"Unlike your Widener stacks escapade? Or streaking at the Game?"

"At least I had an afterglow. My skin is dehydrating out here," Melissa whines. "I could use a cosmo martini right now."

I rest my head against the windshield and search for the *outlaw spirit* billowing through the rock formations. That's when it hits me. Richardson wouldn't just dig a hole straight down. That's too simple. I slide off the hood and open the compass to follow along the base of the mountain. The compass needle spins and points to the mountain wall.

Stoph jogs over. "What's up?"

"Let's push these out of the way."

"You want to move these boulders?"

I tug on a few of the smaller rocks to pull them down. "I think the *mezuzah* is behind these rocks."

"The *mezuzah*?" He starts fidgeting with his man bun.

"There are mysteries about Solomon's Temple regarding the doors. In the book of Kings, it describes the outer sanctum and the inner shrine as having five *mezuzot*. A *mezuzah* is the doorpost. I bet the first doorpost and the entryway are over here behind these rocks. The site plan Richardson drew up is marked here which is this stone wall in front of us."

We gather the Quadsters and the shovels. We all move to the area where I think the door might be and we start wedging the shovel blades into the creases between the rocks. First, the smaller stones wiggle free and tumble to the ground. We move them out of the way and keep chipping away the stones we can manage.

"How deep do we need to go?" Stoph pauses to analyze the small opening.

"Not too deep, unless other rocks fell through creating a barrier. It has been a lot of years," I say.

"If we find the door over here, then where is the ark? In this mountain?" Sheila asks.

"No. It should lead us to an underground tunnel that leads back to the pyramid."

Jill leans against the end of her shovel. "Do you really think they could have dug all that earth out by hand back then?"

"They dragged all the granite out of the mountain to build the pyramid. They certainly could have dug out a tunnel as well."

We continue until we run out of daylight as well as physical strength. I feel like we barely made a dent in creating the opening. We finish setting up the tent and pile sticks to start a bonfire. We cook hot dogs while Stoph's music streams from the van.

"Just sayin', this is the last of the beer," Sheila mentions as she passes around the cans.

"That's okay. I'm so tired I'll be asleep in an hour." I toss back the beer and head straight for my sleeping bag. Stoph said finding the ark will be epic, but all I can think now is *epic failure*.

27. The Tunnel

Stoph and I gaze from the edge of the cliff. His voice breaks my meditative gaze toward the top of the Ames Monument. "Dude, you couldn't sleep?"

"I'm just thinking about Richardson's site plans. I'm convinced the tunnel entrance is here. They put the ark on the train to bring it west. I think it was originally kept in North Easton in the attic room of Memorial Hall. That's what makes the most sense to me. Then they had to move it, possibly because someone figured out it was there."

"Right, and they needed to protect it."

"Maybe Richardson kept the ark in North Easton while he planned the holy of holies in this ghost town. Once he built the monument, then it was moved by rail, hidden in cargo, super secretive operation. Once it got to Wyoming, it was transported underground so no one saw what was going on. Then — the ballsiest move of all — they moved the train tracks! That way no one would come to Sherman because the town no longer exists. Everyone left. Ghost town."

"Brilliant. If it's true."

"I could also be one hundred percent wrong and the Quadsters will kill me for trashing their fall break."

Stoph waves off my negative thoughts. "Don't even go there. This trip has been a blast."

I smile at him. "If nothing else, I love tooling around in the Peace Train. It feels so —"

"Sexy," he says and kisses the side of my neck. "We've hardly had a minute alone though…"

"Okay, but we'll have time —"

"Once we're done being archaeologists."

"Right." I kiss him and announce, "I'm going into town to pick up some food. We can get back to chipping when I return."

He salutes me. "Yes, Sargent Paige."

It's several miles of uninspired flat land before I find a country store. I'm starving. I grab a package of bacon from the refrigerated case. There's a picture of a white hog with lopped ears on the package that says *100% Premium Landrace Bacon.*

"Need help finding anything?" asks the store clerk.

"What's Landrace bacon?"

"That's the best bacon money can buy. Pricey, but delicious. The Landrace pig is used mostly for crossbreeding in the U.S. There's a fourth-generation farm not far from here that controls the monopoly on American Landracers. Gold mine if you ask me."

"What's the name of the farm?"

"Preston's Farms."

I put the bacon back in the refrigerator case and buy some beef jerky. Landracers, I recall that's the name of the company that Captain Biff said the Land Rover was registered to. In the A.O.D. meeting he said Landracer is a company in Wyoming. I wonder if this is just a coincidence. I assumed Landracer had something to do with Land Rover. There's a Daylight's Donut shop next door so I get some glazed and powdered donuts and a box of joe-to-go. It's not made with the magic beans of the Daily Grind, but this is as close to toughy juice as I'm going to find in Wyoming.

On my way out of town, the voice on the van radio forecasts thunderstorms in the days ahead. I pass a motel where two parked cars have Massachusetts license plates — I guess we're not the only nuts who drove cross country — only we're the fools for glamping with sketchy weather on the horizon. It is odd though, that other tourists from Massachusetts are here at the same time we are.

Back at the camp, I see Melissa standing outside the tent with her hands on her hips. I beep the horn and zig-zag the van toward her to be funny. She flips her middle finger at me.

"I thought you took off and left us here."

"Do you have abandonment issues?" I hold up the bags. "Coffee and donuts."

Her face lights up as she takes two glazed. "You're a lifesaver."

After breakfast, we resume digging. Our shovels clang against the side of the mountain. Small chunks crack off and roll away. Then larger pieces start to break away until a boulder finally budges.

I stop to catch my breath. "I don't know how archaeologists devote their lives digging for fossils."

Melissa leans against the wall and sips her coffee. "You mean this isn't a career path for you?"

"Maybe, if we discover the ark."

We strike our shovel blades under a jagged rock to force it free. Sheila shouts, "Hey, what's this?"

We gather around where an iron hook pokes through the opening. "19th Century iron! Dig around this area — open it up," Stoph says. "This could be something."

After a few more hours, we reveal that the hook is attached to a stone slab. We clear away more rocky terrain to find a seam in the stone. "Does anyone else think this is a door?" I ask.

Jill tugs on the hook. "If it is, how are we going to open it?"

Stoph jogs toward the Peace Train, swings it around, then backs up as close to the wall as he can. He takes the bungee cords from the camping gear, hooks them together, and ties one end to the hitch and one end to the iron hook. He leans his head out the van window and shouts, "Balls to the wall!"

He floors the gas pedal. The spinning wheels kick up massive dust clouds and spit pebbles. The door shifts and the Quadsters start cheering. The van struggles to inch forward, then the cord snaps in half. Stoph blasts forward in the van before he jams on the brakes and skids to a stop.

He slams the van door. "Shit. Now what?"

I tell him, "It was working. The stone shifted a smidge."

Jill takes her shovel and tries to wedge it into the seam. The rest of us follow her lead thinking we can use the shovels to pry the door. No luck.

"Let's go to the hardware store and get an industrial strength chain and two crowbars," I suggest.

"Good idea. I'll make the run." Stoph rumbles off in the van.

"Beef jerky anyone?" I pass the bag around.

"Who is going to venture in there if we get it open?" Sheila taps her foot against the door.

Jill nods as she swallows the jerky. "Not going to lie, I'm too scared to go in a cave. What if there's dead bodies or rodents?"

Melissa inspects the wall as if she is window-shopping down Fifth Avenue. "This is Paige's quest. We just came along for the photo ops. I vote for Paige to go suss it out while we wait here. We'll call for help if the shit hits the fan."

Stoph is gone for a long time while we keep digging around the door. I find an old gilt button with worn out lettering that I imagine popped off Richardson's coat. I put it in my back pocket for luck.

Stoph finally returns and parks the Peace Train near our dig site. He is wearing a miner's helmet with a light fastened to the front forehead. He lines up four miner's helmets on the ground along with a can of bright lavender metallic spray paint.

"I got us all helmets. I figured you'd want to accessorize them — hope purple works for you ladies."

Sheila is over the moon with excitement. "I'm on it. Everyone want their helmet painted — matchy-matchy?"

"Hell, yes! Quadster purple head gear," says Jill.

I help Stoph hook up the thick chain to the trailer hitch. "What took so long?" I ask him.

"Couldn't find the right gauge chain in the hardware store. Took forever. The locals move slowly out here."

I notice he smells different, like a short-order cook. "Did you stop and get something to eat?"

"No, I just went to the hardware store and came right back. Why?"

I yank the sleeve of his shirt toward my nose and inhale. "Then why do you smell like bacon?"

"What are you the FBI? I had breakfast; I admit it. I was starved. What's the big deal?"

"How was the Landrace bacon?"

His mouth drops open. "How do you know about Landrace bacon?"

"Because it's the best around. You settle for nothing less."

"Busted," he chuckles.

I'm not exactly amused. I worry that if he's willing to fib about a small detail, then he'll be untruthful about bigger issues. The other thing that bothers me is he fed himself, took his time, and didn't bring back any food for the rest of us. One, dishonest, two, selfish, three, typical one-percent behavior.

Melissa struts around distributing the painted helmets. "Too bad these lights don't blink like a disco ball. Let's do a photo op before we open Pandora's Box. Everyone with the hard hats. Let's go."

Stoph snaps a few quick shots and then fires up the van. Sheila and I wedge the crowbars in the seam while Stoph hooks the chain to the bumper. This time he revs the engine and eases forward instead of gunning the motor. The van fishtails in the dirt before it straightens and tugs on the hook. He pumps the gas as we crank the crowbars. The stone shifts. Suddenly, there's a cracking sound as the hook springs free from the ring and blasts toward the van like a missile. The metal hook dings the rear bumper.

Melissa and Jill rush over to check the tunnel door. There's a jagged hole, almost big enough to climb through. We whack our shovels to break away more chunks of rock.

"Can you see anything?" Stoph collects the chain and tosses it to the side of the van.

I poke my head through. "Not yet."

He peers into the black hole. "It's tight, but I think we can squeeze through. You game?"

"Hold on," I say and head toward the camper. "Need the compass."

I stash the compass in my pocket, fasten my helmet and toss a shovel through the hole. We listen as it clangs against the rock ground.

"Are you sure about this?" Jill says, biting her lower lip.

"Definitely," I say, thinking to myself, this is the dumbest thing I've ever done. "You guys stay here."

It's a tight squeeze. The Quadsters help shove my butt through the opening. The helmet light reveals stone walls that resemble Egyptian hieroglyphics — intricately carved oak leaves, mistletoe, pinecones and swirling ivy with cherub faces intertwined in the wild bramble. We proceed down the corridor, seeing elaborate stone carvings of battling dragons and wild mythological creatures.

"Dude, I've never seen anything like this."

We are immersed inside a maze of an eerie cavernous underworld.

"Some of this looks like the work of the Norcross brothers," I say, knowing that Richardson often contracted James and Orlando Norcross for their elaborate stonework. I recognize two of the carved creatures, Astarte and Bael. "Some of these wall carvings are the spirits of Solomon. I haven't counted them all, but I bet there are seventy-two demons in this tunnel."

"Seventy-two demons?"

"Solomon imprisoned the demons in a brass vessel and tossed it into the sea. The Babylonians found the vessel and thought they discovered a great treasure. When they opened the vessel, the demons and their legions were set free. The Lesser Key of Solomon is a grimoire to the evocation of the seventy-two spirits."

"What's a grimoire?"

I run my hands along the details in the wall. "It's a textbook of magic and spells. A how-to book to invoke supernatural entities like angels, demons and spirits. It explains how to make magical talismans —"

"Why would they carve all this and hide it in a tunnel? It should be somewhere visible like the Million Dollar Staircase that Richardson designed in the New York State Capitol building in Albany."

"Not if you're building Solomon's Temple and protecting the ark of the covenant." I continue down the corridor before I trip over something. I shine the helmet light toward the ground. "Check this out!"

Stoph stoops next to me for a closer look. "Train tracks?"

"For transporting the ark into the pyramid. Follow the tracks."

"This is interesting." Stoph shines his helmet light on carvings of George Washington and Abraham Lincoln with their names underneath. "Were George and Abe demons? What do they have to do with Solomon's Temple?"

I run my hand across the faces. "Washington was a Freemason. Lincoln commissioned the Ames Shovel Company to dig the railroad. Maybe it's a tribute?"

"Maybe."

We follow the tracks deeper into the cave. I stop when I see a carved large-winged crow standing upright that has human arms and legs with talons for feet. He holds a shovel in one hand.

"Fascinating," I say.

Stoph steps next to me. "Why is that fascinating?"

"It's Malphas. One of the major demons."

"Dude, you and your demonology."

"They each have a sigil assigned to them."

"What's a sigil?"

I point out the line pattern above Malphas that resembles doodling, much like the doodle drawings in the oxblood notebooks. "It's a symbol that has magical powers."

Wild scrolls of flowers and bramble lead to carved heads of people that I don't recognize, many of them with bulging eyes and frightened expressions.

"This one looks like a weird zodiac sign. Leo's a lion, right? Check this out."

It's a lion's head with five goat legs. "I'm guessing that's Buer, the president of hell. He commanded fifty legions of demons."

"It's insane that you know this stuff."

"I don't know it. I just remember it. Buer should be your tattoo."

"The president of hell on my ass, check. Sounds good to me."

We follow the tracks up the incline. We reach an area that opens to an alcove. There is a statue of a cat with human arms, hands, legs and feet. The cat is blowing into a French horn.

"This might be a better demon tattoo for you," I say. "Music surrounds Byleth."

"He's cool. Why would they put a statue in the tunnel?"

"Maybe they imported it, brought it in on the train."

"Do you recognize the artist?" He strokes his chin as if he's pondering a masterpiece at an art exhibit.

"Maybe Daniel Chester French, but that's a guess. Let's keep moving."

The hollowed canyon gets steeper and the walls are blank for a long stretch. Stoph says, "If it wasn't for the tracks, I'd think we reached no-man's land."

"It's strange that the walls are suddenly blank. This whole tunnel is so bizarre. I wonder why the carving stopped?"

Stoph passes something etched on the floor. "Here's a naked woman with braided hair."

I look over his shoulder. "Seriously? That's a scorpion. What part of that looks like a naked lady to you?"

Stoph rubs his eyes. "There's her butt, there's a braid —"

"No, it's one hundred percent scorpion."

"Who's the scorpion demon?"

"No clue."

More wall carvings continue — thick trees in a lush forest branch toward a horse creature that is half man, shooting an arrow at a wild boar across the woods.

"It's over here!" Stoph shouts. "Check it out, the wild boar is the Porcellian sign!"

It's over here. The words ring in my head. I freeze. The same words, spoken in the same pitch I heard once before — the night of the break-in.

"Why would there be a Porcellian pig sign in the tunnel? Richardson was hiding the ark from the Porcellian Club. He broke away from them to work with the A.O.D."

"Richardson was a Porcellian, so it's an indication of his allegiance."

"That makes zero sense. The pig is not a demon. Plus, that's not a pig, it's a goat."

He looks closer. "Damn, now I see the horns. You're right again."

"Stoph, what aren't you telling me? What does the Porcellian Club have to do with the ark of the covenant?" I stare at Stoph, aiming my helmet light in his face.

He is wheezing from the dust in the tunnel. "No clue."

"That's bullshit. This has something to do with your overnight punch event, doesn't it?"

He shakes his head. "I can't tell. I'm sworn to a lifetime of secrecy."

"Stoph, we're in this together. We've come this far. You have to tell me."

"You have to swear on your life —"

"I need to know. We can't turn back now. We need to work together to find the ark."

"Swear on it."

"Fine. I swear. Now tell me."

"There are divisions within the Porcellian Club." His voice has a truculent edge. "Certain members have responsibilities passed down from generations as far back as early American settlers. There are several tentacles of other secret societies affiliated with the Porc, including the Ancient Order of Druids, the Knights Templar, the Freemasons. No one needs to know what the other societies do. We are supposed to focus on our own responsibilities."

I pause to let that sink in. "What's your responsibility?"

"Architecture. Finding ancient relics." He shrugs. "Some of the ancient Porcellian relics are hidden in architecture — like when you found the drawings in the clubhouse secret wine room. I'm guessing no one could interpret what Richardson was up to."

"You told the other Porcellian members about the Richardson drawings we found?"

He hesitates.

"You were part of the robbery at the lodge, weren't you?"

He walks away from me. "Seriously, dude."

"I don't have time for your lies. You can get lost!"

He spins back around. "Fine! The lodge incident was part of getting punched. True, I was in on that. I was ordered to figure out the secrets that Richardson hid in his architecture. Richardson was a Porcellian Club member and a druid leader. Things turned tense between the Porcellians and the local druids in the 1850s. Richardson sided with the druids because their focus is on architecture. The Porcellians wanted —"

"They wanted complete control of the biblical artifacts that the druids brought to America! That's why Richardson designed according to Solomon's Temple! He could hide the ark of the covenant from Porcellian."

"The Porcs couldn't believe you figured this stuff out —"

"Wait. You told them what I was figuring out?"

"Relax." He brushes dirt from my shoulder. "It's all good."

I deflect his hand. "Were you just using me to figure out Richardson's architecture?"

"Oh please, Paige. I figured out that Treadwell was researching Richardson in the lodge long before we even met."

He just called me Paige instead of *dude* — he's lying to me again.

I press him. "Oh really? How'd you figure that out?"

"Richardson designed Sever Hall with a secret crypt. But the crypt is empty. Weird, right? He designed a lot of places like that, with odd empty spaces. He was looking to move the relics around. Keep things hidden. There's other Porc members surveying Richardson's buildings. I was assigned North Easton."

"Everything you just said is stuff I figured out. You've been using my ideas and riding my coattails all along."

"Look, you have no clue how deep this society runs."

"How did you know what Treadwell was researching in the lodge?"

"The Porc brothers have been watching him for a long time. I saw steady activity at all hours at the lodge. I knew there had to be important information in there. The Porcellian clubhouse holds tons of early American secrets, documents, and religious relics that pre-date the colonies. But Richardson — the Porcellians want what he hid."

"I bet they took you down to that wine room for the overnight and made you drink whatever is in those wine jugs. More ceremonial mind-bender juice. It's brainwashing. They want to make you think you'll be one of the righteous bros. But it's not brotherhood, it's greed. That's how they stay wealthy and exclusive. You do realize the Bible says the ark has special powers, don't you? If we find it, I wouldn't try to get greedy with it."

He slams his shovel on the ground. "Let's just get back to doing what we came down here to do."

"Not so fast, Stoph. You wouldn't be anywhere near finding the ark if it weren't for me. You've been using me all along."

"How much more do I —"

"Just stop."

He holds my shoulders, looking deep into my eyes. "You know I'm with you, Paige. Let's do this together. What demon are we looking for — Satan?"

I step past him, marching through the tunnel. The ground gets steep before it flattens into a small room. There is a large bronze bas relief sculpture of a fly raised in the same solid bronze as the memorial plaques on the outside of the pyramid.

"Beelzebub," I say, admiring the thick fly that has fanned wings and spooked eyes. "I bet this was sculpted by Augustus Saint-Gaudens."

The room has an arched opening — classic Richardson — and on the right side is a large circular design with a carved Knights Templar cross, a classic symbol of the Temple of Solomon. Above the cross is an engraved pyramid with a floating human eye at the top.

The archway leads to a solid iron door. There are two scrolling iron hinges that stretch across the width of the door. Stoph tries to open it, but it's locked. "Now what?"

"Shine your light by the doorknob so I can see better," I tell him.

I crouch to get closer. "It's just a key hole. A regular key hole. No magic or tricks to it."

Stoph whines, "That would be wonderful news if we had the key. But it was probably buried with Richardson."

"Or stashed in the Porcellian clubhouse." I try the door just to double check it's locked, then go back through the archway. "Let's get out of here. The Quadsters are probably freaking out because we've been down here for a long time."

We backtrack through the corridors. "Dude, this place is a museum. I have loads of new VR ideas —"

And that's when I lose it. "This isn't about you and your lame-ass projects. This is the real thing. We are this close to finding the ark of the covenant and all you care about is your bullshit?"

"Dude, chill out already."

Heat swirls through my head. I'm not giving up, so I sprint back toward the door. Stoph lowers his shoulder to push past me. That triggers me into full soccer mode. I catch the tail of his shirt and tug him back before he pulls away. I chase after him — heels kicking, elbows pumping hard — I haven't run like this since my last soccer game. Stoph is fast, but I stay right on his heels. When we reach the stone steps, he slips and loses his balance. I grab his shirt again to pull him back so I can hop over him — soccer players trump Ultimate Frisbee dudes — and my foot clips his leg. As I stumble forward, my hand that holds the compass smacks hard against the stone wall.

The impact breaks the compass in half. But then I see the polished brass key.

"The Lesser Key of Solomon," I say, huffing hard, and pick up the key from the broken pieces. "New rule. The person who finds the key gets to open the door."

"Who cares who opens the door?" Stoph says, swiping dust from his sleeve.

"I care," I say, slipping the key into the keyhole.

It clicks open on the third twist. The door hinges squeal and swings open. There is a winding spiral staircase in the center of the room. We take the steps two at a time until we reach the top.

"Dude, is this —"

"The holy of holies."

A golden glow radiates from the walls, adorned with carvings of cherubs. There are two massive gold cherubim with wingspans that touch the side walls twenty cubits apart. The creatures appear to be guarding a box that looks like a small gold coffin with two poles on the sides. Positioned on top of the box are two brilliant cherubim with graceful wings reaching toward each other.

Stoph gazes over my shoulder. "Is this what I think it is?"

"The ark of the covenant."

"We're rich."

"Wrong. We're going to take this and hand it over to the druids for protection. This is not about fame or money. This is not about Porcellian," I tell him.

"Paige, you have no idea how powerful they are."

"Stoph, which side of this are you on?"

"Of course, I'm on your side," he says, kissing the top of my head, "which is why you have to listen to me. They have power you cannot even begin to believe."

I know he sides with Porcellian, but I need Stoph's help to get the ark out of the tunnel. Once it's out, then I will deal with him.

The ark sits on a granite stone altar in the middle of the room. There's a door on the other side of the room that doesn't have steps to exit; instead, it has rail tracks leading right up to the threshold.

"It's a mine cart track system. The chassis is right there, so if we pull it in here, then we can slide the ark on top of it. We can use the track system to roll it out of the tunnel."

Stoph tightens his man bun while he thinks. "You think that will work?"

"It's primitive technology but how else would they have transported the ark into this room? They used the mine carts to haul in all the building material and then, ultimately, the ark."

Stoph stares at the tracks. "They must have used the tracks to haul in all this gold as well. This room must be worth billions in gold alone."

"Forget about the gold, Stoph."

"I'm not saying we take it."

"Let's push the chassis into the room." I tug on Stoph's sleeve so he comes with me. I don't trust him to be alone around the gold.

The mine cart has steel wheels that groan when we move it. It's stubborn, at first, but once it gets rolling it's easy to push. We line it up with the end of the ark. Stoph gets on one side and I step to the other.

"It's going to be heavy — the Bible says it's coated with gold inside and out. Plus, the stone tablets are in it."

"How big are the tablets? Don't you want to open it and look inside?" Stoph asks.

"That's a hard no," I say. "I'm not religious. But the ark is meant to be respected. The Bible says God will punish anyone with malice intent."

"You just said you don't believe in all that."

"I believe in respect. We shouldn't mess with a biblical artifact. The Bible says the ark has special powers. All I want is for it to be properly protected."

Stoph shrugs. "Superstitions, that's all. Ready? On the count of three."

We can barely move the ark. The poles are meant for transporting it, but it would require a small army to carry this box around the desert during biblical times. We push it inch-by-inch to slide it off the rock altar onto the chassis. The ark fits with room to spare. We push the wheeled mine cart toward the door and align the wheels onto the tracks.

"We'll have to push it the whole way," Stoph says.

The tunnel walls are narrow and straight as far as we can see. The pyramid is at the highest elevation of the transcontinental railroad, so it's downhill from here on. We begin to push it but it feels like something is dragging. I check the sides to see what's blocking the wheels. He comes to the back and we both kneel on the tracks to look underneath the cart.

"There's a lever. Pull it," I say.

Stoph cranks the lever that releases the cart — it jolts forward and starts rolling — so I jump on the back. Stoph scrambles to his feet and sprints behind the runaway cart and dives onto the back. The cart starts to drop downhill and I get the sensation of being on an old rickety rollercoaster — rattling, jerking, dipping.

We pick up speed almost instantly. When the cart veers around a bend, I release the loudest scream of my life. A flurry of sparks shoots off the rail. The ark slams down and wobbles around the cart. We are moving even faster. I cling to the pole on the ark.

The cart whines against the rusted rails, and we hold onto the ark for our lives. Finally, we burst through the opening in the side of the mountain. The impact sends Stoph flying off the back of the cart while I hold on and shoot out of the tunnel like a cannon ball. The tires kick up the loose gravel before the heft of the cart sinks into the gravel and slams to a stop. My body flies forward and I crash head first against the ark.

I land flat on my back. The impact knocks the wind out of my lungs. I crawl forward, gasping for air. Then I feel dizzy and faint. Everything goes dark…

A thunderclap snaps me back to reality; the rain pours straight into my face. I feel hands pulling me to my feet. I am half-carried, half-dragged toward the tent, but everything is spinning. I turn my head to the side and relieve a wave of sickness.

"Argh! She puked on my boots!" a guy yells.

"Gordy, put her with the others," says Stoph.

My wrists and ankles are tied tight and I am stuffed into the tent. I blink to see the Quadsters, tied up, their mouths taped, with a collective look of wide-eyed terror.

There's a distant chuff-chuff-chuff sound that seems to grow louder. I roll toward the tent door to see the whirling blades on a helicopter rising over the mountain. It angles downward and lands near the ark.

Wind gusts blow against the thin tent walls until it springs free, whipping our shelter away like a kite. The rain pounds against our faces. I blink the water from my eyes to see Stoph, Gordy and two others throw a cargo net around the ark and cinch it tight.

My head is spinning. I see Sheila, wriggling her hands free. She loosens the rope from her ankles and rips the tape from Melissa and Jill's mouth.

Sheila rushes to untie my wrists and ankles. I get to my feet and run toward the ark with the Quadsters yelling at me to stop. Stoph and the other guys get on the helicopter.

"Get back!" Stoph yells, his mouth gaping wide, his eyes bugging. "Just give it up already, Paige."

"Don't," I manage to say in a thick voice.

The helicopter pilot lifts off. The ark pulls away from the ground and dangles like a yo-yo as it gets reeled toward the passenger cabin. Strong winds push back against the helicopter. The ark sways back and forth. Black thunderstorm clouds release hail that pelts against the windshield. In the distance, I see the Quadsters running for the van. Loud thunderclaps give way to lightening that cracks across the sky.

Thunder smacks so loud that I cover my ears and scream, "Holy hell!"

I drop to my knees and shield my head with my arms while the hail pelts against my back like punches. I look overhead to see the helicopter erratically swaying in the wind. I move into the tunnel opening and peer out.

Ahead, strong winds cut across the mountain range and push back against the chopper. The guys wrestle with the cargo net, trying to pull the ark into the open bay. The ark swings away from them. One of them is tangled in the net, and he slips from the helicopter. He grabs the rope with his free hand and hangs on while the others try to reel him and the ark back up.

Another gale sweeps across the mountain top and tilts the chopper almost on its side. A body falls out the opening and disappears down the mountainside. The chopper loses more height and the man swinging from the cargo net careens against the mountain. His body folds in half as he slams repeatedly into the mountain as the weight of the ark swings the cargo net back and forth.

The two guys in the aircraft scramble to pull up the ark and the dangling man. The chopper steadies itself against the storm, lifts higher and starts to clear the mountaintop. Lightning strikes and strong winds force the chopper back down. The pilot forces the aircraft to go nose up, gaining rapid altitude. The wind turbulence overwhelms the chopper; the engine sputters and pops. The chuff-chuff-chuff sound stalls before a booming explosion cracks louder than the thunder. Then it spins out of control and descends rapidly, tail first, cracking against the mountain peak. Helicopter parts splinter off as it collides with the mountain.

The fuselage slams hard into the mountain just above the tunnel opening. The impact frees a boulder, triggering an avalanche of loose rocks. I rush out of the tunnel opening as the earth overhead shakes and crumbles. Massive boulders cascade down, piling up in a thick mound that covers the tunnel entrance.

The ark tumbles down the mountain before it gets wedged between rocks. I climb toward it and hide against the side of the ark before a fireball erupts. A fiery shattering of machinery shoots everywhere. Another massive explosion scatters the chopper remnants.

I shelter against the ark, staring at the wreckage in horror. The Quadsters appear in the van down below and beep the horn.

"Let's get the fuck out of here," Melissa shrieks out the van window. The wipers can't swipe fast enough to clear the rain.

"We need to save the ark!" I wave my arms, bleary-eyed and dizzy, signaling for help. The Quadsters jump out to join me by the ark.

"What the fuck are you doing, Paige?"

"We need to move fast to save it. If we go two of us on each side, we can manage to get it down the mountain and into the back of the van."

"Just leave it. Get in the van," Melissa yells.

Sheila says, "We should see if anyone survived."

Melissa throws her hands up. "No one survived the explosion. They all burned to death."

"What about the guy who was tangled? He should be right over there."

I go with Sheila to search. A piece of the tail is pointing up from the ground like a lawn dart. The main rotor is a hundred yards beyond the tail. It takes a few minutes before we find the remnants of the rope. We follow the rope toward a lifeless body slumped against a boulder. We push him onto his back, but he is already stiff and pale, a deep gash slants across his forehead. He has no pulse.

"He's gone. Everyone else burned. Let's head back," I say.

In the distance, a lone tire tilts on its side. The debris field seems to stretch for hundreds of feet; a scattering of the charred mangled metal mess.

"Anything?" asks Jill.

"We found the guy. But he's dead."

We climb part way down the mountain and manage to straighten the ark to slide it level with the ground. I yell to the Quadsters: "On the count of three, lift! Ready?"

As we maneuver down the mountain, Jill slips and let's go of her side. The ark pulls from our grasp and slides the rest of the way to the ground. We hustle down after it. Melissa backs the van closer to the ark. It takes several attempts, but finally, we fit the ark into the back of the van.

"Let's get out of here," I shout and jump behind the wheel.

"What about our stuff?" Melissa asks.

"We don't have time," I snap. "I guarantee more Porcellians are on the way."

"No way. I'm not leaving without my matching YSL luggage."

I slam on the brakes. While she crams her luggage into the van, I grab the soaked sleeping bags to cover the ark because it is supposed to have a veil. We abandon the rest of the camping gear in the quick exit. I accelerate as fast as the van will allow — at times it feels like I am back on the tunnel rollercoaster flying out of control. Every emergency vehicle in the area rushes past us on route to the crashed helicopter.

"Paige, I think you should pull over — switch drivers," Jill suggests.

I ease the Peace Train to the shoulder of the road.

28. North Easton or Bust

My head is throbbing. I can't think straight with the Quadsters asking a million questions.

"Is this really the ark of the covenant? Or just a replica?" asks Jill.

"It's the real deal, I think. The only way to know for sure would be to open it up and see if the tablets with the ten commandments are inside. There should be a golden pot with manna and Aaron's rod as well."

"We should open it. See if there's eleven commandments. Maybe one got lost in translation."

"Thou shalt not endanger your friends' lives on fall break," Melissa chimes in from the back seat.

Sheila reaches toward the front passenger seat — squeezes my shoulder — and sits back without saying anything.

Jill glances at me. "You okay?"

"What happened at the campsite after Stoph and I went into the tunnel?"

Jill shakes her head. "A black SUV pulled up and three guys —"

Melissa interrupts, "Our age! Super good-looking —"

"If you're into Androids, but whatever," Jill continues. "They acted all nice at first, asking us a million questions about camping —"

"Glamping. I told them we were glamping and they laughed. They were totally into me," Melissa adds. "Too bad they're all dead."

"Did you recognize any of them?"

"Only from my dreams," Melissa says.

"You didn't recognize Gordy? The *bartender* from the Porcellian clubhouse?"

"Wait, what?"

"The guy that dragged me to the tent. That was Gordy."

Stoph's voice runs through my head: *Gordy Preston...he runs Porcellian...comes from the wealthiest family in the country.*

Jill continues, "Dark storm clouds started rolling in. The guys were pretending to be interested in the monument, but I realize now that they were just stalling, waiting for the helicopter. When the chopper flew over the mountain, that was their cue to tie us up and keep us in the tent."

"They were Stoph's Porc bros. When I went into town early in the morning to pick up breakfast, I saw cars with Massachusetts license plates. I bet that was them. I should've realized then. Did they hurt you?"

Sheila says, "They told us to cooperate or else. It wasn't like we could run away. It's so isolated. We just went in the tent and they tied us up and taped our mouths shut. They weren't rough about it. I think they felt bad they had to do it."

Jill nods. "Then they went in the tunnel, but they came running back out. We heard you and Stoph screaming your heads off before you blasted out of the tunnel on that go-cart."

"There's miners' tracks in there. We loaded the ark on a miners' cart and the thing just rocketed as if it had a mind of its own. It was insane how fast it went."

Jill glances at me, her forehead furrowed. "The helicopter landed. The pilot stayed in it with the propeller spinning. I saw you rolling around on the ground. Stoph started to check to see if you were okay, but the other guys yelled at him to get moving with the cargo net. Two of the guys carried you to the tent," Jill says, pausing for a moment. "And you realize the helicopter crashed and burned with everyone in it. Including Stoph?"

"Right."

Sheila reaches to the front seat and squeezes my shoulder again. "You seem to be taking it —"

Melissa cuts her off. "She's in shock."

I know I smacked my head against the ark when we crashed and everything became fuzzy. I saw the helicopter, heard the guys shouting about the cargo net and remember the ark hanging by a thread. How the helicopter struggled against the elements. It feels like a bad dream that I can't wake up from.

Jill takes the next exit to find a gas station. There are street signs at the end of the exit ramp. A separate sign says *Preston's Farm — 5 miles*. Gordon Preston, a fourth-generation pig farmer — how fitting. Now it hits me: Landrace LLC, the anonymous corporation in Wyoming, must be affiliated with Gordy and his family farm.

Two of us stay in the car to babysit the ark while the other two go inside to use the restroom. My hands feel clammy and I have a crazy thirst. Sheila returns with a case of water and a hot pretzel with salt. She breaks a piece off for me. The warm pretzel dough sticks to the roof of my mouth. Melissa returns chomping on bubble gum and blowing bubbles.

"What exactly are we going to do with this thing?" asks Jill, peeking into the back window.

"Return it to those who will protect it," I say.

"And who are *those* that will protect it?" Melissa asks.

"An Ancient Order of Druids Society headquartered in North Easton. The A.O.D. We need to hand it over to them. They'll know what to do."

The storm clouds give way to the sun. Melissa sits on the hood to sun herself. "And what's in it for us?"

"Nothing. Obviously, we should all be happy we're alive."

"True that," says Jill.

I lean against the bumper and close my eyes for a minute to think. Melissa whispers to Jill and Sheila, "What do you think, post-concussion syndrome or PTSD? Her boyfriend just got blown up in a helicopter."

I keep my eyes shut and think here we go again. The post-concussion counselor told me to trust people, share more with my friends. I learned to keep my cool from soccer — tie game in sudden-death overtime and I'm taking the penalty shot — stay focused, aim for the corner of the net, poker face toward the goalie. Bam! Goal, we win, next game, do it again. I'm good at keeping my cool.

"I'm still shaking. I think I have PTSD," says Sheila.

"Is it illegal that we took the ark? I feel like we stole it," Jill admits.

I rub my pounding forehead. "Everyone calm down. I don't have PTSD. I need to focus on one thing at a time. First, we get the ark back home. Once it is in safe hands again, then I will process what happened with Stoph and his friends. He used me to find the ark. He was using me all along."

"Sorry Paige," Sheila says.

It's my turn to go use the restroom. I make the phone call.

"Precinct, how may I direct your call?"

"Captain Biff, please. Tell him it's Paige Moore and it's urgent."

Captain Biff gets on the phone and listens while I explain what happened. "I have the ark," I tell him, "and we're bringing it home to the A.O.D. for safekeeping."

There's a long pause, before he says, "Do you think you're being followed? Where exactly are you? I'll arrange a police escort."

"No one is following us. I think we should just keep going before it gives Porcellian time to sort out what went down."

"Agreed. Come straight to the police department. Call me right away if anything comes up."

I head back to the van and prime my music to take over the driving.

Melissa flips her thumb like an umpire making a call at home plate. "Out!"

"What?"

"You're not driving. Not with your head all —"

"I'm fine. I can take a shift."

"Seriously? You're in denial," Melissa says. "Ladies, never trust a woman who says *I'm fine*."

Sheila gets in the back seat. "What's wrong with saying *I'm fine*?"

Melissa power sighs. "Think about it. How many times have you been pissed off about something and you don't want to talk about it? What do you say?"

Sheila shrugs.

"I'm fine! I'm fine! I'm fine! That's what chicks say when they're ready to blow a mental gasket." Melissa balances her coffee on the hood of the van and flips open her palm. "Hand over the keys. I'm driving. You can't be fine. You just had a concussion. And your boyfriend just died in a fiery crash after he betrayed you to a bunch of studly Harvard goons. So, get out."

I realize I'm not winning this debate so I slide out of the driver's seat and get in the back. Melissa turns down the volume and eyes me from the rearview mirror. The trees blur past my window. I know I'm doing the right thing. I'm trusting my instincts to hand the ark over to Captain Biff and the North Easton druids. But what if I'm wrong — like I was blindsided by Stoph.

The front windows are open, blowing Melissa and Jill's long hair all over the place. A 1960s orange Volkswagen Beetle pulls up alongside the Peace Train. There's an older man in a Grateful Dead t-shirt driving and puffing a joint. He flashes the peace sign at Melissa. I hold my breath thinking she's going to flip the middle finger at him because he's not the one percent. She holds up a peace sign, beeps and waves back at him.

"He was probably really cute back in the day."

Jill leans forward to get a better glimpse. "If we were in college in the late 1960s or early 1970s, do you think we would've been hippies?"

Melissa rolls up her window and fixes her hair. "Sure, I could see us rocking a Parisian peasant look. Maybe bell-bottoms. I could've loaded my closet with Halston dresses. Swap out cosmos for joints."

"I could picture you two doing the folk scene at Greenwich Village," Sheila says. "Not me. I would have been all over the elevator shoes and disco like Soul Train. What about you, Paige?"

I think for a moment. "Bob Dylan. Carole King. Joni Mitchell. Judy Collins. Heavy on the lyrics. Grungy jeans. That'd be me, Kew College 1974."

Sheila looks in the back of the van. "I wonder, if we were friends at Kew in 1974, if we would've taken this road trip and found the ark?"

"Definitely," says Melissa, blowing a bubble until it pops. "We were destined to be total tomb busters."

29. While We Live

The Quadsters are tired from sharing the nonstop driving, so I convince them I can take the last leg of the trip. I say I feel great, scratching the word *fine* from my lexicon. I put on my playlist and when a Tool song comes on, I feel a wave of sadness about what happened — Stoph turned me on to that group. I hit the skip arrow.

When I cross the Massachusetts state line, the New England foliage presents us with an orange-hued homecoming. I tell the Quadsters we are taking the ark straight to Captain Biff at the police department.

"But we're not in trouble with the cops, right?" Jill asks.

"No. We're heroes. But no one will even know about this."

Melissa says, "Watch. They'll sell it to a museum and walk away with millions. *"Quadsters? Who are the Quadsters? Never heard of them..."*

I lower the volume. "The druids will protect it in one of Richardson's other hiding places. He designed loads of them."

"Cool," Sheila says.

I see flashing lights in my rearview mirror and pull over. I open the window to hand the officer my license. He lowers his aviator-style sunglasses and when we make eye contact, I recognize Captain Biff.

"Follow my cruiser the rest of the way. You will be flanked by unmarked squad cars. I will lead you into the station's sally port. Any questions?"

"No, sir."

The cruiser takes the lead as we ease back onto the road. Melissa groans, "Great, here's where I get arrested again — tack on another hundred hours of community service."

"Just chill out. We're not getting arrested." The rearview mirror shows the unmarked Ford Explorers trailing us.

Melissa sighs. "We should have gone to Florida like normal people."

I can't listen to her whining, so I crank a "Peace Train" cover by the 10,000 Maniacs. She takes the hint and shuts up. I feel my jaw unclench as I follow Captain Biff into Shovel Town — we pull into the precinct sally port garage and the doors automatically shut behind us. He walks around to the back of the van, opens the door, and stares at the ark. I join him while the Quadsters sit like mannequins in the van.

He opens the side door. "Ladies, follow me."

Melissa jumps the line to be the first Quadster seen by the hottie young cop opening the main door. She bats her eyes at him. "Thank you, officer."

I whisper to Melissa, "One, he's blue collar, and two, he barely meets the PD height requirement."

"I know," she whispers back, "but I have a thing for men in uniform."

"Betty, call over to Agostino's. These ladies need penne and meatballs," Captain Biff tells his secretary. "A bottle of Chianti, too."

"We're not 21," Sheila admits, then stares at the floor to avoid Melissa's daggers.

Captain Biff clears his throat. "Betty, eighty-nine the Chianti. Just Pellegrino."

A female officer arrives to escort us to the locker room. She hands us fresh towels. "Shampoo and conditioner are in the dispensers. Hair dryers are by the sink. Your robes are in the dressing room — one size fits most."

Melissa looks around. "This is a high-end locker room for a —"

"Police precinct? Captain Biff and a few officers remodeled the station's gym and locker rooms. It helps motivate the crew to stay in shape."

There's a fresh eucalyptus bundle draping down from the shower head. The aroma, combined with hot pulsating water hitting my head, frees some of the tension pent up behind my forehead. I wrap the plush towel around my body, dry my hair straight down, and head for the lockers. There are brown hooded monk robes folded on the bench.

Melissa holds up a robe by the hood. "When Lady Cop mentioned robes, I thought she meant high-thread count Egyptian cotton. What's this? Prison wear?"

"It's druid wear," I say.

"Do we wear underwear with this?" Jill asks.

Lady Cop steps around the corner. "Food's ready. Right this way as soon as you're all set."

We all put on the robes — underwear included — and head for the break room. There's an aerial view photograph of North Easton on the wall. Captain Biff is drinking coffee at the table with a few others who are all wearing druid robes. "Let's eat and talk."

One of the robed men says, "Ladies, you deserve to be recognized as the pride of Kew College. There's no undefeated sports team, scientific breakthrough or Pulitzer Prize-winning professor that would put Kew on the map as a leading institution the way your discovery rightfully should. Unfortunately, this must remain strictly confidential."

I feel Melissa kick me under the table. But I already know who it is…the president of Kew College, a druid.

He continues, "In exchange for your strict confidentiality regarding your discovery of the ark, arrangements are in the works to have your full tuitions waived, full room and board waived, and full graduate school scholarships should you choose to pursue higher degrees at any institution in the world. This scholarship will appear as academic, but it is really in exchange for your discovery."

"Thank you, Dr. Webster," I say. I can't breathe. The thought of not paying any college costs is like Christmas morning on steroids.

Another druid says, "And to express the gratitude of North Easton, you will also have unlimited dining privileges at Agostinos and Wild Ginger Chinese restaurant. Boots-n-Paddles Olde English Pub will also extend privileges once you are all 21.

Melissa nudges me. "Never doubted you for a second, Paigester."

We have not had real food since we left North Easton six days ago. The aroma rising off the meatballs smells like grandma's hugs. The Quadsters dig in, devouring the food, the best Italian I've ever tasted. Captain Biff sets down a loaf of warm Italian bread for us to sop up the red sauce.

"Here's what's going to happen — midnight tonight, you four will be escorted to the Rockery. Then, a ceremonial initiation where you will be sworn in as honorary members of the Ancient Order of Druids. This is a secret society. No one talks about it, ever. You will lead the procession of moving the ark of the covenant to the attic room of Memorial Hall. After that, you go back to college and study hard. Don't worry about the A.O.D. or the ark. There are A.O.D. officers who will take care of those things from now on. Got it?"

We all nod in agreement.

After dinner, Lady Cop says to us, "Follow me to the lounge area."

We hang out on leather club chairs drinking Pellegrino. Melissa lightly kicks Sheila's ankle. "Would be nice to have a glass of Chianti right about now, but no, *none of us are 21.*"

"Sorry about that. But you can't break the law inside a police station."

There's a television in the corner that lulls me into a nap. The robes are comfortable, maybe that's why Richardson wore them to work. Just as Captain Biff explained, we head for the Rockery at 11:45 to be in our places by midnight.

"Moore, you're with me. You three go with Officer Quinn." The corners of Captain Biff's mouth twitch upward, almost smiling.

He hands me the keys to the Peace Train and gets in the passenger side. "Are you sure you don't want to drive — make it more official police business?"

He focuses straight ahead. "It's all you."

I back the van out of the sally port and follow Officer Quinn's cruiser transporting the Quadsters. I drive extra slow with the police captain as my co-pilot. I pause at the end of the driveway and look twice.

"Ready on the right," he says, as if I only have a learner's permit. "While I have you alone, I want to make you an offer. You are invited to train for full initiation as a North Easton druid. It's an honor that I hope you accept and take seriously. It will give you worldwide contacts that open doors in ways you can't even begin to imagine."

"Like being a Porcellian?"

"Bigger than that," he says. "Much bigger."

"Sign me up," I say.

It's a short drive to the Rockery — a good thing because my hands are trembling. There are police detour barricades that get moved for us to pass through. The full harvest moon hangs bright over Memorial Hall. As I pull around the Rockery, I see a parade of hooded druids holding lit candles for the ceremony. They line the street and circle the Rockery.

"Pull up to the front of Memorial Hall," he tells me, then reaches over to pull my hood up on my head.

I put the van in park and follow him with the Quadsters toward the Rockery where there's a bonfire. A man is rotating a rotisserie spit where a whole lamb is roasting. He steps around the bonfire in his Birkenstock sandals. One foot is bandaged. He looks up at me. Treadwell folds his hands prayer-style, bows toward me.

"Impressive work. I look forward to hearing about your discovery," Treadwell says. He bows toward me, then bows toward the altar. "Not in a million years would I have guessed it was in the monument in Wyoming. I am awed by your abilities, young lady."

I look closer at the altar and realize it is the shovel desk from the Archive Department. A fresh animal fur — probably skinned from the roasting lamb — covers the altar top. Treadwell strikes a match to light three fat candles, then fills a large gold chalice with a red liquid from a brass vessel that could be either Chianti or lamb's blood.

There's a gradual buzzing sound — a low-pulse melodic line — as the druids start their ritualistic chanting. The chant rises as the druid circle draws closer to the Rockery.

Treadwell burns the end of a stick to mark the space around the altar with a triangle. Then he collects bramble and dried flowers growing wild near the Rockery boulders. He bunches it like tumbleweed to burn in the bonfire. He lights a torch and passes it to a hooded person who shares the flame to light dozens of other torches held by more hooded druids. He drinks the blood, or the chianti, and passes the chalice down to the next hooded person.

A woman's voice calls out from the top of the Rockery: *"Stand like druids of eld, with voices sad and prophetic...loud from its rocky caverns, the deep-voiced neighboring ocean speaks."*

It's Ms. Montgomery, reciting Longfellow. When she is done, she looks toward the Quadsters, folds her hands, and bows.

"I knew there was a reason I chose you to be my intern. This is truly remarkable," she says to me. "Outstanding work, miss."

There's no time to wallow in the praise. Captain Biff gestures for us to follow him down from the Rockery toward Memorial Hall. As we move forward, the other druids, still chanting, follow the procession to the Peace Train. Four druid honor guards slide the ark of the covenant out of the van to transport it up the grand staircase of Memorial Hall.

Captain Biff tells me, "After the ceremony the ark will be moved to its new home. It will remain protected under heavy surveillance. I have a feeling we'll be staying in touch."

The glorious full moon casts a hint of light over the zodiac tower. I admire and respect the night sky, which reminds me of the constellation of risks in the pyramid tunnel, and I think: *While we live, let us live.*

Brian Sampson on the road

Acknowledgments

The brainstorm for this novel began after Thanksgiving dinner in 2017 when my nephew Brian Sampson shared his epic insights into early American architecture. I was not too familiar with Henry Hobson Richardson's work, or many of the other architects, artists, sculptors, movers and shakers whom he spoke about with great enthusiasm. But I became instantly fascinated with his take on all of it.

I stepped inside Brian's world where his perspective and ideas are not what you read in a book or lookup on the internet. We met on a frigid weekend in Boston for the *Brian Tour* filled with his insights that delve deep into the city's great architecture and art history. After Boston, we visited Cambridge and North Easton to view more Richardson buildings.

And that's when the fun began.

Countless phone conversations, text messages and email exchanges proved that there was a pulse to Richardson's architecture waiting to give life to a novel.

Brian endured many drafts as I grappled with his architectonic ideas, the characters that evolved and the wild ride they took us on. To say we had a blast collaborating on this novel is an understatement.

Brian, a 2012 Penn State graduate, is an architectural engineer who retired at age 30 to embark on his solo bike tour of the world. He's been on the road since 2018 logging over 20,000 miles. He got the idea for the bike tour when he was in middle school and read Patricia Shultz' book *1,000 Places to See Before You Die.*

Follow Brian's bike tour on Instagram: @brian.sampson4 and www.justfeltlikebiking.blogspot.com.

Brian's ideas are endless. The sequel is in the works.

Appreciation

A heartfelt thanks to John Sampson who provided unwavering support, careful critiquing, reading of countless revisions, and sincere enthusiasm during the writing of this novel. I appreciate the space given to pursue this endeavor and the gentle reminders that if nothing more came of the whole process than just the pleasure of writing a novel, that we can still consider ourselves very lucky.

Troy Sampson and Sheila Sampson deserve special thanks for their inspiration and for listening, with great patience, about the writing of this novel.

I owe a huge thanks to my writing guru Dan Pope who provided professional guidance through multiple drafts. I greatly appreciate the trip through Kew Gardens.

Thank you to the brave folks who took the time to read early drafts and respond with insight and encouragement: Robert Leader, Charlotte Forshaw, Margaret Murphy, and Patrick Gustafson. Also, sincere appreciation goes to the Sampson Family, the Gustafson clan, and Corrigan Courier Service.

CPSIA information can be obtained
at www.ICGtesting.com
Printed in the USA
BVHW082246300321
603712BV00001B/75